FIREFIGHT

FIREFIGHT

A Novel

Joseph Ferrandino

SOHO

A portion of Chapter 15 first appeared, in somewhat different form, in
Vietnam Flashbacks, No. 12, (1984), published by Pig Iron Press,
Youngstown, Ohio.

Published in the United States of America by
Soho Press, Inc.
1 Union Square
New York, NY 10003

Library of Congress Cataloging-in-Publication Data

Ferrandino, Joseph, 1948-
Firefight.

1. Vietnamese Conflict, 1961–1975—Fiction.
I. Title.

PS3556.E7252F5   1987   813'.54   87-13052
ISBN 0–939149–09–5

Manufactured in the United States of America
FIRST EDITION

For my father,
Pete the Barber,
who knew intuitively
the truth Tithones discovered
after centuries of harsh experience.

From the epigraph to *Hell In A Very Small Place:*
The Siege of Dien Bien Phu
by Bernard B. Fall
1966

When a nation re-awakens, its finest sons are prepared to give
their lives for its liberation. When Empires are threatened
with collapse, they are prepared to sacrifice their non-
commissioned officers.

Quoted from *The Revolt*
by Menachem Begin
Leader of the Irgun
1951

———————————————
———————   ———————
———————   ———————
———————   ———————

From *A Walk In The Sun*
Harry Brown
1944

One moment he saw himself sitting by the fire at home, the
next moment he saw himself, as though from a great distance,
crawling over a muddy plain. He did not recognize the landscape as a real one. He had never fought in such a place. But
the landscape was familiar for all that. It was the landscape of
a dream. He had been moving through it for years, he would
probably never find his way out of it.

1

Amaro hopped from the Chinook and walked through the swirling dust of the landing zone at Duc Pho, the forward base camp of the First Brigade. The area was defoliated, bulldozed flat across a former rice field. The compound was a squat of tents and sandbags, its back to the South China Sea and its eyes fixed inland on the enemy-held highlands.

Amaro tossed his gear onto the back of a deuce-and-a-half and jumped on. He sat on his duffel bag and the truck lurched into gear heading for Charlie Company.

The truck passed a large wooden sign with the division's shoulder patch painted on it in black and white: an eagle head. The words NO SLACK were printed in block letters above it.

Red crosses painted on tents marked the battalion aid station. Fifty-five-gallon drums surrounded a sign that said TRIAGE. They were empty for now. Beyond the aid station was an outdoor movie screen and a landing zone. Rockets were piled high on pallets at the far corner of the LZ. The truck traversed the road separating Headquarters Company from Alpha Company, made a quick turn at the Charlie Company sign, and shuddered to a halt in front of the command post.

Charlie Company was westernmost on the outer perimeter. The flats extended a few hundred meters farther like a warning track, and then rose into lush green hills beyond the concertina wire.

The command post was at the center of the company area.

A large tent served as combination supply and orderly room. To the rear of the CP, a row of smaller tents billeted the officers and NCOs. Facing the CP were sandbag rectangles, with pup tents pitched in the first few spaces. The rest of the tent areas were vacant. Past them, spaced at twenty-meter intervals, stood bunkers along a low sandbag wall.

When the wind was easterly, a sea smell wafted over the area. From the west the wind brought the scent of jungle mulch.

Sergeant Watts, the company supply sergeant and clerk, met them in front of the CP. He cradled a clipboard. The bottom of it rested on his pistol belt.

"Welcome to Charlie Company," he said. "Put everything you own, except the clothes on your back and your web gear, into your duffel bag and forget about it." He handed each guy a large manila tag. "Put your name and service number on it, tie it to your duffel, and stack your shit on the pile in the orderly room. My name is Watts. Listen up for yours." He said this while staring at his clipboard. He never looked at the replacements.

"Corporal Amaro and Lee . . . first platoon. Haws and Everly, the second. Red Cloud or Bitah or whatever the fuck your name is . . . Well? What is it?"

"Bitah is my first name, Sergeant," the dark guy with the even darker eyes replied. "Red Cloud is my last name. It's Navajo Indian."

"Well, Chief. You're assigned to the third platoon. Pitch your tents and stay in the company area. The Mauldicker will give you an orientation when he's good and ready." Watts turned and walked into the CP.

They filled out tags and, in the orderly room, added their duffels to the high wide stack along the length of the canvas wall. They drew shelterhalves and pitched tents back in the bivouac rectangles. Amaro and Lee worked together. A tall, big-built trooper and a short, seedy-looking guy sat lounging on the top step of the commo bunker, smoking and joking and shaking their heads. A runner summoned them all to the orderly room.

First Sergeant Henry Fluett sat behind his desk in the orderly room as the five soldiers shuffled over and stood at attention in front of him. His scalp shone through salt-and-pepper stubble as he bent his head forward to scan the orders on his desk. Fluett shifted his eyes from the orders to the faces of the replacements.

"At ease," he said. He stood up, ramrod straight. He was a tall man, well-built but not muscular. His skin, the color of leather, was pulled tight over the muscle and bone of his face. The lines at the corners of his eyes were traced with white because of the squint he wore outdoors.

"Vietnam is not like any other place on earth," Fluett said. His voice was flat and deep. "You are expected to adjust and act accordingly. When you meet an officer you will execute a smart airborne salute and shout the greeting, 'No *fucking slack, sir.*' Is that understood?"

"Yes, First Sergeant," they answered.

"This is the No Slack Battalion and no fucking slack will be tolerated. Do you read me loud and clear?"

"Yes, First Sergeant."

"That goes for you, too, *former* Sergeant Amaro. You understand me, *former* Sergeant Amaro?"

"Yes, First Sergeant."

"I don't care what you've done before or what you intend to do when you leave here. You are *here* now and *that* is all that matters. You are no longer boys or men or even human beings. You are the meanest goddamn soldiers in the world. You are the meanest goddamn soldiers in the meanest god-damn *outfit* in the world. You are expected to act accordingly. Do *not* expect any of the courtesies normally reserved for members of the human race. You will receive only the courtesies due you as soldiers. No more. No less. Do I make myself clear?"

"Yes, First Sergeant."

"Good. You may find the going rough at times. At these times you may feel the need for sympathy. If so, you will find it here." He picked a dictionary up from his desk and held it overhead. "You will find sympathy here—between *shit* and *syphilis,* and nowhere else in this goddamn country. I know there are no questions . . . Dismissed."

The men turned and strode out of the orderly room.

"Holy shit," Lee said. "I feel like I been reamed with a bore brush."

"He shits brass," Amaro said.

"He ain't nothin'," Haws said. "Hot damn, I got a grand-mama back home jus' chew him up and spit him twenty feet."

"He has an Indian name, you know," Bitah said.

"Say what?" Lee asked.

"Indians are named after the first thing the baby's father sees after it is born," Bitah said. "My father saw a red cloud. Fluett's papa saw a big prick."

"You got that right," Everly said.

Amaro said, "I'm glad my old man wasn't an Indian. He'd of called me Broken Rubber."

Out back they rummaged through a pile of bullet-torn and bloodstained rucksacks trying to find some that were still serviceable. They were issued twenty magazines each and an equal number of ammo boxes. They would each carry grenades and three hundred rounds of machine-gun ammo. Amaro and Haws had drawn claymores and detonating devices. Lee, the Chief, and Everly packed tripflares in their rucksacks.

They drew three days' worth of Cs, which they pushed into socks and stuffed them in or tied them onto their packs. Each man selected five plastic canteens and Watts instructed the cherries how to fasten these to their rucksacks with D-rings. Brigade Standard Operating Procedure demanded each man in the field carry two ammo pouches and one canteen on his web gear; everything else was distributed in or on the rucksack according to personal preference.

They removed the slings from their weapons and clipped general-purpose straps to the carrying handle at the top of the M-16. This let the weapon hang loosely from one shoulder.

The replacements sat on the sandbag wall around the pup tents and pulled maintenance on their equipment. They broke down the weapons, cleaned and covered the metal with a light coat of oil. The magazine springs were checked, oiled, reassembled. Twenty rounds were pushed into each. Finally they were done.

When the line companies were in the field, perimeter guard duty was pulled by rear-echelon troops who never left the camp. Just before sunset, Amaro and Lee watched these guards change in the bunkers. During daylight only one guard manned the position. At night, three rotated sentry duty.

Sergeant Watts came over to the replacements and invited them to the orderly room for a poker game. All of them accepted his invitation.

Inside the huge tent they sat on the wood floor around a footlocker, handling the cards and adding or subtracting from their respective piles of piasters as the game began. Watts had never been to the field; his repertoire of war stories was depleted after the first few hands.

Two scruffy guys strolled into the tent and sat on the stacked duffel bags. Pot smoke clung to their fatigues.

"Hey, Crawford," Watts shouted to one of them. "Come here and show the cherries your souvenir."

Crawford leered. He unsnapped a chain from around his neck. The chain had a plastic pill bottle on it. He handed the pill bottle to Amaro. Amaro passed the bottle to Lee.

"Where'd you get it?" Amaro asked.

"Off a fuckin' gook. Where do you fuckin' think?" Crawford said.

Lee dropped it when he realized what it was. Red Cloud reached over, picked it up, and stared at it in the glow of the bare bulb.

"This was the first one, so I kept it," Crawford said.

"The first one?" Lee said. "There were more?"

"Yeah." Sergeant Watts nodded. "He sells them to the gook barber that works around here sometimes. The government pays a bounty on them."

"Only for right ears," Crawford said. He looked over at Moose. They both laughed.

Haws took the bottle from Red Cloud. "It's mighty small, ain't it?" he said to no one in particular. "Looks like a dried apple."

"The formaldehyde makes them shrink," Crawford said. "I take some of that shit with me to the field. When I get back I trade what I got to the barber for . . . Well, I trade them to the barber."

"That's funny," Amaro said. "When I was a kid in my old man's barbershop there was this old guy named Joe working a chair. The other barbers used to tease this guy and tell him he fed his dog with the ears he cut off customers."

"This gook don't feed nothing to his dog," Moose said.

"Fuckin' A," Watts said. " 'Cause he done *ate* the goddamn dog."

Amaro nodded. "They do like dog."

Everly refused his turn when Haws offered him the bottle. Crawford took it and snapped the chain back around his neck. He looked at Red Cloud.

"Hey," he said. "You're an Indian, ain't you?"

"Yes," Red Cloud replied. "Full-blooded Cherokee."

"Cherokee?" Amaro said. "This afternoon you told us you were a Navajo."

"Whatever," Crawford shrugged. "I got something you'll really appreciate." He walked over to the duffel bags and started throwing them around the orderly room.

"Clean up this fuckin' mess when you're finished," Watts shouted.

"Yeah yeah yeah. Fuck you," Crawford said over his shoulder. "Come on, Moose. Give me a hand."

Crawford found his duffel and ransacked it for a few minutes. He came back to the footlocker pulling a length of long black hair from a plastic bag. The hair shone blue-black in the weak light. Crawford held it by the leathery oval of skin and shook it in the air. He gently smoothed the tangles with his fingers and handed it to Red Cloud. "Ain't it beautiful?" he asked.

Red Cloud looked at it but refused to touch it.

"A second-looey forward observer called in artillery on this family we caught in a freefire zone," Crawford said. "Did it for fuckin' practice. I moved in for souvenirs. The barber offered me two thousand P for it but I says, 'No way. What are you, crazy? Fuck off,' I says to him. 'I'm gonna take it back to the World and give it to my girl.' "

"Why?" Amaro said. "Is she bald?"

"She's gettin' balled by every swingin' dick in Northwest Philly," Moose said, laughing.

Everly ran out of the tent. They heard him puke.

"He's gonna go far," Crawford said.

Watts shuffled the deck. "I'm glad he didn't do that in

here. Ante up, boys. Five-card stud and the Jack of Spades runs wild."

Shots were fired on the perimeter. Watts shut the light and screamed, "*Incoming*. Go. Get the fuck outta here. Hit the bunkers."

Amaro heard boots thud on the planking and made to run. But he could not find his piece where he had left it. He groped for it blindly. He tripped over the duffels. The snapping of the firing intensified. Someone must have moved it. He walked toward the desk and found his piece by kicking it to the floor. He picked it up and sprinted to the closest bunker, cursing.

The rifle fire lasted for ten minutes. White flares bathed the flats in stark light. Amaro saw nothing but dancing shadows. He did not fire his weapon. After a tense half hour the all clear was passed along the perimeter.

"Hey. Look there," Haws said, pointing out toward the hills.

"Look where?" Lee said.

"There. Up there," Haws said, sighting along an outstretched arm. "See them fires?"

Fires twinkled in the distance.

"That's Victor Charlie," Amaro said, "sitting up there day and night, just watching and waiting."

"Don't that beat all," Haws said. "Jus' like moonshiners back home. Hot damn, you can see their fires by night but, by God, the guv'mint people can't never find hide nor hair of 'em come daybreak."

In the pup tent Amaro lay on the dirt wrapped in a poncho. He tried to sleep but adrenaline kept him up. He was wide awake and nervous. He sat up and unclipped the GP strap from the carrying handle of his weapon. He snapped one hook onto the lower stock swivel, the other hook to a loop on his pants. Then he lit a cigarette.

He saw the explosions flash red in the darkness but did not hear their sounds. No noise or vibration. Just flashes of blood red. He rolled sideways for cover and kept crawling because the blackness around him kept changing color. He stopped when he reached the wall.

The firefight must be in the next valley. But where is all the noise?

He looked around and as the contours of a sandbag wall came into focus, he realized there was no firefight at all. He sat with his back to the wall wiping sweat from his face with his hands. He tried to remember. Tried to figure it out. But he had no idea. He felt scared and absolutely alone. The flashing red light became his heart, pumping blood to the worn and lumpy stuffing of his organs. And he became his own mind, shivering in dark space, wondering where the hell he was.

It was nearly daylight.

2

Medevacs blew up dust around the battalion aid station. Amaro watched the corpsmen run to the choppers with stretchers to pull what looked like piles of dirty laundry from the Hueys.

"Looks like somebody hit some shit," Watts said as he sat in the shade fanning himself with his clipboard.

They were working at the landing zone off-loading crated rockets from a deuce-and-a-half and stacking them on pallets. It was their third day. They worked bare-chested in the sun and heavy, still air. Amaro found it hard to breathe. His sweat felt thick and sticky. During a smoke break Amaro pulled on his jacket and walked to the aid station. The barrels out front had bloodstained fatigues in them. There were a couple of boots lying alongside. And some equipment. He looked through a window flap, turned his eyes away, and walked.

Late in the afternoon a pickup drove onto the landing zone and off-loaded three black plastic bags. These were placed in line on pallets at the far side of the LZ.

Before chow Amaro took a saltwater shower but he did not feel clean. He changed his socks and pulled on his fatigues. It was too hot to wear skivvies. He broke a sweat walking to the mess tent. For dinner he ate cherry pie and drank a glass of warm iced tea.

After dark the five of them went to the evening movie. Vic Morrow in a "Combat" episode. Television put onto film is what it was.

"Hey. Smell that?" Amaro said.

"Sure do." Lee smiled. "And it smell real good."

"We should try to cop."

"I did. But these dudes, man, they look at you like to say, 'Who the fuck are you, man?' Know what I mean?"

"I hear you," Amaro said.

"I talked to a guy in Bravo Company today. It was them got hit. Seven wounded, man. Three KIA."

"Yeah, huh," Amaro said. "Come on. Let's get out of here."

They stood up and stepped carefully through the crowd sitting on the dirt. Haws joined them. Everly and Red Cloud sat staring at the screen as a GI tommygunned two dozen Nazis.

"He makes it look easy," Haws said. "Jus' like pissin' on a rock."

They wandered back to their tent area and came upon Sergeant Watts.

"What are you rushin' around for at this hour, Sarge?"

"Y'all be goin' to the field in the morning," Watts said. "First call at oh-four-hundred hours."

Amaro spent the night in private thoughts. He repacked his rucksack and cleaned his piece a third time, then sat in a corner of the orderly room and under the bare-bulb light he wrote two long letters home. He did not mention going to the line. He decided to tell of it when he returned.

He sat with his back against the sandbag wall outside his tent and smoked one Lucky after another. He felt the same way he had felt on his first jump. Sitting up against the skin of the aircraft, regretting being there. Wishing he were somewhere else.

He almost did not jump. He almost refused to stand up and hook up. Fuck you, he almost said to the jumpmaster. Almost. But, he thought, you asked for it: you shook the tree, now you got to eat the fucking apples.

Stand up and hook up.

And he did. He locked the static line on the metal wire and slipped the safety pin in place.

Check equipment.

: 10

He went through the motions. He patted the chute in front of him, not noticing anything about it. He was worried about his own chute. About himself.

"Sound off for equipment check."

"Okay," he said. Okay, and he felt a slap on his thigh and he slapped the guy in front of him. "Okay," they said. "Okay. Okay." But he knew none of them knew what the fuck they were talking about and he did not care. Okay. Okay, he said. It will open or it won't. Simple, really.

"Shuffle down and stand in the door."

He pushed the static line forward. Took the awkward ducksteps, with the foot near the skin of the aircraft always in front of the other. Why? *Who cares?* That's the way it's done. Who cares why. He watched the red light, the wind rushing past the open door, deforming the jumpmaster's face as he leaned out to scope the drop zone. The light turned green.

"Go."

I'm going, I'm going. In the door without thinking. The prop blast pushes legs above head. *One* one thousand. *Two* one thousand. Clutch the reserve. *Three* one thousand. The chute opens and he sees it between his boots. The risers jerk him right-side up. Dangles and swings in the silence. "Fuck you," he screams, "fuck you."

Amaro jerked upright. It was two hours after midnight.

The landing zone used for troop movements was out on the flats between Bravo and Charlie companies. Before dawn, Watts made several trips out there with the three-quarter from the company area. He stacked boxes of ammo, C rations, and sundries on the pallets along the edge of the landing zone before the replacements had finished chow. Each box was marked by platoon.

Amaro, Lee, Crawford, and Moose lined up their rucksacks in front of the cartons marked FIRST PLATOON. Amaro placed his steel pot on his rucksack and leaned his weapon up against it. He lit a Lucky and watched the sunlight spread upward. He fussed with his equipment. Although he had eaten chow, his stomach felt empty and tight. He took a few sips of iodine-tasting water to moisten his mouth.

Rotors thudded in the distance, coming closer. Then they were over the camp, flying low: twelve of them. Amaro felt their throb deep in his chest.

They helped the crew chief of their bird load cartons onto the Huey. Fluett supervised the operation personally. He glanced at his watch. "Time to suit up," he said.

They pulled on their rucksacks. Amaro checked his weapon. He locked and loaded a round.

Watts handed him a green laundry bag. "Give it to Sergeant McGee," he said.

Amaro struggled to seat himself on the deck. The others looked for something to hold on to.

"Relax," the crew chief shouted. "It's a cold landing zone. Hold on to something and don't fall out the fucking door."

He said a few words into the microphone and the chopper lifted and veered off, following a course northwest into the high mountains. Amaro admired the jungle below as the chopper climbed. He saw the shadow of the Huey rise and fall on the contours of the land. Rain forests of emerald and blue-green stretched outward toward the horizon. Sunlight reflected from thin blue-white ribbons threading several valleys. Ancient terraced hillsides appeared as clam-shaped steppes.

Rugged mountains, primitive and uncultivated, rose upward along the horizon. In valleys were villages and rice paddies. Then came rolling hills and green canopy topped by protruding layers. This part of the earth seemed unchanged since the time of the great reptiles. Amaro expected to see something being eaten alive down there under the chopper's wasplike shadow.

Forty minutes out the Huey began its descent. Amaro saw the grassy hilltop but did not realize it was the landing zone until the chopper came down to treetop level directly above it. The troopers below were concealed by the canopy, blending into the foliage like chameleons. Displaced air flattened knee-high grass in a circle as the Huey touched down.

When the replacements jumped from the chopper, several troopers approached, knees bent and shoulders hunched. The noncom in charge was black. MCGEE it said on his name tag. He had E-7 chevrons pinned on his lapel, a black metal pin.

McGee welcomed Crawford and Moose with a nod. Amaro handed him the laundry bag. The troopers off-loaded supplies.

"Sergeant Watts told me to give this to you," Amaro said.

The sergeant took the bag and dropped it on the dirt. He took a pad and pencil from his trouser-leg pocket. McGee was in his early thirties, average looking, quiet, competent. Amaro liked him right off.

"My name is McGee—your platoon sergeant," he said. "Give me your names and service numbers," and he wrote the information on his pad. "Lieutenant Graham is the platoon leader," he said, turning his head from side to side. "He's around here someplace."

The E-7 squatted over the laundry bag and pulled out four string-tied packs of letters. He stood up and handed Amaro the stack marked FIRST SQUAD. He handed the mail for the second squad to Lee. He pointed to a tall, heavyset guy in his twenties. "That's Russell, your squad leader," he said to Amaro and Everly. "Bring him the mail and he'll square you away."

Amaro turned to Lee as McGee sauntered off. "See you later," he said.

"Yeah," Lee replied. "Be cool."

Sergeant Russell wrote Amaro's name and service number in his notebook, too. Then Everly's. "You're lucky," he said. "McGee's the best platoon sergeant in the outfit. He's a good guy. You got any troubles, come see me and we'll talk it over with the Sarge. Lieutenant Graham ain't worth the shit it took to make him and the Old Man is even worse. But you didn't hear that from me. McGee is the chief honcho around here, as far as I'm concerned. He's a *good* guy."

Amaro and Everly followed Russell along the perimeter. The troops were rummaging through the boxes of supplies, fighting over cartons of Marlboro and making deals for their favorite candy. They loaded up on envelopes and writing paper, packets of iced-tea mix, bottles of redhot sauce, and ammunition. Russell stopped in front of two guys busy dividing a case of Cs between them.

"This is Amaro, your new roommate," Russell said. "C'mon, Everly."

The guy with dark eyes and a four-day stubble on his chin looked up. "I'm Martin," he said. "And this is Fitzgerald."

"How you doin'," Amaro said.

"What a fucking question," Fitzgerald said, without looking up. All Amaro could see of the guy was curly orange hair.

Amaro dropped his rucksack and leaned against it as he sat on the grass. None of the squad paid any attention to him. He was the new guy, living confirmation the guy he was replacing would not be coming back.

Amaro scanned the jungle: the soil, dark and rich; the earth, dank and mildewed. Thick canopy blocked sunlight. Vines from the rain-forest floor wound around rough-barked trunks of bizarre trees. Palm fronds waved shadows over the lower-growing shrubs. It all seemed vibrantly alive.

Martin and Fitzgerald listened up for their names during mail call. Fitzgerald's sullen face brightened: a letter from home. Amaro had moved around. His mail hadn't followed. He hoped it would catch up with him soon. He knew he needed some sort of contact with someone he loved and who loved him. Funny. He was never really alone, yet he was often very lonely. He sat back and composed his next letter home in his head.

The platoon medic walked the perimeter, stopping at each position. "Who the fuck are you?" he asked when he reached Amaro.

"My name's Amaro. I came out on resupply."

"I'm Spector. The *bak-si*. You take your salt today?"

"No. I forgot."

Spector shook two salt tablets from the large white plastic container in his hand. "Here. *Bon appétit*," he said, then turned to Martin and Fitzgerald. "How about Martin and Lewis? You guys need some?"

"No," they each said.

"Well, see you gentlemen in the morning. *Au revoir*." He walked away.

"What a fuckin' asshole," Fitzgerald said, loud enough for Spector to hear.

The medic kept on walking, giving Fitzgerald the finger behind his back without turning around.

Russell came up to the neighboring hole where Everly

was and gave the word to stand by. Everly stood and pulled on his rucksack.

"Didn't Watts give you any machine-gun ammo?" Russell said.

"Yeah."

"Where is it?"

"In my rucksack."

"A lotta fuckin' good it's gonna do in there," Russell said, shaking his head. "Square the cherry away."

Amaro showed Everly how to adjust the ammo in two bandoliers. Then Amaro pulled his rucksack on and crossed a bandolier over each shoulder. Everly followed suit.

Amaro fell in with Martin. Fitzgerald rolled his eyes. "Keep between Martin and me," he said. "Try not to get lost." Under his breath he muttered, "Fuckin' new guy."

Martin led them to their humping position behind the gun crew. The company formed up and moved off the hillside in a single file. Amaro only saw the guys immediately in front of and behind him. He had no idea at all of where he was. He stood in an unfamiliar place bracketed by strangers.

Amaro felt apprehensive and alone as he stumbled off the hilltop and descended the slope into the darkly shadowed valley.

The company split up when it reached the valley bottom. The first and second platoons crossed the valley and humped parallel to the third and fourth platoons, following the contours of the land as the unit swept the sector.

The air was humid and still under the canopy. Light did not travel in a straight line but wavered in space. Everything seemed to shimmer.

The saltsweat burned. He pushed vine-tangled branches from his path and kept his footing on the slick green leaves as he scanned the canopy and understory for snipers.

His rucksack grew heavier as the day wore on. A sharp pain stabbed his lower back. The heat and heavy air closed on him. He listened to their dull footsteps, the murmur of voices, the rattle and clink of the march. He had trouble breathing, trouble just standing up. The rain forest was far from beautiful when you were trapped inside it.

During a short smoke break Amaro slumped to the damp ground and leaned on his rucksack. He closed his eyes and tried to think.

"*Snake,*" Fitzgerald yelled.

Amaro tried to jump to his feet but the weight of his rucksack pulled him off-balance. He struggled like a turtle on its back.

"Relax," Martin said. "He just meant you should keep your eyes open."

"Fuck," Amaro said. He lit a cigarette, not knowing what else to do.

"You'll get used to it again," Martin said in Everly's direction. "It takes a few days of gettin' used to. Sometimes humpin' gets so bad you hope to make contact just so you can drop your rucksack for a while and lay down in the dirt."

"That's for sure," Fitzgerald added. "But you never get used to it."

Martin looked at his watch, then at Amaro. "We'll be settin' up for the night soon. You'll feel better after chow and some rest. The hardest part is still ahead of us."

"What do you mean?" Everly said.

"After humpin' all day we climb the highest fuckin' hill in town and set up a perimeter. Somethin' about it bein' easier to defend the high ground or some such bullshit."

"Bullshit is right," Fitzgerald said. "It's a real ballbuster. If you think you're tired now, wait till we get ready to set up."

The platoon prepared to move out. Martin stretched a hand to Amaro and helped him to his feet. "Keep your eyes open," he said. "I can smell Charlie."

They moved uphill. Amaro found himself constantly leaning forward to keep from being pulled backward by the dead weight of his rucksack. The climb became so steep he had to grope with both hands for roots and vines firm enough to pull himself up with.

The incline leveled off gradually and the file halted just before reaching the crest of the hill. The two platoons were deployed in a circle around and just below the hilltop.

They set up in three-man positions at ten-meter intervals. Martin selected a spot next to some bushes. The machine gun was set on the right flank; a rifle team to the left. They dropped their rucksacks and sat down, lighting smokes and staring downhill.

The air felt a little cooler and smelled fresher. Amaro drew several deep breaths and gazed at the scenic view: the darkening gray-green hills across the valley and the textured roundness of the emergent layer on the slopes and ridgelines in the distance.

"You got a tripflare or a claymore?" Martin asked.

"A claymore," Amaro said.

"Good. Get it out and come with me."

Amaro followed him out to a point ten meters directly in front of the position. Martin took the claymore and set it, convex side downhill, away from them. He inserted the metal fuse and walked the wire back up to the position. Amaro knelt behind the claymore and scanned the foliage. Martin set out again and Amaro followed him to a point several meters farther downhill. Martin took the ends of two separate lengths of thin metal wire and twisted them around a skinny tree trunk six inches off the ground. Amaro took one of the wires and stretched it out across the claymore's blast pattern. He tied a cylindrical flare to another tree, fastened the loose end of the wire to a ring on the flare, and straightened out the cotter pin. Martin turned to Amaro.

"Whatever you do, don't trip it," he said. "Those fuckers up there will light us up sure as shit."

Amaro carefully avoided the tripwire as they walked back along it to set up the second flare on the other side. Up in the position Martin took the detonator and set it on a rock.

"If you see those flares go off during the night the first thing you do is squeeze the detonator. Got that?"

Amaro nodded.

Fitzgerald made a stove from a bread can. He poured some water into his canteen cup, untied the knot in the top of a sock, and measured out some captured rice in the palm of his hand. He dumped the unhulled rice into the cup, lit the blue heat tab in the stove, and set the canteen cup on the fire to boil.

Amaro cooked a can of beef and potatoes. He spooned soft rice into his canteen cup, poured in the Cs, and doused it with hot sauce. He felt hungry enough to eat anything.

After chow, Fitzgerald sat leaning against a tree writing home in a pad resting on his lap. Martin nudged Amaro with his foot. "Come on," he said. "I'll introduce you to the neighbors."

They walked over to the gun position. Vernon, the machine gunner, sat behind the gun clipping together ammo belts collected from the squad. He had a triangular, flat face and a head that seemed too small for his body. His nose was bulbous and fleshy, like a clay figure-eight someone misplaced in the middle of his face. His mouth was small but his lips thick, locked in perpetual pucker. A two-inch-wide band of hair, cut Mohawk-style from front to back, separated the stubbled halves of his head.

"*This* is Vernon," Martin said. "The ugliest motherfucker in the world."

"And the number-one meanest," Vernon said.

"My name's Amaro."

Vernon looked up with cold blue eyes under pale brows. "Howdy," he said. His lips barely moved when he spoke.

"I told you he was ugly," Martin said. "And crazy. This is his second tour."

"No lie," Amaro said.

"No lie." Vernon smiled. "I was here with the One-seventy-third when y'all was still shittin' yaller."

"He loves it here," Martin said.

"Fuckin' A tweet." Vernon started to sing: "*I love it here, I love it here. Fuckin' A, I love it here . . .*"

Martin turned to the guy with the round face and the broken nose sitting next to Vernon. "Hey, Tigerbaum," he said. "Meet Amaro. Tigerbaum is the brigade's token Jew."

"It is my lot in life to lead you slobs out of bondage," Tigerbaum said.

"Are y'all comin' by later?" Vernon asked.

"Yeah," Martin replied. "Where's Johnny Vanilla?"

"Out somewheres hearin' voices I reckon. We'll find an errand for him to run if he comes back too soon." Vernon spit his plug on the ground and started working a fresh chew.

"Who's Johnny Vanilla?" Amaro asked, as they walked back to their position.

"The third stooge," Martin replied. "A doofis guy from

North Carolina. He's the ammo bearer. You know, the guy that came by before to collect the belts."

"Oh, yeah."

"His name's Goober or Gore, or somethin'. Was raised on a mountain by his dear old mother, a spinster aunt, and three old-maid sisters. He didn't believe Tigerbaum was Jewish because he thought Jews had horns."

"How'd he wind up here?" Amaro asked.

"That's what he'd like to know. He's been here a couple of months and he still looks like a fuckin' glass of milk. No beard. Don't shave. His voice never changed and he don't get a tan. None of us believe he's fuckin' human."

Martin and Fitzgerald left the position and walked over to the gun. Amaro sat near the detonator. He heard muffled laughter coming from the right flank and smelled the aroma of potsmoke. It smelled like primo reefer, light and flowery. Amaro wished he had a joint, but he had no stash and no one as yet offered to duke him into any.

Amaro heard footsteps approaching from the right. He looked up and saw Johnny Vanilla, white-faced and eyeglassed, standing next to him.

"Evenin', neighbor," the young man said, his voice soft and high-pitched.

Amaro smiled. "Yeah. Well, clean your feet on the rug and sit a spell," he said.

Johnny Vanilla sat cross-legged on the dirt. "Vernon and Martin told me to come over here to keep you company, seein' as how you're a new guy and all."

"I appreciate it," Amaro said.

"My name is John Storz. You're Amara, right?"

"Yeah."

"Martin told me you're I-talian. Are you I-talian?"

"Yeah." Amaro fought back a smile. It was hard for him to believe Johnny Vanilla was for real.

"Them guys tell me all kinds of things. It's gettin' so's I kin hardly believe a word they say."

"What do they tell you?"

"Oh, Lord. Dreadful things. Just awful. They're such hateful people. I never met the likes of them before. Always cussin' an' a takin' the name of the Lord in vain. An' Vernon always a spittin'. No sir, I never met their likes before. They're bound for hell, no doubt about it."

Amaro nodded. "Looks like we're already here."

"Yes. I do believe you may be right. Sometimes I feel like that when I'm alone with those two heathrens. Lord, how they do torment me so. Do you pray?"

"No."

"You should, you know. You really ought to."

Martin and Fitzgerald stumbled into the position.

"Time to go home, milkface," Fitzgerald said.

Johnny Vanilla jumped to his feet. "Good night, Mistah Amara. It was a pleasure to make your acquaintance."

"Yeah. Good night."

Johnny Vanilla left.

"Christ," Amaro said.

"Exactly," Martin said. "We expected to come home and find you guys just a kneelin' an' a prayin'."

"Or barkin' at the fuckin' moon," Fitzgerald said. "Praise da Lawwwd."

"He's really a case, eh?" Amaro said.

Fitzgerald snickered, "You ain't said snack bar, son. Wait till he tries to save you. He thinks it's a sin to meet a backslider and not try to save him."

"Especially out here," Martin said. "He feels real close to his maker out here. He don't want to die with no sins on his soul. He takes this savin' business serious. Even Vernon and Tigerbaum can't wear him down. And they really try hard."

"I'll bet," Amaro said, shaking his head.

The company settled in for the night. The watch started around nine. Each man stood guard for ninety minutes while the other two slept. Martin took the first watch. Amaro unrolled his poncho and sat on it. He started to unlace his jungle boots.

"I wouldn't do that," Martin said. "If we make contact you'll be runnin' around here barefoot."

"Just scratching an itch," Amaro said. He snapped one end of the GP strap to the swivel on his piece and hooked the other to a belt loop. He propped his rifle against the trunk of a tree, laid back on the poncho, and fell instantly into a deep sleep.

Martin shook Amaro awake. Amaro's eyelids felt heavy. His mouth was dry and foul tasting. He splashed water on his face and swallowed a few sips. He felt cranky and annoyed.

"Here," Martin said as he handed him the watch with a luminescent dial. "Wake Fitz at midnight. Keep your eyes open and if you gotta smoke do it under a poncho."

Martin crawled off and fell asleep on the dirt. Amaro took up a position behind the detonator. He lay down on his stomach but it felt too comfortable. He nodded once or twice, then sat upright. He fought off the urge to fall asleep and forced his eyes open.

The jungle was alive. During the day the animals shaded up and rested. At night, when the air was cooler, they came out. Rats and other rodents scurried across the rain-forest floor. Treeborne monkeys chattered and howled—eerie shrieks. Birds of prey circled above, shadowed and silent.

Amaro heard the rustle of branches and the snap of twigs—maybe the muted snap of bones bitten through—and he was frightened more than once by the sounds of life and death. He listened to the snores and murmurs of the guys in his squad.

Amaro felt hungry but was afraid to eat. He wanted to smoke but was afraid to light up. So he sat and watched and listened. Under the cover of night noise and starless black anything could happen, but the darkness felt safer. It was no doubt a foolish belief, like the one he clung to in his first firefight: if he didn't kill any of the enemy, then none of them would kill him. Kind of a tacit spiritual agreement. But of course it hadn't worked that way.

3

First call was before dawn. The perimeter came to life with slow, shadowy movements. Amaro felt clammy and damp. Everything was spotted by drops of condensing moisture. He sat up on the dirt and scratched his itchy scalp.

They prepared breakfast in silence. Amaro opened a bread can and made a stove out of it. He spread peanut butter and jelly on the bread as some water came to a boil. He stirred an envelope of cocoa and one of powdered milk, and three packets of sugar, into the boiling water, then set his canteen cup on the dirt to cool. He bit the bread, not caring that ants had gotten to it first. They crawled all over it.

Spector walked into the position. "*Bon jour, tout le monde,*" he said while giving out salt tablets.

"Fuck you," Fitzgerald said, popping salt in his mouth and washing it down with Kool-Aid. "You ever been to fuckin' France?"

"*Certainement.* Many times. In my soul. In my dreams. I spent last night at my villa in Bordeaux with Brigitte and sweet Monique."

"You're an asshole," Fitzgerald said.

"Perhaps. But you, *vous êtes un cafard, mon ami.*" Spector ambled to the next position.

"He's as crazy as a shit-eatin' rat," Fitzgerald said.

"Maybe," Martin said. "But he's a good guy to have around." He turned to Amaro. "Spec'll do anything for a guy who gets hit. He's got balls."

Amaro felt the hot cocoa working in his bowels. He shoved a small roll of toilet paper in his pocket, picked up his weapon, and walked out of the perimeter. He chose a spot between two thin trees on the safe side of the claymore and kicked a shallow hole in the duff with the toe of his jungle boot. He propped his rifle against one of the trees and dropped his fatigues to his ankles. Holding the trees for support he squatted and leaned back as far as he could to keep from crapping on himself.

He felt ridiculous and scared to death. It would be embarrassing to get blown away like this. Would the telegram from the Defense Department make note of it? Amaro, John P., killed in action while taking his morning shit in the mountainous region northwest of Duc Pho, Republic of South Vietnam. His friends back home would have a laugh about it over beers in Tobin's Bar. They'd say, Johnny got it while shooting a moon at them Congs. That's what they'd say, then have a beer and watch the game and scheme how to get laid. It never happened to John Wayne. No one ever had a bowel movement in a war movie.

His watery stool spurted and squirted in the dirt. Amaro wiped himself, pulled up his pants, and kicked loose dirt over the slimy waste.

Back at the position they pulled in the claymore and tripflares, packed their rucksacks, and collected the machine-gun ammo belts from Johnny Vanilla. They sat smoking cigarettes, awaiting the word to move out.

Russell approached them. "First squad's got point today," he said. "Martin and Fitzgerald up front. Amaro, you hang out with the gun crew until you get to know what's happenin'."

The guys saddled their rucksacks and shuffled along the path. Amaro fell in behind Johnny Vanilla.

Fitzgerald moved to the front of the file and took the point. Martin took up his slack, scanning the flanks while the point man concentrated on the trail.

The point team started down off the hill following the same trail they walked up the night before, Fitzgerald first, Martin ten meters behind him. Russell, Evans with the radio, and a rifleman named Flowers, followed at a thirty-meter space. Tigerbaum led the gun crew, then came Vernon, Johnny Vanilla, and Amaro. Jesse Farias, a small Mexican rifleman, humped behind Amaro bringing up the rear.

Sergeant McGee, his radioman, and Spector headed the main body of the file behind the point. The column moved slowly down off the hill, then stopped.

"What's goin' on?" Johnny Vanilla asked.

"How the fuck do I know?" Vernon answered.

A sharp crack echoed in the valley. Martin yelled, "*Medic, Medic,*" above the small-arms fire. They all fell flat and got tight. They listened to the gunfire.

"Come with me," Russell said. They jumped to their feet and trotted forward.

He led them to the spot where the slope dropped steeply. Down below Martin sprayed the trees. "*Get a medic down here,*" he screamed.

Vernon set up quickly and fanned tracers downhill, splintering the trees in his field of fire. Tigerbaum clipped ammo belts together as Johnny Vanilla dropped them next to the gun. Spector ran forward carrying his first-aid pack.

They dropped their rucksacks and Russell led them at a run downhill. A couple of them fired as they moved. Everly lost his footing, tripped, and fell, slamming hard into Fitzgerald's body. He lay there and stared at the hole in Fitzgerald's chest. Open-mouthed, orange-haired, lifeless Fitzgerald never knew what hit him or what happened after that round stopped his heart.

"*What* are you waitin' on?" Russell hollered.

Everly rolled over and got up on one knee. He clicked off the safety and fired a round between Flowers and Farias. The Mexican turned around.

"What the *fuck!*" he screamed. "Do that again an' I kill your dumb ass." Farias turned back and continued to fire on automatic. "Motherfucker *dumbass* cherry," he screamed, slapping a fresh magazine in the well.

Amaro crawled up to the line and fired into the bush. He could see nothing to aim at.

"He's bought it," Spector said. He clicked his weapon to automatic and joined the others spitting rounds in every direction. Johnny Vanilla fired from above with the grenade launcher.

"*Eat shit and die,*" Vernon shouted over the hammer of the sixty.

The machine-gun firing stopped. There were no more explosions. Russell gave the ceasefire. The squad remained still, scanning the jungle. Nothing moved. Amaro once again felt his heart beat.

"They gone," Flowers said.

"I think you're right," Russell said. "A sniper."

McGee and the second squad came downhill carrying the gear the point squad had left behind.

Farias cut down two saplings with his machete and made a litter with a poncho. Amaro looked at the blood-smeared body wallowing in its own shock-released waste and felt something strange, something he could not explain to himself.

Spector reached down and closed the wide-open eyes of the corpse. Amaro turned away and shut his own.

He was afraid of the suddenly dead. Not of the body but of what it meant. And then he felt calm—cold. If that's what it is then that's what it is, he said to himself. What it is, man. Jive me five. What it *is*, motherfucker. What it is *is* a motherfucker. What it is. And the coldness spread from within to touch his skin.

He stared at the poncho-wrapped body waiting in the shade for dustoff back to the world.

The company regrouped in the valley and humped back up to the landing zone that had been used the day before for resupply. No one spoke. They rested, opened cans of fruit, smoked cigarettes, wrote home. But no one spoke.

Amaro thought about being dead. He knew at some point they would all be dusted off. At different times, from different places.

They climbed another hill that night. Martin and Amaro cooked their Cs and set the claymore and flares. Amaro felt like talking but kept it to himself when he saw the way Martin just stared into space. He wrote a letter home. Occasionally he looked up at Martin and tried to figure out what the guy was thinking about. He guessed it was the sniper and Fitzgerald.

Amaro thought back to the firefight. It hadn't been much really. No bodycount. No enemy seen. Just the jungle, and it was the jungle at which they fired their weapons. The bullets ripped through the tangle as if it were animate and responsible for the death.

Other guys died. They figured in the statistics. Not him. He could not imagine being dead. He was too alive to even sleep.

He ran his fingertips over the plastic front stock of his piece. He felt the nicks and scratches, felt the ridges with his fingertips. He pressed a palm in the dirt—dry, spongy. It gave a little when he pushed. He leaned forward and touched the soles of his boots. Hard rubber cubes. Then the firm leather and scratchy canvas. Laces crisscrossed and tightly tied. He touched his hair, the skin on his face, his fatigues, an ammo pouch. He touched these things and recorded the textures, measured the differences between them.

He was fascinated by all the things around him, by the details of himself. He wanted to touch everything he could reach, like that rock near the detonator. Not any rock, that particular rock—gray-black, smooth, with a wedge chipped from it, as if hit by an ax.

It was important to him, that rock, because it was there with him in this very space at this specific time. That meant something to him, a kinship he had never felt, not even with friends or family. That rock was with him now, sharing this jungle night, the both of them surrounded by shrubs doing slow dances in the darkness. Wavering, slithering. He heard a muffled laugh from a nearby position.

A tree monkey screeched. His stomach fluttered, his heart beat fast, pounding hard inside his ribs, threatening to explode a hole like that ugly mess in Fitzgerald's chest.

He did not feel the way he was told a soldier ought to feel. He did not feel the way he was told a man ought to feel. All he knew for sure was how he felt when he stared at the dead guy with the silly orange hair and that ugly hole where his heart should have been.

Amaro knew he was no soldier. Now he knew he was no hero, maybe not even much of a man. He'd have to live with that. Being alive and able to feel disgusted with himself was better than being dead and not feeling anything at all.

He looked over at Martin and knew what the guy was thinking. Amaro smelled the jungle and his own odor. He listened to the night noise of the rain forest. He saw again Fitzgerald's eyes staring blankly skyward. The coldness returned.

"If that's what it is, then that's what it is," he said. Martin said nothing.

Amaro knew it was Monday because Spector handed out Dapsone along with the salt.

"Tastes awful," he said.

"I know." Spector nodded agreement.

Amaro pulled off his damp jacket and tried to dry it by waving it around. It had rained and his clothes were wet. They clung to him all night, cold and heavy.

"That won't do any good," Spector said. "Wait for the sun to get hot."

"Yeah," Amaro said.

"Except that by then your shirt will be soaked with sweat," Spector said. "You can't win for losing."

"Hey. You want some cocoa?" Amaro said to Martin.

"No."

"How about some jelly and bread?"

"No thanks."

"I got fruit cocktail."

"You eat it," Martin said. He turned away.

"What a lousy night. I'm going to catch pneumonia or some damn thing," Amaro said.

Martin did not answer him.

"You know you got to eat something."

"Why don't you shut the fuck up," Martin said.

Amaro pulled in the claymore and flares. He packed his rucksack and started another letter home. He belched and tasted bitter quinine in his throat.

They humped a wooded area, more like forest than jungle. The first squad marched somewhere near the middle of the file. Pho Dot Province, Amaro had heard someone say. Pho Dot Province. So what? Amaro said to himself. It all looked the same. The names meant nothing. He never really knew where he was. I'm in my boots, he'd say to himself.

The bush got thick on some of the hills. Plants with spikes and thorns ripped his fatigues and scratched red welts into his skin. Razor-sharp elephant grass, tall as a tree, sliced clean cuts on his hands and arms and face. They walked through a sea of it between hills. In the shade of a bamboo grove the company stopped for chow.

"Eat quick," Russell said to Amaro. "You're goin' on water run."

Amaro wolfed his pound cake and washed it down with peach juice. He left half of the peaches for Martin.

Amaro and Farias reported to Russell carrying the squad's empty canteens hanging from D-rings and GP straps over their shoulders.

Sergeant Romo of the third squad led the detail off the hill. Romo had a *Playboy* bunny inked on both sides of his helmet. Ears, pointed nose, even a sharp bow tie, were cross-hatched on the cloth camouflage.

A stream ran through the shallow valley just beyond the bamboo. As half the detail stood guard, the rest filled canteens. Some washed up and shaved, others soaked their feet.

Amaro took a mouthful from the creek and spit it back out. It tasted rotten. It reminded him of the way a sewer smelled back home in autumn, clogged with fallen leaves, after a hard rain.

"Are you stupid?" Farias said. "Don't drink this stuff till it's treated."

"*Hey,* Sarge," a trooper shouted. It was a guy Amaro did not know. "There's a dead water buffalo upstream."

Romo shook his head, his dark round face twisted with his thoughts. He hated to make decisions. "Fuck it," he said. "Don't tell nobody about it up top."

Back in the grove atop the hill the troopers dosed their canteens with Halazone and, if they had some, iced-tea mix and Kool-Aid.

Amaro relaxed against the bamboo, brushed ants from the rim of the can, and ate the hot peaches Martin had not touched.

They marched in the rut of a dry streambed. It was shallow except where monsoons had washed away the clay, making the banks shoulder high. Amaro lit a smoke.

He saw Vernon pointing to his right flank. The gunner stopped in his tracks, hawked phlegm and spat it toward where he was pointing. Johnny Vanilla passed the spot and tipped his helmet brim.

When Amaro reached the spot, a place where the stream bank rose almost straight up, he saw a field shelter dug in the mud. It was carved like a pocket in the bank among the roots of the growth overhead. Empty ration cans, candy wrappers, bullets, bits of paper, salt tabs, dirty socks, a pair of ripped skivvies, and other trash had been chucked into the shelter, littering the black and bloated body of a VC.

It lay on its side, head resting on arms, knees pulled up to its chest. Amaro saw white maggots bubbling in its eyes. They swarmed on its nose and crawled where lips used to be. The stink was oddly familiar. It smelled like the gristle in the cracks of the floor at a butcher shop. Amaro flicked his cigarette butt, hitting the dead thing square in its chest.

Back in Duc Pho the company stood at attention for reveille and the dead. Six pairs of jungle boots were lined up before the formation. Six rifles, inverted, stood behind them, each topped with a camouflaged helmet. Taps hung in the air.

After chow Amaro and Lee drew clean fatigues, then waited on line at the shower point. The saltwater shower burned the cuts on Amaro's skin, but he got used to it. It felt good to be clean. For a while the ant and mosquito bites on his hands and face did not itch.

When he and Lee returned to the company area there were Vietnamese civilians about.

"What's going on?" Amaro asked.

"Them's KPs," Vernon replied. "And that one there is the barber." He pointed to an old man in faded fatigues standing next to a wooden chair under a tree. A crooked table had a bowl of water and some barber tools on it. A rectangular mirror hung from the trunk of the tree by a string.

Amaro's hair was curly. Hard to comb.

"You want number-one hakkut, Joe?" the barber asked. His skin was parchment, his few teeth were the color of dirt.

"Use the clipper," Amaro said, sitting in the chair. "Make it real short, papasan."

"I give number one hakkut," the old man said.

The handheld clipper pinched his neck and seemed to pull hair by the roots. The haircut was uneven, with lines like a fresh-mown lawn. But it would do.

He paid the barber and walked to the platoon area looking for Spector. He found the medic sitting on the sandbags next to his pup tent.

"Yo, Doc. You got to help me out," Amaro said. "This itch is driving me crazy."

Spector looked at the lesions and said, "Take these." He shook a couple of tablets from a bottle. He poured calamine lotion onto a cottonball and dabbed it on the bites. "This will help for now."

Amaro felt the lotion dry and cool his skin. "Thanks," he said.

"Try not to scratch at them too much. It might cause an infection or impetigo." Spector looked up. "I recommend thirty days in Arizona."

"Sounds good."

Johnny Vanilla approached them carrying his weapon on his shoulder like a fishing pole. Spector said, "Here comes Opie."

"Mornin'," Johnny Vanilla said. "Sergeant Watts is a lookin' high an' low for ya, Amara."

"What for?"

"He didn't say. But he's waitin' on ya in the CP."

Amaro thanked Spector for the help and went to his tent. He ate a can of pears then strolled to the CP.

"Where you been?" Watts asked.

"Shit, shower, shave and a haircut . . ."

"That so? Grab your web gear and get back here in five minutes. You're on trash point detail."

Amaro gathered up his stuff and climbed onto the back of a pickup with a half-dozen other guys. One of them lounged against the cab, the bright light bouncing from his sunglasses.

His skin was clear and tanned. He had a decent haircut and wore new fatigues and looked like a new guy, except for his boots. These were worn and scratched. This guy had been around, too.

The truck drove through the forward base camp, passing the other battalions, the support groups, and the rock-outlined tents of brigade headquarters. They were like different neighborhoods. The truck stopped in the low-rent district at the edge of a wide, sprawling garbage dump.

Amaro and the guy in sunglasses were assigned to the same bunker. Not a bunker really. More a waist-deep foxhole with sandbag sides coming up to shoulder height.

The two guys they replaced walked quickly past them without saying a word and hopped on the truck.

The guy in the sunglasses dropped his gear in the hole and sat back against the sandbags facing the sun, soaking rays.

Amaro scanned the hills of trash. Just one big hole, ringed with bulldozed dirt. He could make out empty C-ration cartons. The dump was filled with them. Here and there the sun glinted off a shiny number-ten can. He saw Vietnamese climbing over the piles of garbage.

"Hey. There's gooks out there," Amaro said.

"There's always gooks out there," the guy said without looking.

"What do we do about it?"

"We're supposed to fire a warning shot over their heads. If they don't move, kill them."

"They look like kids."

"They are kids," the guy said. He took off his sunglasses and rubbed his eyes. "According to MACV they use empty cans to make land mines."

"No shit?"

The guy laughed and shook his head. "Why, when the VC can get claymores and grenades right off the docks? Those kids are looking for something to eat. If they get lucky maybe some clothes, too."

Amaro watched the children rummaging through cardboard and tin, running barefoot over the sharp metal. One of them, one of the taller kids, carried what looked like a burlap sack. He waved something over his head and shouted to the others. They joined him and dug quickly around where he was standing, finding things and tossing them into the bags they carried.

"Your name's Amaro, ain't it?" the guy asked.

"Yeah."

"From New York. That right?"

"Yeah. Brooklyn. And you?"

"Jersey. Carlstadt."

"I know where that is. What's your name?"

"Malone."

Amaro reached over and shook his hand.

"How long you been in country?" Amaro asked.

"Six months. I just got back from R and R in Bangkok."

"I heard that's a pretty nice place."

"It's a great place. The food, the women . . . goddamn, I hated to come back." He glanced at Amaro. "And you? How long you been in this shit war?"

"A hundred years."

"You were demoted."

"Yeah," Amaro said. "I was demoted."

"Amaro, you get high?"

"Yeah. But not lately."

"Some guys can't handle it here," Malone said.

"It's not that. I can't seem to score any reefer."

"The guys are careful. This outfit is chickenshit when it comes to guys getting high. Always sending CID to bust us."

"What for?"

"Who knows? But if they pop you, it's six months in the Long Binh Jail. It's all bad time, too. When you get out of LBJ you still got to put in your full three-sixty-five in the boonies."

"I've smelled it around here but nobody's offered to turn me on."

"You never know who's CID and who ain't. Lieutenants and captains making out to be privates. It's a fucking joke," Malone said. "Couple of months ago we killed one sneaking up on a field position at night."

Malone pulled two units of Cs from the field pack on his web gear. He held them up over his head.

"Hey," he shouted. "You slant-eyed soon-to-be-gook motherfuckers. Come here."

The tall kid approached carefully.

Malone showed him the Cs. "You got *dinky-dau* cigarettes? You bring *dinky-dau* cigarettes. I give *sop-sop*."

"Sure, Joe, sure," the kid said. "I bring. You wait. Number-one *dinky-dau* smokes, Joe."

"Better be, slopehead. Or I'll feed you to the rats."

"No worry, Joe. I bring number-fuckin'-one top stuff. You wait. Okay?" The kid ran along the edge of the dump and disappeared in the bush. The younger ones returned to the garbage.

"You can cop from the barber and some of the KPs, too," Malone said. "But make sure you get ready-rolls from them. Sometimes the loose stuff is shit."

"I'll remember that," Amaro said.

The kid came back and held out a sealed plastic bag with five thick joints in it. "You give *sop-sop* now, Joe," he said.

Malone handed him a unit of Cs.

"Two box *sop-sop*," the kid said.

"Bullshit, dink. Two bag *dinky-dau*. Two box *sop-sop*."

The kid reached under his shirt and pulled out another bag.

"That's better, little Ho."

They made the exchange. The kid ran away.

Malone ripped open a pack and took out two joints. "Hold these," he said. Then he got up and walked away from the bunker. He kicked a hole in the dirt, stashed the other eight, and covered them with a piece of cardboard. "If it's more than thirty feet away they can't prove it's yours," he said.

They sat facing each other, covering their backs, and fired up the joints.

"So you made four the hard way," Malone said.

"Yeah," Amaro wiped his eyes. "I made E-5 right away. Shit. It happened even before I knew what was going on. Guys getting hit. Company understrength. They handed out stripes like ice in the Arctic."

"So what'd you do? Get popped holding tickets to a magic carpet ride?"

"No. I know a couple of tricks when it comes to that," Amaro said. He took a long toke and held it in. "They'll never catch me dirty. No. It was right after I made five. Me and my squad went out on a night ambush. We set up, didn't have the slightest fucking idea. Anyway, we set up near this trail and waited. Hours. Then we heard them coming and it chilled our shit. And there's all these guys, guys in the squad, and they're looking at me like, hey, what are we going to do? and I said to myself we ain't going to do nothing unless we have to. Why look for trouble? Why bust chops? Know what I mean?"

"I hear ya," Malone said. "It's fucking crazy to pick a fight at night on their turf."

"Exactly. So I held fire and the fuckers walked right past us, big as could be. I was in tight with my squad after that."

"So why did you get busted back to E-4?"

Amaro looked around the garbage dump. Kids climbed trash hills along the distant rim. "Because the gooks we were supposed to ambush stumbled right into the fucking perimeter and a whole bunch of grief broke loose."

Malone laughed out loud. "The humbug is the one fucking thing there's no protection from. I'll be damned if it don't fly up and bite you on the ass the minute you think things are cool."

The reefer hit Amaro like a truck. He felt his head get light, his mouth go dry. The heat was more intense. So was the garbage stink. His skin burned and itched but he did not scratch it.

Sunlight lined the hill of garbage. In his unfocused eyes the stripes doubled, tripled, seemed to move up and down. He shut his eyes tight. Reopened them. The yellow stripes still moved.

He followed the stripes to where they fell across the emerald mountain under a brilliant cobalt sky. He imagined the green canopy scattering sunlight into small and shapeless patches. Leaf-pattern fragments dappled the ground; shadows wriggled over his skin. He felt them move, cool wherever they touched, wriggled, leaving a cooling slime trail. He admired the sluglike shadows, wrapped in their own excretions, protected from knife-edged obstacles and the drying, biting wind.

The scent of herbs filled the air—flowers and rich, moist earth. It tickled where the insects nibbled. He smiled.

"Where the fuck are we?" he said.

"Fucked if I know," Malone answered.

4

The operation began with a heliborne assault in deep swampland. The landing zone was cold.

Amaro splashed in knee-high mud, trying hard to keep his balance, not wanting to get covered with muck. Some of the guys fell in. They cursed and rinsed their hair with fresh water. The others laughed.

"Who farted?" Malone asked.

"It's swamp gas," Vernon said.

Amaro smelled the stink of rotten eggs. It burned his throat like lighting a stick match too close to his nose. He thought it came from the slimy layer of green algae coating the stagnant water. As the troopers slogged waist deep through the slime, they broke the scum surface and stirred the mud. The stink made their eyes tear.

They cut a trail through the algae, passed tall reeds and moss-covered trees. The air was still, heavy, and moisture filled. The canopy blocked any breeze.

Sweat poured and clung, rolling in their eyes, dripping like rainfall off their faces. They humped in silence to the cadence of sucking mud through cloud swarms of mosquitoes.

Then the mud firmed up underfoot. The swamp water grew shallow, the scum less thick. A slight breeze reached them. The jungle air smelled springlike and fresh. Amaro pulled in several deep breaths and slowly came out of his stupor.

On solid ground in a bamboo grove, shards of sunlight

broke through. It was around noon; in the swamp it had seemed like twilight.

"Take twenty for chow," Russell said.

They dropped their rucksacks and lay back exhausted. Amaro did not feel like eating. He was too tired even to light a smoke.

"Open your shirts and drop your drawers, gentlemen," Spector hollered. "I have to check your bods."

Amaro stumbled to his feet and dropped his pants.

"You got pets," Spector said. "Look at this."

Amaro turned and stared at the backs of his legs. From midthigh down past the soft spot behind his knees to his calf, shiny brown-black leeches stretched long and fat, gorging on his blood. His legs were smeared, crusted brown.

"*Fuck,*" Amaro shouted, sick to his stomach. "Get these fuckers off me, man." He reached for a stick to scrape them off with; he did not want to touch them with his hands.

"Easy, my friend," Spector said. "Let's do it the right way."

He squirted mosquito repellent the length of one leech. It slowly released its grip on the skin and began to peel off. Blood flowed from groups of tiny holes.

Amaro used the repellent on his right leg as Spector worked on the other. When the leeches were off his skin and writhing on the dirt, Amaro stomped them with his boot, pulling the ridged soles across, tearing them to shreds. Blood spurted from them like ruptured tubes.

"*God damn it* to hell, that burns," Amaro screamed as Spector poured alcohol on his legs.

"I know," Spector said.

"Yo. *Bak-si.* Come here on the double," Flowers shouted.

Amaro pulled up his pants. The bloodstains dried stiff and black.

Farias sat naked against a tree, his groin covered with blood.

Flowers said, "We got the leeches off his balls but the blood won't stop."

Spector wiped away the blood with a field dressing but more pumped out through the sucker holes.

"Call Russell," Spector said. "We got to dust him off A-SAP."

Russell hustled over. "Can't you do nothin', Doc?" he asked.

"Just use direct pressure to slow it down until the chopper gets here. It's a bad spot. He could bleed out."

"I'll get on the horn to Dutch Uncle and arrange it," Russell said. He got up and walked over to the radioman.

The guys in the squad carried Farias's equipment. The little Mexican walked naked, except for boots and steel pot, pressing gauze and field dressings on his crotch. Blood streamed down his legs and he rolled his eyes and he mumbled something over and over again in Spanish at the dustoff coordinates. The bird came in fast and took him out.

When the medevac left, the company saddled up and started a sweep through some rice fields. Amaro walked on the earthen dikes whenever he could, not wanting to wade through the rice paddy. Abreast, they walked on line in company strength.

The villagers stared from their hooches. Amaro saw old folks mostly, and women and children. The men worked the fields in straw hats and rolled-up pants. When the troopers approached, they moved to the hooches. The women and children huddled around water buffalo laden with baskets of firewood.

Amaro looked at them and wondered what they thought. What they thought about him and the guys and helicopters and jets. They had no plumbing. No electricity. No sinks or stoves or beds or TV sets or anything. Just planted rice today so they could eat tomorrow. He wondered if they'd ever seen ice or tasted beer. Did they know who he was? Who the guys were? Where they all came from? Did they know an invisible B-52 could make a mountain disappear?

Tigerbaum said, "Recon says there's gooks in the treeline. Pass it on."

Before Amaro could relay the word, mortars thumped. Shrapnel and muddy water sprayed the troops. They took cover behind the dikes. Bullets kicked up dirt and whizzed into the water. Some skimmed like flat rocks. The company opened up loud and hot on the treeline.

Something picked Martin up by the head and slammed him backward into the water. Malone lunged after him and pulled him to the dike. He stuck a finger in the hole in Martin's neck, shouting for Spector. The rest of the squad stayed low and put out firepower. Amaro just pointed his piece and squeezed rounds at the woodline.

A curtain of purple smoke rose up in front of them, marking their forward positions, and the Phantoms screamed in low from behind, firing rockets and dropping antipersonnel ordnance. The treeline exploded. The jets banked and circled for another run, vapor trails streaming out after them. Amaro watched them streak over the line, so close he could reach up and touch them. And the ordnance, loosed, falling, slamming the woodline and blowing it to splinters.

Phantoms came in from the flank over the woods, dropping napalm canisters like kegs of beer that tumbled end over end. When they hit, a wall of black smoke went up, and orange flames erupted in a line from the bouncing thing and spread crossways.

The Old Man pulled the fourth platoon back to dry ground to set up a command post. Amaro saw them move out as he sprayed rounds at the jungle. Flowers and Malone low-crawled through the paddy dragging Martin to the aid station.

After the airstrike, the company swept the woodline. There was nothing left but charred jungle and broken trees. No enemy dead. No sign of him at all. Only the dead and wounded guys back in the CP proved there had been any gooks.

They herded the villagers into a group. None of the guys spoke Vietnamese so orders were given with hand signals and rifle muzzles.

The medevacs came in and dusted off the casualties. They left a few five-gallon cans of fuel behind. The Old Man strutted back and forth in front of the villagers. It was the first time Amaro had seen the company commander; he just knew the Old Man called himself Dutch Uncle.

Dutch Uncle puffed on a cigar stub—his AR-15 assault rifle slung barrel down over his shoulder—and yelled at the Vietnamese who stared blankly at him and the guys surrounding them.

"So you think you're smart?" Dutch Uncle screamed. "You think you're so fucking smart? I'll show you what smart is, you stupid sons-of-bitches. I'll teach you to play fuck around with me." He waved to a detail standing near hooches.

Amaro watched the detail search the village. Some weapons were found. They held them up over their heads.

"*See?* See that?" Dutch Uncle said to the villagers. "And you *don't know* what's going on? *When* are you people going to learn?" He turned toward the detail. "*Do it up,*" he shouted.

The detail poured gas on the hooches and zippoed the dry straw. The villagers stood expressionless amidst the crackle and black smoke.

The guys loaded up on the captured rice. Some of the officers grabbed the AK-47s for souvenirs. Charlie Company moved out.

The high ground was too far to hump before dark so they set up on some rocky hills. The air was fresher but still carried a slight sulfur stink from the swamps nearby.

Amaro, Flowers, and Malone set up on a slope between some big rocks. They cleaned their weapons and ammo before starting to cook chow.

Russell said to Malone, "Spector told me what you done out there today."

"I didn't know what else to do," Malone said.

"Doc says you saved Martin's life. I'm puttin' you in for a Bronze Star."

"I'm glad Martin's gonna make it," Malone said.

Amaro said, "That was damn quick thinking."

"Who was thinking?"

They sat around after chow and tried to relax. Amaro noticed Flowers had a gold sleeve slipped over his top front tooth. There was a heart-shaped cut in it and bright white enamel showed through when he smiled.

"Why is the heart upside down?" Amaro asked.

Flowers shrugged. "I don't reckon I know."

At twilight the mosquitoes began swarming. Amaro covered himself with repellent, but as he lay with his feet braced against a rock to keep from sliding downhill, they buzzed in his ears and nose and inside the steel pot he was using for a pillow. He squirted on more repellent and rubbed. It did not help. He tried waving them away and smacked them on his skin. They kept coming. He wrapped himself in a poncho but the heat was too much. He broke a sweat and thought he wiped all the repellent off, so he put on some more. Nothing worked. All night he lay there and listened to the buzzing and felt them biting his skin.

Replacements brought the mail on resupply. There were two thick stacks for Amaro. He thumbed through them quickly, putting them in postdated order. They were from his parents and his sister. He put the letters in two plastic bags and buttoned them into his trouser-leg pockets.

He picked out envelopes and writing paper and bags of M & M's from the sundry box. He took a carton of unfiltered Luckies for himself and packs of Marlboro and Salem to trade with the other guys for cans of fruit or dope.

Two new guys sat together watching the others rummage the sundries. Their boots were still black, their fatigues unstained.

A flare went off in somebody's rucksack. *"Fire in the hole! Fire in the hole!"* Everyone flattened. Two grenades exploded and sent the contents of the rucksack sailing around the perimeter.

In the confusion afterward, Amaro cracked open two cases of C rations and took the fruit from the B-1 units. Then he sat down and read his mail.

His mother had taken a job at Sears to keep herself busy, she said. And his sister just got her new glasses. A letter from his father described the new car: a beauty with a black vinyl top. Amaro smiled. It was the first new car his father ever owned; the others had been used.

"Saddle up," Russell said.

Amaro put his mail away and pulled on his rucksack.

Charlie Company worked a sweep across the rugged ridgelines. Sergeant Romo and the third squad had point. The first squad took up the slack behind Romo's.

There was an explosion up ahead. Then two more. And

rifle fire. And someone screamed, "Help me, dear God. Please help me."

Amaro took cover. He saw Evans, the radioman, dive to the dirt, and a bright green blade of grass wriggled S-shaped, tightened up, and snapped out straight, biting the radioman's cheek. Evans jumped to his feet, his hands on his face, yelling, "Oh shit," and his hands exploded, and his face exploded. He spun around, his helmet flew off, and he landed hard on his chest, spread-eagled.

The other squads came up on line. A couple of guys tried to reach the point but one got hit. The other crawled back.

Sergeant McGee shouted to the point, "Keep down. Keep low. We're firing over your heads."

Help me help me help me. Somebody up front was screaming.

The squads on line low-crawled, firing as they moved. Amaro saw Sergeant Romo curled up on the dirt covered with blood but moving—trying to crawl back to the line. A medic and two other guys dragged him to the CP. Romo's steel pot lay near the dead point team, the big *Playboy* bunny had a chunk of shrapnel protruding from its head.

Amaro took cover behind a tree. Bits of bark splintered above him. Branches jumped and fell all around as rounds slammed the tree.

Vernon set the gun up behind the dead point team. They had all bought it. Johnny Vanilla crawled crablike, dragging ammo belts. Tigerbaum tossed grenades. Amaro, Flowers, and Malone dropped their rucksacks and fired uphill.

"They're in bunkers," somebody shouted.

A guy popped smoke but it hit a tree and bounced back behind the line. The gunships came in low and fired on the smoke, hitting the guys on line. A round hit Flowers in the hand and shattered his M-16.

Caught in the crossfire, they were stuck. Malone crawled to the radio strapped to Evans's back.

"Whiskey One to Dutch Uncle . . . Whiskey One to Dutch Uncle . . . Call off the gunships, goddamn it. They're hitting *us* . . . Because we're *in front* of the smoke, that's why . . . Call them off . . . Yes, sir . . . Yes, sir, we're Cougar Company . . .

We're tired, hungry, dying cougars, you asshole. Call off the gunships and come get the wounded."

Malone slammed the handset to the dirt. "If he got off his ass and came up here, the dumb fucker would know what's goin' on."

The gunships made another run over the line. Bullets churned the dirt between Amaro and Malone. Purple smoke went up twenty meters in front of them.

"It's about time," Amaro said.

Russell low-crawled into the position. "Can you walk?" he asked Flowers.

"No sweat, Sarge."

"Good. Listen. You two lend a hand and get Quinlan, the new guy, to the CP. He's hit in the back. Fuckin' gunships."

Amaro and Malone each took one of Quinlan's arms and stretched it over their shoulders. They reached across the guy's back and walked him to the aid station in the CP. They laid him down next to the other wounded.

Dutch Uncle sat behind a wide tree, his back to the line. He was on the horn to whoever. His RTO kneeled next to him.

Malone said, "That's why he don't know what the fuck is goin' on."

Engineers packed strips of C-4 explosive in a semicircle around some tree trunks blasting a landing zone in the jungle.

"Fire in the hole!" they shouted, then detonated the plastique. The trees fell like spokes in a wheel.

Amaro saw Haws's dead eyes staring up at the sun. All the dead guys seemed to be wondering what had happened.

"Hey, Amaro," Lee shouted. "Goddamn it, come over here." He was on the dirt propped on his elbows, a blood-stained field dressing around his calf.

"What a lucky fucker you are," Amaro said.

"No lie," Lee said, forcing a smile. "You got any smokes, man? Lef' mines in my rucksack."

"Sure do." Amaro handed him a pack.

"Oh, shit, man. These are ugly."

"Give them back if you're particular."

"That's okay. Guess they'll do."

"Take care, man."

"I'll be thinkin' 'bout you, man."

Malone said, "Come on. Let's help off-load. It's better than goin' back up there."

They carried cases of ammo and grenades from the landing zone to the perimeter. They unloaded a couple of dozen LAWs from the slicks ferrying ammo in and wounded out.

"You two carry these rockets to the line," a lieutenant said to Amaro and Malone.

"Who the fuck is he?" Amaro asked.

"Graham, the platoon leader," Malone said.

"No shit? What's he doing back here?"

"That's why McGee is the main man."

They carried as many LAWs as they could back to the line where McGee was set up. The incoming was heavy.

"Graham says to use these on the bunkers," Malone said.

"Ain't that some hot shit," McGee said. "Now all he has to do is show me where the fuck these bunkers are." Some rounds whistled and cracked overhead.

"Go easy and stay low," Russell said. "Word is, after the dustoff is finished, we're pulling up outta here." Amaro and Malone low-crawled back to the squad.

Airstrikes slowed down the incoming. They also covered for the medevacs so the choppers came and went unharmed. The explosions shook the ground and sent fragments whizzing all around.

"Okay," Russell shouted. "On me. We're movin' out. Grab your shit and git."

The guys moved in a crouch back toward the CP. The last dead and wounded had been dusted off. All that remained were empty boxes, scattered ponchos, and blood puddles in the dirt.

The airstrikes increased in intensity. There seemed to be more and louder explosions.

"The flyboys are bringin' scunnion," Spector said.

"Sounds like it," Amaro agreed.

They heard a whistling getting louder and louder, then an explosion that shook the whole valley. Whizzing bits of metal hit the trees like hatchets. Fragments ripped Amaro's sleeve. Some hit his chest, his arms. Spector caught some in the back. The planes roared off.

"Let me take a look," the medic said. With a tweezer he pulled several small chunks, the size of match heads from Amaro's arms. "The rest are too small to get at. They'll pop out on their own. But, hey, we just got our Purple Hearts."

"That's great," Amaro said. "I'm deeply moved."

They climbed a nearby hill and set up for the night. Charlie Company regrouped into two platoons. Bravo Company humped into the perimeter just before dark to pull guard.

"Get a good night's sleep," Russell said. "We're goin' to take that fucker come sunup."

The fucker was called Hill 187.

Amaro ate cans of fruit and some pound cake and split a joint with Malone. Then he crawled off to lie down. But he could not sleep.

After dark the airstrikes stopped and a battery of 175s took over. All night the artillery shells whistled and exploded on the bunker system. Amaro tried to count the hits but he could not keep up with them.

With Amaro on point and Malone taking up the slack, the survivors from the day before led the reinforced company up the slope of Hill 187. Amaro kept his eyes locked straight ahead, depending on Malone to scan the flanks.

The trees low on the slope were white scarred near their tops. There was dust all over: on the rocks; on the ferns and moss. As Amaro climbed higher his boots slipped on the layer of fresh dirt thrown over the hillside—dirt with small white stones in it like from an excavation site. He stepped over fallen tree trunks and dislodged boulders. He saw daylight under the treeline. The loose dirt became deeper, the splintered trees more numerous. He crawled on his knees for the last thirty meters and looked out on the blasted hill. Everything was flat.

Trees, split and splintered and ragged, lay on the dusty rubble. Some were bent and broken, their ends bristled like straw brooms. Here and there a dust-covered tree stump or low bush stood alone in the deep, loose dirt. Craters, ten feet down and thirty wide, pocked the rolling contours of the crest. Amaro waved Malone to his side.

"Look at this," he said.

Malone tipped his helmet back and whistled.

"It looks like the fuckin' moon," Amaro said. "Like we landed on the fuckin' moon."

The reinforced company got on line, ten men abreast, and searched the area. All they found was dirt and tree shards, and boulders blown to stones. Not a scrap of a Goodyear sandal or black pajamas, or a grain of rice or a finger or an AK, a sandbag, or anything. Only rubble. Dirt and dust.

They spent the best part of the day sifting the hilltop with entrenching tools, vainly looking for traces of the enemy. Up on another hill that night, Amaro and Malone set out the claymore and tripflares. A guy they didn't know from another platoon sat in the position with them.

There was a flat rock, like a bench, in front of a tree. Amaro sat on it, prepared chow and wrote letters. He leaned back, stretched his legs, and blew smoke rings. "This is livin'," he said.

"All the comforts of home, eh?" Malone said.

"There should be something like this in every position. All I need is a table."

"Wanna doodle-oo a jaybird?" Malone asked, low enough so the other guy could not overhear.

"Soon as I get back," Amaro said. "I gotta tap a kidney."

He picked up his rifle and strolled out of the position. He pissed on a tree and the urine burned.

A shot rang out. Amaro hit the ground and low-crawled back up so as not to get caught out of the perimeter when the shit started flying.

"What happened?" he said, slithering back into the position.

Malone said, "Look for yourself."

The stranger sat on the bench leaning up against the tree, his eyes bulging. His tongue stuck stupidly out of his mouth while a bloodstain spread between his shoulder and his chest.

"The wound don't look fatal," Amaro said. "Is he dead?"

"Dead as he's ever gonna be. He just stared down at it when he got hit, like he didn't believe it. I think he died of shock."

For a while they scanned the treetops for the sniper but could not find him. Then they closed the guy's eyes and wrapped him in a poncho.

5

They stood down for three days in Duc Pho. The company piled onto a convoy of deuce-and-a-halfs for a ride to the beach and a cookout: a day of barbecued hotdogs, all they could eat, and lots of hot beer and soda.

Amaro did not like to swim in the ocean. He soaked neck deep for a while, letting the cool saltwater work on his sores. Then he backed up to the water line, lay down, and closed his eyes. He heard the surf bubble and hiss, felt the wet sand shifting underneath, slipping out from some spots, piling up in others. He spread his arms and legs and felt himself sink in the sea edge. The saltwater helped his skin, and he liked taking the sun, but he did not like the cookout. It was too noisy and crowded. After a hotdog and a can of warm beer, he felt bloated and sick. But it did remind him of Manhattan Beach back in the World: the squall of radios, each blaring a different tune; the scent of coconut oil and baking skin; the girls glancing to see who was checking them out. He liked to see them in swimsuits and high-heels up on the boardwalk. And at night the noise gave way to the slapping surf and a crowd huddled around a small fire drinking coolered beers, and somebody played a guitar and somebody else sang. The sky, black and star-specked.

Amaro rose and dove into a breaker to wash off the wet sand. Back on the beach, stretched out on a towel, he fell asleep.

The latrines in the forward base camp were made from fifty-gallon drums: three drums cut in half. Three halves supported a four-by-eight plywood board with holes cut in it and dowels next to the holes. There was never any toilet paper on the dowels. The guys had to bring their own from the C rations.

Amaro and a new guy who called himself Jose Las Vegas lifted the board and leaned it up against the low sandbag wall in front of the latrine. Then they pulled the filled half-drums to the side.

"Goddamn it, be careful," Amaro said. "Don't let the friggin' thing bounce."

"Roger on that," Las Vegas said. "Don't want to get splattered by this."

Las Vegas was from the Lower East Side and claimed to be a singer. With the Jokers, he said. "From the Peppermint *poppa poppa shew wop* Lounge, motherfucker."

"Line up the empties while I get these going," Amaro said. He poured diesel fuel into the first full can and touched it off with his lighter. Using a bamboo pole he stirred the thick mess under the flames.

"Goddamn, bro. That stinks. *bad*," Las Vegas said. "*Bruto.* Know what I mean?"

"It's worse when they serve liver and onions."

"How long this gonna take?"

"A couple of hours. Then we serve it in the officers' mess."

"*Bueno,* bro!"

Las Vegas torched the second shitbucket and they both stood in the sun, bare-chested and sweating, stirring and burning the waste. Las Vegas sang. ". . . *Glo-ri-a . . . not ma-ree-ee-ee . . .*"

He had a nice tenor voice. Amaro thought he told the truth about being a singer.

Malone, Vernon, and Tigerbaum walked through the smoke.

"Time to party hearty," Malone said. "Let's do a few bangalore torpedoes."

"Right *here?*" Las Vegas said.

"Why not?" Vernon said. "Ain't nobody gonna smell nothin' while y'all burn the shit."

"So let's burn some good shit," Amaro said.

They squatted on their haunches upwind of the smoke and lit joints. Thin tracings of gray smoke drifted into the larger dark cloud and spread over the company area.

"Now I know why you didn' mind this detail," Las Vegas said to Amaro.

Tigerbaum opened a tin of salve, dipped a finger in it and rubbed some on his forehead.

"Let me hold some of that," Malone said. He rubbed it on his own head.

Las Vegas screwed up his face. "What's that?"

"Tiger Balm," Amaro said. "It's like a menthol thing. Helps you identify your middle eye."

"I can dig it. Hey, man. I thought you was Tigerbuns."

"I am," Tigerbaum said.

"His real name's Isaac Feigenbaum," Vernon said. "See why he changed it?"

"Of the Kluczbork Feigenbaums, late of the Warsaw Ghetto," Tigerbaum said.

"You don't say," Las Vegas raised his eyebrows. "Hey, let me try some of that." Malone rubbed some on his forehead like a priest giving the last rites. "It burns, man."

"Just groove on it," Tigerbaum said.

Crawford and Moose approached the latrine. "What's up?" Crawford said.

"We're preparing a recon of higher levels of consciousness," Tigerbaum said.

"Far out." Crawford smiled. "We brought some transportation." He held a pack of ready-rolls. "Better than C-4."

"Commence firin', motherfucker," Malone said.

"I read in the *Stars and Stripes* where the Chinese want to turn Nam into another Florida," Tigerbaum said.

"Absolutely," Amaro nodded. "Develop it. Build hotels and condominiums for the retired Chinese."

"I heard the same thing," Malone said. "A consortium of slick gooks in shiny sharkskin suits see this as the Gold Coast of the Orient."

"Hot damn," Vernon half-shouted. "A place to sun up when it's winter in Manchuria."

"We should buy in," said Crawford, "instead of fighting them. Pump some foreign aid into the Duc Pho Deauville. Change the name of Highway One to the Dixie Highway."

"There you go," Las Vegas gave him five up. "A place where the elderly can play fantan and fool around. We'll serve prechewed rice to the toothless."

"And fish heads to the wealthy," Malone said.

Vernon said, "I'd give 'em squeezed swamp slop and leftover Cs."

Las Vegas made a face. "That's what *we're* eating tonight."

"Yeah," said Amaro. "Las Vegas can line up the entertainment. He can warm up the crowd for Chen-Li Youngman and Buddy Chin."

"A Borscht Belt extravaganza," Tigerbaum snorted. "This is right up my alligator alley."

"Miami is in his blood."

"And run dog races. Think of all the dinks in black pajamas with palm trees and stupid blue dolphins printed on them."

"Instead of chasing a rabbit, the gooks can chase the dog. It's perfect. The winner eats the fuckin' thing."

"I'll tend bar at the Chu Lai Jockrot Club."

"Or come back to burn shit."

"Me and my brother can make a fortune building circular drives around hooches."

"Here comes the first shirt," Vernon said.

"Fuck him," Amaro said.

"Be cool, bro. The man is covered with stripes."

"So's a zebra's ass," Amaro said. "Toss the roaches in the shitbucket. I'd love to see him stick his arm in there up to the elbow to bust us."

Fluett came up and stood among them. Next to him was a guy with fairly long hair and new fatigues.

"This is Conroy," Fluett said. "An AWOL returned from Saigon. He is restricted to the company area awaiting court martial. No one is to speak or associate with this sorry excuse for a soldier. You, Amaro, will guard him twenty-four hours a day. If he tries to make a run for it, blow him away. Get your shirt on and sling your weapon, soldier. Vegas can finish this detail himself."

Fluett about-faced and marched back to the CP. Crawford and Moose drifted off.

"What a fuckin' drag," Amaro said.

"I'll see you after chow," Malone said. "Maybe we can tie him up in a bunker or something and go catch the flick."

Amaro buttoned his shirt. "I'll talk to you later," and turned to Conroy. "Let's go up to the tents and get away from this stink."

"Good idea."

Together they lumbered to the tent area. Amaro sat down and smoked and wrote some letters home. He said nothing to Conroy but was aware of his presence.

"Why don't you take a nap or something? It's a pain in the ass you sitting there," Amaro said.

"Not tired."

"Why don't you write a letter."

"Don't feel like it."

"Want something to eat? Some candy or fruit or something?"

"Not hungry."

"Well, goddamn it, do something instead of just sitting there staring."

"I'm not bothering you."

Amaro sealed the letters. He put his paper and pencil away. He felt tired, heavy-headed from the heat and reefer.

"How long were you in Saigon?" he asked.

"Eight months."

"Damn. How'd they catch you after all that time?"

"A raid. They checked my prints and found out I belonged here."

Conroy bummed a cigarette and told his story. He had been a squad leader. During a standdown he slipped out of his company area and hopped an outbound chopper. He did not know where the bird was heading; he didn't care. It landed at Tom Son Nhut, and Conroy drifted to Saigon.

There were streets, buildings, cars, motor scooters, pedalos, rickshaws. The war seemed far away. He sold his M-16 to a cabdriver, and with the money he bought some civilian clothes and rented a hotel room on To Do Street.

There were a lot of Americans in the city, most of them dressed in civilian clothes. Conroy moved among them unnoticed, selling reefer to GIs in town for in-country R and R and PX goods to black-market traders.

He made connections in the Saigon underworld with Vietnamese black marketeers and foreign opportunists. He was arrested in a warehouse while selling crates of claymore mines to an Australian national posing as a journalist. In custody Conroy refused to speak. Only afterward did the military police discover that he was an American absent without leave from a line unit in the north.

"Had a hell of a good time. Lived in a fancy hotel and wore civvies. CIA thought I was CID. CID thought I was a journalist. Reporters thought I was a spook. Nobody questioned me at all. They all had their own secrets to keep. I just came and went as I pleased."

"Sounds great."

"It was okay."

"Come with me," Amaro said. He walked to the CP and dropped his letters in the mail bag. Then he headed for the mess tent.

They ate in silence. Conroy just pushed at the food on his tray, not eating or drinking much of anything. Amaro did not want to talk to Conroy when Fluett could see. It felt awkward, uncomfortable. After his initial annoyance, he found Conroy wasn't a bad guy, and his stories about Saigon were interesting.

After dark, most of the guys went to the movies and the company area was almost deserted.

"Let's go for a walk," Amaro said, leading the way out toward the perimeter wall. They stopped near the latrine. Amaro lit a joint.

"I'm locked and loaded," he said. "If you're CID and make a move while this is burning, you're a dead man. After it's gone, well, fuck you. Go and prove it."

Conroy said, "Can I have a hit?"

Amaro shrugged and smiled. "Why not?"

They sat on the sandbag wall facing the company area, passing the joint.

"You're okay," Conroy said. "Thanks for the turn-on."

"Don't mention it."

"I'm going to do you a favor. There's this outfit in Saigon with good connections in Europe and Australia. If you want, have your folks send fifteen hundred dollars American to this address in Sydney." He handed Amaro a slip of paper. "Then hook up with the people in Saigon. Their address is on the other side. They'll get you out of here and fly you to Sweden."

"Christ."

"It's something to think about. That's all."

Amaro folded the paper and slipped it in his pocket. Then he hopped off the wall and took a piss, his back to the company area.

He didn't see Fluett come up until it was too late. He buttoned his fly but could not get back to the wall where Conroy and his M-16 were.

Fluett snatched the weapon and shoved it in Amaro's face. "What's *this?*" he screamed. "What's *this?* You're supposed to be guarding this prisoner and I catch *him* sitting with *your* rifle while you're twenty feet away."

Amaro was angry with himself for letting the first sergeant sneak up on him like that.

"So what?" Amaro said. "We're in the middle of nowhere. Where in the fuck is he gonna run to?"

"Who do you think you're talking to, trooper?"

"I'm looking straight at you."

Fluett pulled his .45. "Get back to your tent. You," he said to Conroy. "You come with me." He pulled the magazine from Amaro's M-16, ejected the chambered round, and tossed the rifle behind him. Then he marched Conroy to the CP.

From his tent Amaro heard the guys coming home from the movie. He heard the laughing, the chatter, Las Vegas singing: "*Shew dew tin shew bee doo . . . shew dew tin shew bee doo . . . In the sti-yill of the nigh-yite . . .*"

6

The first part of the operation passed quietly. For days there was no contact. No booby traps or ambushes. Just non-stop humping over steep hills while hacking dense jungle with machetes.

The guys were without water for two days. Good water was hard to find in those hills. They made a run to a small stream, but decomposed bodies lay bloated on the rocks around it. The contour maps showed no other sources.

Heat, hard humping, and lack of water wasted a couple of guys. They keeled over, cramped and hyperventilating, their skin pale and clammy. Even the scout dog, assigned to the company to sniff out the enemy, growled and snapped at its handler. The handler thought it wise to take the canine back to the base camp before it went wild.

They loaded the heatstrokes on a chopper. The scout dog and his handler climbed aboard.

"Hey, Sarge," Amaro shouted. "How come the dog and not me?"

"The dog's more valuable," McGee said.

Amaro turned to Malone. "Ain't this a bitch?" he said.

"The dog's smarter, too. Got any good *nook?*"

"Not a drop."

"Give me a can of peaches."

"It'll only make it worse."

"I gotta have something."

Amaro turned his back to Malone. "Take it out yourself."

Malone dug through the rucksack and found what he was looking for. "Close it tight," he said.

Amaro's tongue felt swollen, leathery in his mouth. His split lips hurt when he talked.

The chopper left behind two plastic five-gallon balloons. The water in them was gone in a day and the guys were ready to drink saline.

"It's the worst thing in the world," Spector said. A guy had asked him for a bottle. "The salt will drive you crazy. You might as well drink seawater."

Afternoon brought torrential rain. It hit the leaves overhead with a sound like applause and dripped down as if from a leaky roof. It lasted thirty minutes at most, but long enough to soak the troops and turn dirt to slick red mud.

Some of the guys used steel pots and canteen cups to catch the rain. Amaro walked with his head tipped back and his mouth wide open. The drops on his tongue tasted good. He collected a couple of mouthfuls in his cup and swallowed it quickly.

After the rain they set up in a circle around a field of elephant grass. A chopper came in dropping plastic balloons from treetop level. Two or three of them broke and guys held up the corner pieces trying to squeeze drops. When they left the landing zone each guy had one full canteen.

"Go easy on it," McGee warned. "Don't know how long it's gotta last."

They halted on a hillside to take ten. Russell stood over Amaro scanning the valley with binoculars. Amaro lit a smoke and looked around. At first he was not sure he saw what he thought he saw. He squinted and focused on a spot low on the next hill.

"Yo, Sarge," he said, hitting Russell on the shin. "I think there's movement over there."

"Where? Over where?"

"At two o'clock. Down low, near those rocks."

Russell shifted the binoculars. "I'll be goddamned," he said. "Who needs field glasses with you around." He got on the PR-10 to Dutch Uncle and reported what he saw.

"Let's go," Russell said. "Try to be quiet and careful. They might not of seen us yet."

They moved downhill and stopped in what seemed to be the valley bottom. McGee ran up the line, setting the ambush positions.

Amaro, Las Vegas, and Malone took the prone on the gun's right flank across a narrow footpath. They were told not to smoke or talk but just keep their eyes open. Johnny Vanilla hustled around collecting bandoliers. From where he lay, Amaro could see the gun. He waved to Vernon. The gunner smiled back and gave a thumbs-up sign. Tigerbaum clipped belts together, stacking ammo neatly next to the gun.

"Here's the poop," McGee whispered, crawling between Amaro and Malone. "You guys are the trigger point. We're on line up the left flank. Don't fire that way. Just out front and to the right. If anything breaks on that trail light it up. Got that?"

McGee and his radioman took up a position between the gun and the rifle team.

They waited in silence, each guy keyed in on the jungle in front of him. Amaro felt his heart pounding. He listened to himself breathe. There was no other sound. No breeze, no rustling leaves or snapping twigs. No birds, monkeys—nothing at all.

He thought of playing in the back of Cuccarulo's bakery, climbing over flour sacks killing rats with carpet guns shooting little squares of linoleum with a rubber band. Out in the vacant lot behind the stores with a broomstick for a rifle shouting, "Bang bang you're dead," and Anthony, the baker's kid, yelling, "No fair shootin' through weeds." He hid in the grass behind Mr. Grimaldi's hedge, playing hide-and-seek and Salvatore called, "Tap, tap, Johnny behind the hedge, one two three." What time was it back home? What day? Yesterday. Or is it tomorrow?

Amaro's body jerked into a knot when the firefight exploded in the next valley. The guys stared at each other. Word passed along the line: Alpha Company hit the shit.

Amaro saw a gook turn the curve in the trail, walking slow, like on eggs, scared eyes jumping side to side. Amaro and Malone fired at the same instant and the gook disappeared as if yanked up and backward by a cable. The gun opened up. Everyone fired. Rounds popped and grenades exploded, and black shadows ran through the jungle. Incoming snapped overhead. The ground shook and trees jiggled. Fragments and rocks ripped by.

"Get ready to move out!" Russell yelled. "Assault on line when McGee gives the signal."

"Are you fuckin' nuts?" Malone said.

"It sure ain't my idea. Word is, Alpha needs help. We gotta break through and get over there."

The guys pushed fresh magazines into their ammo pouches. They shoved ammo wherever they could on their web gear and fatigues. The firing lightened up on the left flank.

"Move out," McGee shouted.

They stood up in a low crouch and ran forward, firing from the hip. A lot of them got knocked backward. Amaro hit the dirt ten meters forward of where he started. So did Malone and Las Vegas.

"Fuck this," Amaro yelled.

Vernon sprayed the bush in a wide arc to cover the medics who had moved up to tend the wounded.

"No fuckin' way, Sarge," Russell shouted above the fight. "We can't move up anymore."

"Then stay put," McGee said.

"That's a fuckin' *rog*," Malone yelled as he crawled behind a rock for cover. Amaro joined him there.

"We're in a bad spot," Malone said, pointing to the slope rising out to their front. "Charlie's got the high ground." Rounds kicked the dirt next to his leg. He scooted closer to the rock. "We're gonna be here for a while."

Amaro leaned out and squeezed rounds at something moving on the slope. Green tracers streaked over his head and slammed the tree behind him.

Purple smoke was tossed out front and the gunships came in. They made several dry passes, then pulled back. The rounds zipped in, cracked past his ears, kicked dirt in his face. He clicked his rifle to rock-and-roll and sprayed hell out of the jungle, putting up a wall of lead. "Fuck 'em if they don't want to be reasonable."

"Goddamn it, things are too tight," Malone said. "There's not enough room for the gunships to work."

"Now what?" Amaro said, his helmet braced against the rock.

"Now we move up an inch at a time. Where's Las Vegas at?"

"In Nevada, bro," Las Vegas said, waving a hand from behind a wide tree.

"Let's keep the fuckers honest," Amaro said.

"Good idea," Malone replied.

They tossed grenades as far as they could in front of them. A dozen or so rounds hit the rock.

"*Fuck you,*" Amaro screamed.

"How you guys doin'?" Russell asked.

"Okay so far," Malone said.

"Good."

Amaro said, "What's goin' on, Sarge?"

"Near as we can figure, Alpha hit the deep shit," Russell nodded in the direction of the fight raging over the ridgeline. "We hit the VC rearguard. Second platoon got wiped trying to get around them."

"We got them surrounded and they got us pinned down. What a fuckin' joke," Malone said.

"Yeah. Well, what the fuck," Russell said. "Dutch Uncle wants us to move up on our bellies."

"Let's *not* and say we did," Las Vegas shouted.

"Yeah. Well, like I said: what the fuck."

Two guys crawled up dragging cases of grenades. Amaro and Malone grabbed as many as they were allowed and continued to lob them out front. The incoming was moderate but steady.

"Looks like a standoff," Malone said.

Russell came back again. "Are you guys still here?"

"Nope," Amaro said. "We pushed this rock ahead of us."

"Each of you take an hour apiece in the CP for ammo and chow," Russell said. "Two of you stay here at all times. We'll probabily be doin' this all night."

"Go to the CP, man," Amaro said to Las Vegas. "Me and Malone will watch the store."

Amaro and Malone took turns on guard. While one looked out and fired a round now and then, the other rested. They listened to the heavy fighting in the next valley.

"Poor bastards," Malone said.

At dusk mosquitoes swarmed. Amaro rubbed repellent on

his skin. Las Vegas returned and Amaro left the position. He low-crawled to the CP, not taking any chances.

The CP was not much safer than the line, just farther from the enemy. The guys stayed low and behind cover when they could. Most of the dead and wounded had been dusted off.

Amaro sat down next to Crawford, opening some pound cake and applesauce. It was his favorite meal, one he ate every day when he could trade cigarettes and candy for cans of fruit and cake. He had been lucky so far—he was neither dead nor seriously wounded—and he knew it was a combination of things that protected him. Smoking Lucky Strikes, for one. None of the guys who got hit smoked them. Another thing was the pound cake and applesauce, it protected him—the pound cake and applesauce and the heavy clove scent of the Tiger Balm he wore on his forehead to identify his middle eye. These things kept him safe, warded off bad vibes and stray bullets, kept snakes from biting and snipers from taking aim. He believed this in his guts with a conviction stronger than any religious faith he had flirted with as a child. The food was real. He could touch it, taste it, see it. He could smell the Tiger Balm, feel it hot, then cool, on his skin.

He reloaded his magazines while he ate, taking extra boxes of ammo and stuffing them in his rucksack. He looked around for more grenades. The night air smelled of cordite.

"Listen to that," Amaro said, nodding toward the sounds of battle.

"Better them than us."

It was Crawford's voice. Amaro turned, startled at hearing someone say that out loud. He felt a hint of kinship with Crawford, some slight awkward comfort in not being the only one to feel that way. Though he wished someone else besides sleazy Crawford had said it, someone he trusted and respected. Malone or Sergeant McGee.

"I guess we'll be okay as long as they don't get behind us," Amaro said.

"We'll be okay until daybreak," Crawford said. He stood up and walked away.

Amaro finished his chow and packed his rucksack. He stretched out on the dirt and tried to nap. He heard the rumble of the fight and wondered if they would have to reinforce. Too nervous to relax, he saddled up and crawled back to the line.

The incoming kept him awake that night. He watched the tracers, white and green and orange, crisscross the black space between him and the enemy. He scanned the bush, waiting for them to come.

In the distance Dragonships, looking for targets, dropped flares, and the ridgeline rose in silhouette against their white light and the clouds of smoke climbing out of the next valley. Amaro fired at shadows he thought were attacking him.

At dawn choppers flew in, bringing reinforcements. Amaro did not know where they came from but he felt better knowing they were there.

He drank water for breakfast. He tried eating some bread but he could not get it down. He leaned against the rock and smoked. No one spoke.

The order came to attack.

The troops ran toward the slope trying to keep on line, firing straight in front of them. The VC resisted and a lot of guys got hit, but the assault moved forward. Amaro stepped over some dead bodies. He saw one crawling and hit the dink with a burst. Another ran across his path and he hit him in the chest. He fired reloaded fired again unaware of anything happening around him. He fired reloaded fired and ran up the slope. Up on the ridgeline the troopers who made it cheered. They regrouped and swept down into the next valley.

Most of Alpha Company were dead, gray bodies lying twisted on the jungle floor. Parts of bodies were scattered about. Some of the wounded cried and groaned. One guy tried to stuff his guts back into the hole in his stomach.

There were boots and rifles and scraps of fatigues and spent brass and blood-black mud. Guys screaming and crying were still taking cover. Small fires burned. It all smelled of cordite and meat-rot and shit.

Amaro and Malone worked together. They picked up bodies and carried them on a litter to a landing zone blasted out by engineers. They laid them down in ranks for others to check dogtags. After the dead were picked up, Amaro and Malone were sent to collect pieces. Amaro did not mind touching the bodies, but dismembered arms and legs made him sick. When he stumbled over a loose head, he stayed on his knees and puked.

Choppers came and went in a constant throbbing of rotors. The dead were flown to the Duc Pho bodypoint to be tagged and bagged. The wounded and crazed were flown out to field hospitals. A detail filled sandbags and stacked them in a large rectangle.

They policed the enemy dead from both valleys and piled them on the sandbags as they were told to do.

"Why don't we just let these motherfuckers rot?" Amaro said.

Malone shrugged. "Who knows?"

The guys laid litters down and kicked the gook bodies over onto them. Some rolled them over with tree limbs. Crawford knelt next to an NVA with his hunting knife. He kicked a body in the stomach and blood spurted from its mouth.

"Give me a count," Dutch Uncle said to Graham. "And hurry them up."

They dropped some bodies around the sandbags high enough to cover the burlap. The rest were stacked on top of the rectangle, heads and hands and feet hanging loose from the pile.

"We count sixty-five," Graham shouted.

"There's more than that, Lieutenant," Dutch Uncle shouted back, chewing on a cigar stub. "Looks like a hundred and twenty at least."

The guys sat around the battlefield among the bullet-scarred trees smoking cigarettes, eating Cs, or just taking a rest. Dutch Uncle and a couple of bird colonels posed in front of the stacked enemy dead. Dutch Uncle stuck a fresh cigar in his mouth as the public-information officer snapped photos for *Stars and Stripes*.

After the press left, a squad poured diesel fuel on the bodycount and touched it off. A cloud of foul black smoke curled upward across the valley.

No one had stayed awake on guard that night. The last thing Amaro remembered was making himself comfortable on the dirt and closing his eyes. No thoughts. No dreams. Nothing at all.

"How do you feel?" Malone asked the next morning.

"Why?" Amaro said.

"You don't look so hot."

"I'm tired is all."

"Me too, bro," Las Vegas said. "I slept all night and I'm just as tired now as when I fell out."

"Salt tablets," Spector sang out.

"You got water to go with them?" said Amaro.

"*Je n'ai pas d'eau potable, malheureusement.*"

"Come on, man. You got any water?" Amaro repeated.

Malone looked at Amaro. "He said no. At least I think he did."

"He said no." Las Vegas sighed. "Shit, bro. Takin' salt without water is like kissin' without lips. No can do."

"I'll be back after resupply," Spector said. "We'll get some good *nook* then."

"He's a cool dude," Las Vegas said, after the medic walked away.

"I like him," Amaro nodded. "Spec's okay."

Las Vegas said, "I gonna fix him up good with my sister. Back on the block we could use a good bullet-hole specialist."

After a short hump they reached the landing zone. There was fresh water, food, ammo, candy, writing paper, cigarettes, and mail call.

Sergeant McGee walked over with a guy in clean fatigues who came out on the resupply. He wore a LURP hat and had a camera around his neck.

"This is Paul Hartman," McGee said. "A reporter. He wants to talk to the guys. Mr. Hartman will be with us for a few days."

"Hello, men," Hartman said.

"Hello."

"Hello."

"*Que pasa?*" Las Vegas said.

"Excuse me?" Hartman asked.

"*Que pasa?*"

"Jose doesn't speak English," Amaro said. "He was drafted from Puerto Rico."

"*Si. Si. Puerto Rico me encanta. No habla inglese,*" Las Vegas shrugged his shoulders and shook his head.

"Oh. I see." Hartman pushed the soft hat back from his face. "What are your names?"

"Snider," Amaro said.

"But we all call him Duke. "I'm Billy Balls," Malone said.

"I'll bet they call you Buster," Hartman said, lowering his pad and slipping his pencil in his pocket.

"Sometimes."

"I heard back in Duc Pho that it was pretty rough out here for the past few days. That right?"

Amaro said, "Like a Sunday dinner when Pop's been suckin' on a wine bottle."

"*Que pasa?*" Las Vegas said.

"Shut up, you dumb fuck." Malone slapped his sleeve. "The army'll teach you some manners yet."

"Well. Nice meeting you, gentlemen. I'll come back and talk to you some more later on." Hartman waved and walked away.

"I'll bet you will, bro," Las Vegas said.

Amaro watched him go. "What do you think?"

"Might be CID," Malone said. "We'll have to wait and see. I'll go tell Vernon to cover his ass until we figure where Mr. Nosy is at."

"*No comprende,* eh? You fuckin' loon," Amaro said.

"Not a bit, bro. Not a bugfuckin' *tee-tee* bit."

Amaro had slept stretched out on the ground the night before. When he woke he was damp, covered with dew, same as ferns, palm leaves, rocks half buried in mud. He rubbed bugs from his face, scratched his matted hair, ate some pound cake and applesauce. Then he walked several meters from the position and took a crap. It was no big deal now. Nothing awkward about squatting in the jungle, scanning the canopy, pinching a loaf near a tree. Screeching monkeys did it all the time. So did panthers. And wild pigs the size of ponies, with curved and ugly tusks. He stood up. Buckled his fatigues.

Walked away without kicking loose dirt over the pile he left behind. No need to. Things rotted fast in the jungle, rotted and turned into something else. A feast for beetles. Or the stem of a tender plant.

He knew how simple it was. Eat when hungry. Sleep when tired. And if anything threatened, kill it. It surprised and fascinated him, this simplicity. It had taken him months to lose all the old rules that kept him from seeing it clearly. All the old rules that got in the way, cluttered his head, distracted him from seeing exactly where he was and precisely what he was doing there.

He did not speak to anyone that morning. He went about his business in silence, concentrating instead on the smells of the jungle and the shapes of moving shadows cast by ever-shifting light.

Even when Malone told him they were on point, Amaro just nodded and strapped up, ready to take his place in file behind Malone, who led the way.

Malone stopped on the dirt trail, waved an arm to Amaro, taking up the slack. Amaro crouched and moved quickly on the animal path, trampled in the duff for thousands of years. Animals had the time to find the easiest way around.

Malone was now squad leader. And when the squad had point, Malone himself walked up front. Amaro would have picked someone else if he had the stripes and authority. He'd put Johnny Vanilla or Las Vegas on point, let them stumble into the deep shit, sound the alarm so he'd have time to take cover. But not Malone. Instead of having someone else play target, he chose to do it himself. Not because he was sharper, better, more alert than anyone else. It was easier for him to take the point himself rather than tell somebody else to do it. It was easier. That's all.

And that was the difference between Amaro and Malone. Amaro knew that he'd send a hundred privates to walk point before he'd do it himself. He knew. He had been there, behind that dike in the rice paddy, close enough to Martin to hear blood bubble from his neck. But it was Malone who reached without thinking and stuck a dirty finger in the bullet hole. It was not something an animal would do, stop another from pumping itself in a greasy slick on paddy mud. It was not something he would do. But Malone, he just reached up, just like that, and saved gunshot Martin's life. There were guys like that in the war. Amaro was not one of them. So he kept his distance. Kept tight within the safety space of his own blistered skin. Outside was out there. He lived in here.

Amaro watched Malone move along the trail.

The trail was narrow, only twelve inches wide at most. There were no ruts, no tracks, nothing but pebbled dirt where moss had been worn away. It wound around tree trunks and thick-stemmed shrubs, detoured boulders shoulder-high and ridges of slate stacked like plates on a waiter's tray. It ran parallel to slit streams, not more than puddles until heavy rains would swell them. Amaro pushed through the tangle of leaves arched over the path. He saw how, for smaller animals, the path made a perfect tunnel under the brush. Nothing to push out of the way or have snap back in the face. All that had been removed many hundreds of years ago by myriad small animals crossing this hill.

Amaro understood the terrain better now. Learned it from paths like this. They were roads, city streets, connectors to other places. This hillside, sloping down, was part of the valley below. Beyond that, another hill, the start of another valley. He knew there were virtual highways made by elephants where half-tracks drove around. There were avenues made by the haunches of tigers. And there were side streets, the narrow paths like this one, made by the scratching claws of nocturnal prey.

Parts of the jungle were neighborhoods. Instead of people hanging out there were monkey-eating eagles who took the collector's juice. Lorikeets perched on branches, like clothes strung on a line. And monkeys, unseen, chattered like children in a distant schoolyard. He walked through this neighborhood. He felt comfortable thinking of it in that way. It started to make some sense, a simple understanding. He walked clumsy on this path meant for smaller animals.

Malone, up ahead, stopped. He waved an arm. Amaro walked to his side.

"What's up?" Amaro whispered. He held his rifle ready, thumb on the safety.

"Look at that," Malone said.

"At what?"

"That tree."

The trunk was massive, ridged with tough gray bark. Weathered roots bent overhead like the knobby knees of the very old—skinny, almost bone. Malone pointed upward, to the trunk over the viny rootwork arch. A small flower clung to the bark. Purple. Violet. Yellow spots. Two speckled wings outspread. At first Amaro thought it was an enormous butterfly or a moth big enough to eat mice.

"An orchid," Malone said. He tried to climb the roots, high enough to reach it, but the soles of his boots slid down the rotting bark.

Behind them there was a steady snapping of twigs. The rest of the platoon. The clink of metal. Voices. Cigarette smoke.

"Every gook in the valley can hear us coming," Amaro said.

"Noisy bunch of fuckers." Malone slung his rifle and got ready to move out. "I wish they'd make even more noise to scare away the hard of hearing."

"Yeah. With our *mazel* we'll stumble into some deaf son-of-a-bitch in the open and we'll all be forced to play guns."

"I know the guy you're talking about," Malone said. "Got his head blown off in *Phouc Ahnay* and can't hear a goddamn thing."

"That's him. Can't eat enough rice or fruitcake to cork his ass. Don't trip over the bastard."

"If he's dumb enough to do it in the road, I'll put three big ones in his chest and—"

"*Hey,*" somebody said behind them.

They dropped to the ground and waved their rifles.

"Whoa. Lighten up. It's me," Tigerbaum said.

"Don't sneak up on us like that," Amaro said.

"You guys are walking the point," Tigerbaum said. "You're not supposed to *let* anybody sneak the fuck up on you. Sarge wants to know what's up. Why'd you guys stop?"

"Look at this flower." Malone got up and pointed to the orchid.

Amaro saw a shadow move through the bushes. He switched to automatic and fired a burst. The weapon jammed on the fourth round.

: 66

Malone and Tigerbaum hit the dirt.

"What the fuck!" Malone yelled.

"Relax," Amaro said. "Only a monkey." He sat up and pulled the magazine out of its well.

Sergeant McGee came up on the double, holding his rifle in one hand, his helmet on with the other. He dove down on the dirt next to Malone.

"Whatta we got?" he said.

"A monkey, Sarge. No sweat," Amaro said. He slipped off his rucksack and rummaged through it, looking for his cleaning kit.

"What do you mean, a monkey?" McGee said.

"Me and Malone thought we saw something out there so we stopped to check it out," Amaro said. He disassembled his M-16 and slid a cleaning rod through the barrel. An expended shell had jammed in the chamber.

"We saw something move," Malone said.

"Right. So I lit it up." Amaro grunted. "Look at this shit. A fucking space-age zap gun and I gotta prime it like a flintlock." He popped the jammed round out of the chamber with the tip of the cleaning rod. "It must be the powder or something. This fucking gun don't eject right."

"How do you know it was a monkey?" McGee said. "And why you sittin' around on your ass? Those shots woke up the neighborhood, chump."

"Come on, Sarge," Tigerbaum said. "The dinks have known where we are since the choppers dropped us off two days ago. They're letting us chase our tail."

"It's a good fucking thing it was only a monkey," Amaro said. "My shit woulda been in the wind if whatever it was shot back."

Amaro slid the bolt in place and seated the trigger mechanism.

Tigerbaum said, "A guy in Bravo Company said that happened a lot to them. It's the ammo. Fouls the whole fucking thing."

"Go see what this asshole shot at," McGee said.

Tigerbaum got pissed. It showed in his face. But he got up and moved carefully to the spot Amaro pointed out.

"How did you know it was a monkey?" McGee asked.

"I heard it scream," Amaro said.

"That's right," Malone said. "It shouted, '*Sweet Mother of Mercy, can this be the end of J. Fredd Muggs.*'"

Amaro slapped Malone five.

"Oh Christ," McGee said. "I'd expect that from him but not from you, Malone."

Tigerbaum came back holding a shred of bloody fur. "This is the biggest piece left," he said. "The fucking thing is nothing but hairballs and chunks of meat."

"Does it count as one confirmed, Sarge?" Amaro said.

"Fuck you," McGee said. "Give me ten minutes, then haul your asses outta here. I got to find the Old Man and tell him to come out from wherever it is he's hiding."

"Good shot," Malone said.

"Yeah," Amaro said. "These fucking rifles can do the trick, when and if they work."

"Scary. Ain't it?" Malone said.

"No," Amaro said. "I'm pretty sure that monkey was out here all alone."

Malone walked up ahead. Amaro waited. Twenty meters. Then moved out to take up the slack.

Amaro felt dizzy while setting the claymore and tripflares. He felt a chill although sweat poured from him. His head ached and his joints seemed on fire.

"Come and get it," Malone said.

"I'll pass," Amaro said. "I'm not hungry."

"Are you nuts? This is number one *sop-sop*. My mom sent me a package today."

"No thanks."

"It's Campbell's, man. Campbell's chicken noodle."

"Okay," he said. "Give me some."

He forced the first mouthful down and felt it pushing back up. He swallowed hard to keep it in. A sour taste burned his throat.

"Take it back," he said. "I just can't eat it."

He crawled on the mud next to his rucksack and laid down on his side. Red ants nibbled on his skin, mosquitoes buzzed and bit, but he did not have the strength to brush them. His eyes pushed hard against the lids. His stomach turned. He swallowed.

He felt swollen twice three times his normal size. His muscles pressed against the skin, the skin pulled tight ready to rip at the weakest spot and he would burst out of himself in drops, in wet red pieces for the rodents and lizards and owls to scavenge. Under the poncho he shivered, covered in sweat.

He felt Malone shake him by the shoulders. He heard him ask, *How you doin', man? What's the matter?* But he could not answer. He was afraid to open his mouth. Afraid that what was pushing up from inside would explode and leave him empty on the dirt. He was swollen. Distorted.

The spinning room caught him in a corner near the ceiling and held him pinned there.

"He's burning up," Spector said. "Let's get him out of that poncho."

Amaro fought them. He wanted to stay wrapped in that plastic skin to hold himself in so the animals could not eat him alive.

"I'm gonna bust," he screamed and choked on a wet burp and forced it back down, trying to spit the foul sour taste out of his mouth. He felt cold.

Spector filled out the tag and twisted the wires through a buttonhole on Amaro's fatigues.

Amaro felt them pick him up and carry him to the chopper. He sat slouched over, his chin on his chest, and the crew chief cinched a web belt around his waist. He heard the voices, the pulse of the rotor, the sound of a baby laughing. The motion of the chopper forced it out of his mouth. He leaned forward cramped with spasms. Some of it blew back in his face.

"Shit," the crew chief yelled.

They touched down at the battalion aid station and Amaro felt them carry him to a tent. They pushed something in his mouth down under his tongue. They tagged his rucksack and weapon. "*One-oh-five point . . . Jesus Christ,*" he heard someone say, "*get him in an ice bath.*"

They stripped him naked and stretched him out on a plastic sheet over a canvas cot. They poured water on him. It reached up to his ears. Someone shoved chunks of ice between his legs in his armpits against the sides of his neck and on his chest and stomach. He shivered and felt cramped. A tall floor fan pushed air across his body and they poured alcohol on him. "Don't smoke in here goddamn it," someone said, and Amaro tried to wave his arms to get them away from him. *Stop it,* he said, *it hurts . . . I'm so cold, please stop it . . .*

They did not dry him, they just put his fatigues back on and strapped him in another chopper for another flight.

Then there was a room. He was in a hospital. He felt himself carried, this time up steps. Stripped again, he sat on a wooden stool in a stall shower and cold water speared his skin. *I've had enough,* he said, pounding weakly on the shower door. *Please, this is horrible . . . horrible. Please let me out of here.*

1

When he tried to stand up, his legs gave out and he had to hold on to the bed. He walked slow, holding the wall, but fell when the room twisted quickly upside down. Blood spurted from his arm where the IV needle jerked out.

"Stay put," a corpsman said as he reinserted the IV. "You're not ready to get up yet."

"Where am I?"

"The Sixty-seventh Field Hospital in Qui Nhon, on the coast."

"How long?"

The corpsman looked at the chart at the foot of the bed. "About five days," he said.

For the next two days he lay in bed with dextrose in his arm, then two days of aspirin, quinine, Darvon, and orange juice. He tried some solid food but could not keep it down. His head ached. His joints felt stiff. He was always covered with sweat.

The guys in the other beds kept to themselves. They all seemed too sick to talk. Amaro saw some patients on the far side of the ward who had dull yellow skin and glassy yellow eyes.

After he held in his first solid meal, they removed the IV. He felt calmer, able to think. On the bedstand next to him was a Red Cross kit with a disposable razor, shaving cream, soap, toothpaste. He felt his stomach rumble; he heard it growl. Walking carefully, he took himself to the latrine.

It was a real bathroom. Sinks. Tile floor. Showers. Commodes with partitions. He caught a glimpse of someone in a mirror and stopped in his tracks. He walked slowly toward the wall.

The hair was wild: matted and curled. The skin, dark as leather. Pus-filled sacs pocked the face. The eyes were ancient. Over the left, between the lid and brow, a blister drooped down. There was another at the corner of his mouth and dozens of harder bumps covered the drawn and sunken cheeks.

He raised his hands to touch himself, to make sure it was him. The hands were red and swollen. Pus seeped from the knuckles.

He stood there and stared at the stranger reflecting back at him as diarrhea dripped down his legs to the tile floor at his feet.

Back in his bed he checked the chart to see what his name was. He tried to remember what had happened. Jumbled impressions made his head hurt. He asked for more aspirin.

Dressed in hospital blues, carrying the Red Cross package under his arm, he shuffled in cloth slippers to a bus. Transferred from the bus, he was strapped to a stretcher in a C-130 for the flight to Cam Ranh Bay.

Ward H in the Sixth Medical Center was an army barracks. Bunk beds lined either wall. A nurses' station was in the middle.

Amaro's temperature was taken four times a day. In addition to quinine for malaria and Darvon for pain, he was given penicillin for skin infection and a sticky white salve to rub on his sores. Smears were taken every day, blood tests and stool samples several times the first week.

Amaro rarely left his rack. He got up only for chow once a day and the latrine. He felt tired. Confused. He just wanted to sleep.

The Korean Marine in the bunk next to Amaro had tried to make conversation as best he could but Amaro ignored him.

Amaro opened his eyes in the morning and the Marine was sweeping the dirt from under his bunk. He stopped and smiled, and offered Amaro the cup of hot coffee and red apple he had brought back from the mess hall.

Amaro sat up and took the coffee. "Thanks," he said.

"You eat," the Korean Marine said. "You sleep. I clean."

The Marine's name was Kim. Amaro liked him for a friend though neither of them understood the other.

Amaro went to the mess hall with Kim and his buddies. He noticed the Koreans often walked hand and hand or with their arms around one another. A lot of Americans thought they were fags but they did not strike Amaro that way.

Kim sat down with a tray piled high with beef stew and noodles. He and the other Koreans poured a thick layer of sugar over their chow.

"What are you guys doin'?" Amaro asked.

Kim said something Amaro did not understand.

"You guys are weird. Sugar on beef stew. And you wear bathing suits in the shower."

Kim smiled. One of his friends said something and they all laughed. So did Amaro.

A guy walked by and brushed the back of Amaro's head with his tray.

"Watch what you're doing'," Amaro said.

"What are you gonna do about it, gook lover," the guy said.

Amaro jumped to his feet but Kim was quicker and stood between him and the guy.

"No fight," Kim said. "Much trouble."

"Out behind Ward H at seven, big mouth," Amaro said.

"You got it, punk," the guy said.

The Koreans jabbered at the table.

"Don't worry," Amaro said.

The guy showed up with a couple of his buddies. "Let's get to it, punk," he said.

"In a minute, big mouth," Amaro said. "First I want to show you something."

He set up two cinderblocks three feet apart. He laid a couple of two-by-fours across the blocks, one on top of the other, and nodded to Kim.

The Korean took a breath and kicked his heel down through the boards, cutting them cleanly in half.

"All of them can do that, shithead," Amaro said, pointing to the half dozen ROK Marines who stood around him.

The guy and his friends walked away.

At mail call Amaro received two weeks' worth of letters and a package from home. He ripped the paper off the box and smiled.

"Yo, Kim," he said. "Come on, man. We're gonna eat good today."

The Korean stared at him blankly. Amaro grabbed his arm and pulled him out the door. "Come on, man. Good *sop-sop*," he said, pointing to the box, then his mouth.

They walked to the beach. Amaro spread a sheet on the white sand.

"Sit down, Kim," he said.

Amaro opened the box. The loaf of Italian bread was covered with green mold. "Number fuckin' ten," he said.

Kim wrinkled his nose and shook his head, Amaro tossed the bread to the gulls.

"Here's some Kool-Aid. And iced-tea mix," he said, holding envelopes in the his hand.

"Wot dat is?"

"Douche powder, stupid. Look see. Like this." Amaro mimed pouring an envelope into a glass of water. He rubbed his stomach. "Ummmh," he said. "Number one *nook-dah*."

"Ahh," Kim said, nodding.

"It's the good shit, too. Sugar and lemon already added."

"*Shoo-gahr*. Yes. Me like."

"Holy shit, look at this," Amaro shouted. He held a quart-size preserve jar over his head. "Know what this is? Huh? Do you? Do you know what this is?"

The Korean shook his head.

"It's veal and fuckin' peppers, you grinnin' idiot. Fuckin' veal and peppers."

Amaro read the note attached to the jar, then laid it aside. He tossed utensils and napkins to Kim. "Set the table, Hop Sing."

Amaro spread the contents of the carton on the sheet. There was a box of Ritz crackers, a round provolone the size of a softball and sealed in wax, three sticks of pepperoni, two cans of olives, a jar of artichoke hearts in vinegar, and a full quart of Four Roses wrapped in a towel.

He left the cans of fruit and soup and envelopes of drink mix in the box along with the writing paper, then opened the jars and set the food out on trays from the mess hall.

"We got to be careful," Amaro said. "This note from Mom says if the veal and peppers pops up out the jar, it's bad."

Kim shrugged.

"Here goes." Amaro flipped the metal wire up and loosened it. He wedged a knife between the glass top and the rubber washer and twisted it. The top opened with a *thhopp* but the contents did not move.

"*Awwright,*" Amaro shouted. "We're gonna eat good tonight." He spooned veal and peppers onto both trays. "Eat up, man. *Buon appetito.*"

"Good," Kim said with his mouth full. "Wot call you dis?"

"Poon-tang."

"Ahh. Poon-tang number one."

"You got that right, Charlie Chan."

Amaro cut a chunk of cheese and held it under Kim's nose. The Korean pulled his head away.

"What are you jumpin' for? It smells like your feet, but it's good."

Kim shook his head.

"I don't believe this. You eat fuckin' fish eyes. Look see," Amaro said, taking a bite out of it. Kim took a nibble and grimaced. Amaro laughed. "You'd like it better with sugar on it," he said.

Amaro and Kim sat on the beach drinking rye and eating pepperoni and cheese on Ritz crackers. They popped olives and artichokes in their mouths with their fingers. Phantoms took off from the deck of an aircraft carrier anchored in the bay. The jets dropped off the end of the runway out of sight for a second then climbed almost straight up and out.

"Ain't that amazing?" Amaro said.

Kim said something in Korean. Then, taking his time, trying hard to say it right, he said, "Dis very good. I want t'ank you *Mah-Row.*"

Amaro clinked his coffee cup of whiskey with Kim's. "Any

time, Kimshi, or whatever the fuck your name is. It don't matter. You're a good guy and I don't understand a fucking word you say, but goddamn it, I always know just what you mean."

They sat and finished the bottle of rye. They watched stars twinkling in the cloudless sky and stared at the blinking lights on the carrier offshore.

Amaro bought himself a few extra days in Ward H by rubbing the thermometer against his pantleg to fake a temp. But he did not know the fever cycle and the medics caught on quick to his scam. They transferred him from Ward H to Cycle 2.

He was not able to sleep in. The racks were empty after first call. In the morning there was physical training and minor details were assigned. Sometimes it was KP, or area police call or cleaning in the lab. Amaro showed up, did as little as possible, then disappeared to the beach.

The medication and soaking in the saltwater had helped to clear up his skin. Most of the seeping sores were gone. Dry brown scabs marked where they had been. He sunbathed when he could and when it rained he slipped into the library to read Perry Mason cases and mysteries by Ross MacDonald.

He lost contact with Kim after changing wards and kept to himself most of the time. He felt like getting high; the relaxed atmosphere around the convalescent center was conducive. But that meant making connections, getting next to a corpsman or permanent party, and Amaro did not feel like talking to anyone. He had nothing to say to them and knew they had nothing he cared to hear about.

He had written only one letter home since getting dusted off. Back in Qui Nhon, on Red Cross stationery, he wrote a short note telling his family he had malaria, was in a hospital, and not to worry because he was out of the line, safe and sound.

He had started other letters but did not finish any of them. He had trouble remembering who he was writing to and why. When he read his mail he sometimes could not understand the words. *Who were these people?* He could not recall the faces of those who wrote the letters. He no longer heard their voices talking to him from the page. Only his own voice now—the face of the stranger in the mirror. So he stopped reading his mail. He tossed the envelopes, unopened, into the cardboard box, along with the cans of fruit and soup and packages of drink mix.

On the chow line he just pointed at the things he wanted, laid his tray down on an empty table, and walked over to get a cup of iced tea. He sat down and stared at his food.

"Didn't you hear me callin'?" a voice said.

"What?" Amaro said.

"I was callin' you from over yonder," Johnny Vanilla said as he pushed a chair back to sit at Amaro's table.

"I didn't hear you."

"How are you feelin'?"

"Okay."

"Me too. Sure am glad to see somebody I know. Gets awful lonely not havin' a body to talk to."

"You get used to it," Amaro said. He stared at the soldier and suddenly remembered who he was. "When did you get here?"

"I got dusted off 'bout a week after you did."

"What's happening back in the company?"

Johnny Vanilla played with his cup of iced tea, making rings on the table with the bottom of it. Interlocked rings, like the links of a chain. "There ain't no Charlie Company," he said. "Leastways not like you'd remember it."

"What are you talking about?"

"Two or three days after you left we was a'walkin' up a hill in the same sector Alpha Company got hit. Only the VC got up there first and we just kinda walked right smack into 'em. We turned to hat up and they was behind us, too. Lord, it was awful. Just as awful as could be.

"Crawford's dead. So's Sergeant Russell, and Vernon. . . . I never thought I'd miss *him* but I do."

Amaro stared at the table. "How's Malone and Spector and the rest of the guys?"

"They're okay. Malone got taken away to honcho the second platoon. We lost over sixty percent of the unit. I was with Bravo when I got sick. No tellin' what's gonna be when we get back there."

"What difference does it make?" Amaro asked.

"Who knows. Dutch Uncle got promoted to major and got a job in Battalion. And Graham is the new company exec. He was actin' CO when we got hit."

"That's going from bad to worse."

"Sure is," Johnny Vanilla said.

"Yeah. That's the Army for you. How's McGee?"

"He took some frag but he's okay. He's still out there, thank the Lord."

"I'll see you later," Amaro said. He walked out of the mess hall and scraped his dinner off the tray into a garbage can.

He sat in the library with a book but could not read. He just stared at the page and the lines got dark. He sat on his grandfather's lap cursing in Italian through the window at the people below like his grandfather taught him. The old man laughed. He pulled on crooked eyeglasses peeled from an orange in a continuous spiral strip. His grandfather knew how to do that.

The lights flickered on and off in the library.

"Ten minutes to lights out," someone called. "Get where you belong."

Amaro walked across the compound to his ward.

He spent the next day avoiding Johnny Vanilla. He did not feel like talking, or listening. His final blood test and stool sample came back negative. "You'll be leaving in the morning," the doctor said. "Your brigade has assigned you to a few weeks of light duty at brigade headquarters—P Squad."

They handed him travel orders and the box containing his personal effects. He had thirty-six hours to get there.

He did not want to put his fatigues on. They were the same ones he had worn in the field and they smelled of mildew and stale sweat. The white saltstains were scratchy and stiff. He tried to brush them off but could only shake some of the powder out. He rubbed the material into a ball trying to loosen it up.

His socks were worn thin and had holes in the heels. He scrounged a new pair and pulled his boots on.

He showed his orders to the dispatcher at the airstrip.

"Go sit over there," the dispatcher said, pointing to a bunch of guys sitting in the shade.

These guys were still in standard fatigues with yellow chevrons and colorful shoulder patches. The white name tags were like their skin. They wore black all-leather combat boots with spitshined toecaps. A few guys had a tan; the rest looked pale, washed-out. They rested on their duffel bags, drowsy in the humid heat.

Amaro sat cross-legged digging through his box. He opened a can of peaches and drank the juice. He emptied his pockets and sorted out the mess. A cigarette from a month-old pack of Luckies still tasted fresh and he laughed when he realized the whole country was a giant humidor.

He took mud-stained letters out of their plastic bags and tossed them in the box with the unopened ones. There was a small slip of paper in his breast pocket with the address of someone in Australia. He tried to remember what it was, and when he did, he refolded it and slipped it back in his pocket.

Tired of waiting, he went outside and looked for another door, the entrance to the operations bay. The shingle was pure white in the harsh sun.

A rush of cold air hit Amaro when he opened the door to the ops. The cold air raised chill bumps on his damp, over-heated skin.

He watched the clerks in starched fatigues bustle from desk to desk. They moved with the hum of machinery, the snowy glow of flourescent light cold as the air that tingled and pinched his skin. His stomach tightened. He started to shake. The orders fluttered in his jittery hands when he gave them to the clerk. Amaro did not know if he trembled from nerves or from the terrible cold. He crossed his arms over his chest and pressed them hard against his ribs, trying to hold back the spasms that wrenched his spine and jerked his shoulders back and forth. Frozen needles pierced his belly and iced upward to his heart, spreading cold like bits of frost instead of liquid blood.

"Corporal, have you got anything I can hitch a ride on?"

"There's an F-4 Phantom going your way," the clerk said, faceless, a voice in green fatigues. He leafed through the papers on his clipboard. "But a major has priority on it. Too bad. That would have been one hell of a ride."

"What else is there?" Amaro asked, forming the words carefully and forcing them through chattering teeth.

"Let's see," the clerk said, thumbing the papers. "Let's see what we've got."

Amaro shivered in front of the desk.

"There's only one other flight scheduled for today," the clerk said. "A C-130, stopping at Chu Lai, then going on to the Philippines."

"Can I get on it?" Amaro asked.

"Well, I don't think you'd want to. It's . . . it's a cargo plane."

"Okay," Amaro said. "I'll take the C-130."

"There's a regularly scheduled bird leaving at nineteen hundred," the clerk said. "You could be on that. No problem."

"I don't want to wait," Amaro said. "I'd rather be on the move, if you know what I mean. This waiting around . . . it's shit, man. You know?"

"It's up to you," the clerk said. He scribbled something on a standard form and hit five copies with a rubber stamp. "Go have a seat over there," the clerk said, pointing to a row of folding chairs lined up against the wall.

"Mind if I wait outside?" Amaro asked. "I'm freezing to death in here."

"Just stay close," the clerk said. "I don't have the time to go looking for you."

"I'll be outside the door," Amaro said. "You won't have to look for me at all, man."

The tall ramp lifted slowly at the back of the back of the C-130. The white light washing the deck diminished inch by inch as if swallowed by the shadow of that clamping monster jaw. Shrinking. Getting narrow. Light slipped quick from the aircraft until it thinned to a single shining stripe falling across the palleted stacks of dull gray military coffins. Coffins stacked in solid squares, like bricks in a pile, the substance of per-

manent crypts. Amaro heard the hydraulics hiss. The tail ramp
sealed.

He could not see the crew chief in the suddenly blinding
dark. Small dots of red and green broke the solid black.
Outside, the engines growled louder, chewing at the air. When
they took a big enough bite, the aircraft lurched forward.
Forward and up, vibrating.

"You best strap yourself in," the crew chief said.

Amaro could see him as a shadow in the dim reflection of
blinking lights. He was green. Red. Pale ghostly white. Amaro
felt around on the webbed jumpseat until he found the belt
ends. He snapped them together and pulled tight. He saw the
crew chief sitting across from him, near the stern of the
aircraft. He sat with his legs out in front of him, crossed at
the ankles. Headphones bulged on his ears.

The engines got loud as the plane gained altitude.

"That's a rog," the crew chief shouted over the mouth-
piece. Then he dropped the headset around his neck.

"You want a sandwich or a cup of coffee?" the voice asked.

Amaro opened his eyes, saw the crew chief standing in
front of him. The plane bounced. The crew chief steadied
himself by reaching up and grabbing on to a steel cable.

Amaro shook his head.

"Sorry to bother you," the crew chief said. "But it ain't
often I've got somebody to talk to on this trip."

"This is your job?" Amaro asked.

"It's what I do," the crew chief said, sitting on the jumpseat directly across from Amaro. "Want some coffee?"

"Black. No sugar," Amaro said.

The crew chief poured coffee from a thermos into a
Styrofoam cup. "Good," he said. "That's the only kind we got.
We make this trip four, five times a week. I spend the
weekends in Manila. Sometimes Subic Bay."

"How do you handle it?" Amaro asked. "I mean . . . all that
fuckin' noise and shit. Don't it scare you at all?"

"Shit no," the crew chief said. "You get used to it. Them
engines always sound like they're about to fall off."

"No. I mean them," Amaro said, nodding at the cargo.

"Oh. It used to give me the creeps at first but now I don't
even think about what's in the boxes. They just bounce around

a little when we hit turbulence. My only fear is one of them fuckers popping open one of these days. Want a sandwich?"

"What would you do if one of them did?" Amaro asked.

"What—want a sandwich? I'd give it to him. We got plenty."

"No. If one of those lids did pop open."

"I'd hook up my safety belt and kick the son-of-a-bitch out the door in a heartbeat, Jim. Ham, cheese, or peanut butter and jelly?"

"Nothing," Amaro said. "Nothing."

8

Chu Lai was a military city. It seemed to have no boundaries. Amaro strolled past motor pools with jeeps parked side by side so close to one another, a guy could walk across them for maybe half a mile. There were rows of trucks, trucks of all kinds, and lots of activity on the road. Marines in their funny fatigue hats, some of them wearing flak jackets; pilots in flight suits, helmets under their arms; lots of GIs in starched fatigues. Amaro was surprised to see so many Americans wearing civilian clothes. He tried to remember the last time he saw anyone in civvies.

What struck him most about Chu Lai was the ever-present smell of hot asphalt. Rows of Quonset huts and wooden barracks stood like houses on a street.

He walked into a PX and wandered through the aisles lined with cameras and watches, stereos, clothes. Pretty Vietnamese girls, dressed in silk, stood working behind the counters. He was amazed to see people shopping in the middle of a war. He bought an orange soda and a bag of oatmeal cookies.

He noticed people staring at him. These people—guys mostly, but there were some American women—all wore clean jungle fatigues. There was polish on their boots. Amaro gazed at them, then thought of himself, and realized how out of place he was. His jungle fatigues were torn. They were stained with mud and caked with the salt of sweat. He was filthy, needed a shave. He knew he smelled bad, although he was used to his odor. His skin was pocked with sores and greasy white spots. He paid for the items and walked quickly back to the road where he felt more comfortable.

He found what looked like a quarry off to the side of a long empty stretch of dirt road. It was a small hill in the middle of the flats, and half of it had been dug up and hauled away. In the shadow of the hollow hill he saw cranes and steam shovels, backhoes and dump trucks. The sun was setting; the work crews were gone.

He sat on the ground with his back up against a huge tire on one of the earth-moving machines and stared at the exposed interior of the hill. It seemed to him obscene, as if he were looking at something he wasn't supposed to see. He lit a cigarette and sucked the smoke in deep.

Lizards scampered over the rotting roots. Rats scratched at the rubble. He followed the slanting lines of the different-colored rocks that rippled across the torn-open face of the hill. The bands narrowed as they neared the top. Covering the peak was a layer of rich, muddy dirt.

The cookies were dry. The hot soda burned his throat. As the sun went down behind the shell of the hill, he sat there smoking. It was quiet. He felt comfortable alone inside the hill, alone with the rats chewing on the cookies he had thrown away. He wanted to shoot them but scattered them with stones.

Back on the road, he walked in the direction he had been headed earlier. The road curved to the right and descended, and he could see the lights of what seemed like a battalion compound sprawled out in the distance. He lit a cigarette and followed the road toward the center of the glow.

A half mile along he heard music playing, loud and out of tune, and decided to find out where it was coming from. In the doorway light of an enlisted men's club he saw guys standing around drinking beer. The club, on the road between two company areas, rocked to the live music playing inside. He nodded to the guys. They did not nod back. He walked inside past them.

Red and green Christmas lights were strung from the bamboo ceiling. Along the bar guys in T-shirts and cutoff shorts were talking and swigging brew. There were booths along the opposite wall, and in the center of the floor guys danced by themselves.

A spotlight with a revolving disk flashed colors on the stage where a Filipino band played American rock-and-roll. The lead singer was a tall girl in a flower-print miniskirt and high heels. Amaro recognized the tune—"Get Off of My Cloud"—but could not understand the words. He stood staring at the singer.

"You think she'd do it?" he heard someone say.

"Bet your ass she would," another said.

"Fuckin' A, if you offered her enough dough."

"It's murder. I'm getting a cramp," a guy said, grabbing his crotch.

"Yo. Johnny! Johnny Amaro," someone shouted. Amaro was startled by the call. He turned and squinted, shading his eyes to see who was coming from behind.

"What are you, fucked up?" the voice said.

Amaro stared at the guy for a second and then he remembered.

"Louie," he shouted. "I'll be goddamned. Louie, you ragged old fucker." He ran to the guy, giving him a hug. "How long you been here?"

"Couple months. Man, I'm glad to see you. I heard you was dead," Louie said.

"Only socially. I'm really glad to see you," Amaro said, his hands on Louie's shoulders. "What the hell you doing here?"

"Easy duty in the rear, my man, for services rendered above and beyond. Connors is here too. So's Armstrong and Daley and little Willy Faye. We all got rotated to the rear for the duration."

"Shit. That's almost the whole damn poker game," Amaro said.

"Just about. The other guys went to the five-o-deuce."

"I know. That's where I tried looking for you before I got re-assigned. Some asshole said he knew you and you was KIA."

"Not that I heard," Louie said.

"Lussier is in Bravo Company, I think. Oxendine, too." Amaro said.

"What about Vince Affrunti?"

"I don't know what happened to him."

"Come on, man. Let's do a number."

"You got shit?" Amaro said.

"Is a pig's pussy pork?"

Louie and Zeppy lived together in a room in a Quonset hut. It had a window and four walls. A door that locked. Bunk beds took up some of the space, but they had a wall locker each, plus three footlockers they shared between them. There was a paper lantern over the lightbulb and a split-bamboo shade in the window. A red-and-gold rug covered the concrete floor. Matching bedspreads covered the bunks. There was a square souvenir pillow on one of the beds, with a green-and-yellow dragon embroidered on it. VIETNAM was stitched across it in white silk to match the tassel-fringed edges. A hand-woven tapestry of blue sky and emerald mountains hung on the door. Zeppy clicked a tape into the cassette player and they listened to "Shake Me, Wake Me" by the Four Tops.

"Man, you guys got it made in the shade," Amaro said, stretching his legs on the rug. His full belly felt good. He was still high and the music seemed to dance in the corners of the room.

"Yeah, but the boredom is a motherfucker," Louie said.

"Right on, Jim," Zeppy said. "Without drugs and music we'd go fucking nuts."

Amaro let his eyes take in everything in the room. Only the curved, corrugated outer wall broke the illusion of being in a small apartment. "I can't believe you guys live like this."

"Yeah. Fucking Disneyland. Hey, Zeppy, did I ever tell you about them girls and the wild nights in Qui Nhon?" Louie asked.

"No," Zeppy said. "But I got a feeling I'm going to hear all about them now. I hope it's not another one of your come-on-her-chin stories."

"Uh-uh. And you know I won't be blowing smoke," said Louie. He held out the palm of his hand and Amaro slapped him five.

Amaro stretched out and fell asleep. He had not taken his boots off.

Red lights flashed in Amaro's eyes. He tensed his body, waiting for the shock. Something hit him on the leg.

"I brought you some breakfast," Louie said.

Amaro rolled out of range of the sunlight that poured through the raised shade. He sat up in the shadows, rubbing his eyes. Then he reached for Zeppy's rifle.

"Don't shoot. The eggs are real," Louie said. "*Mangia. Mangia,* like Mama used to say."

Louie placed the tray on a footlocker. Amaro sat on the edge of Zeppy's bunk.

"What time is it?" Amaro asked.

"I don't know. About eleven, I guess," Louie answered. "Sorry the toast got cold."

"It's good anyway," Amaro said, dipping the hard bread into fried egg yolks. "Real fucking eggs, I can't believe it."

"The bacon is top shelf. I save the lean pieces for my running partners."

"Hey. There's pulp in my orange juice."

"Oh. Did you want it strained, sir? This ain't the fucking Plaza Hotel."

"No. I mean it's fresh."

"Squeezed it myself. It's so fresh I had to slap it."

"Unfucking real," Amaro said, wolfing down the food. With his last slice of toast, he wiped the tray clean. "That was number fucking one," he said, sipping coffee.

"The benefits of knowing a cook," Louie said.

"What time did you say it was?" Amaro asked.

"About eleven-fifteen, I guess."

"Shit."

"You're fucked up. Here's some shaving stuff and a clean towel. The neighbors are starting to complain. The latrine is just down the hall."

"Good idea," Amaro said, walking out of the room.

Amaro stood under the hot water, his eyes closed. He shampooed, soaped up, and rinsed twice, then he let the water needle his back and shoulders until it started to turn cold. He dried himself and wrapped the towel around his waist.

He wet a Q-Tip and cleaned his ears. It sounded scratchy in his head. He felt like his ears had popped.

He lathered his face with shaving cream, then slid the lather off with his thumb so he could shave around the healing sores. He sprayed on deodorant, splashed on some cologne, and powdered his feet. He rubbed his fingers through his hair so it would dry curly. Then he used a Q-Tip to spread salve. Being clean felt good.

"Can I borrow a pair of socks?" Amaro asked when he got back to their room.

"That ain't gonna help," Louie said. "Try these on. We scrounged up a pair that might fit."

Amaro pulled on the new jungle fatigues. He rolled up the cuffs and sleeves, slipped his belt through the loops, and transferred his belongings from the old pockets to the new.

"This is living," Amaro said.

"Man, you are fucked up," Louie said. "Hang out in here for the rest of the day. Play tapes, but keep it low. I'll lock you in and bring you some chow later on."

"I think I'll just go back to sleep," Amaro said.

"Whatever you want," Louie said. He stopped at the door and brought the boots back inside. "Just don't burn no reefer in here. Some of these motherfuckers will rat you out in a New York minute."

Amaro heard the lock click on the other side of the door. He stretched out on Zeppy's bunk, then suddenly jumped up. He carefully folded the bedspread and placed it on a footlocker. He clipped the GP strap to a belt loop, laid Zeppy's rifle on the floor under the bunk, fluffed the pillow, and stretched back out.

He stared up at the rectangles made by the springs under the bunk overhead, those rectangles stuffed with soft mattress. He gazed at the lowered bamboo shade, the dust motes floating in the slanted light, the mountain tapestry hanging on the door, the metal waves of the Quonset roof.

He heard a jeep grinding gears outside the window. He heard voices, the sound of voices. He could not make out the words.

In the drone of the busy camp, in the heat of that quiet room, he cupped his hands behind his head and closed his eyes. Feeling safe, clean, feeling far away from the war, he crossed his bootless ankles and fell asleep.

"We got cold brew in the cooler," Zeppy yelled from the cab of the three-quarter-ton truck.

Louie pulled a few cans from the ice and passed them around. He handed one to Amaro. Then he gave one to a guy named Clyde, a heavyset blond kid who worked in supply. Sitting next to Clyde was a tall, thin guy named Carney. He was the company clerk.

Amaro remembered seeing them in the EM club on the previous night.

"This is the regular crew," Louie said, sipping foam from the top of a can. "That's Jones in the cab with Zeppy. He's a truckdriver, too."

The truck lurched forward. Amaro and the others lost their balance in the back.

"Yo, Zep," Louie shouted, banging on the cab roof. "Watch what the fuck you're doing, man."

Zeppy shot him a bird through the back window.

"Louie told us you're from a line unit," Carney said.

"Yeah," Amaro replied.

"Fuck a bunch of line units," Clyde said, tossing an empty can on the bed of the truck. He popped open a fresh one. "That sure ain't for me."

"It's where you belong," Louie said. "All you squirrel-shooting assholes belong in the line. Not city boys like us," he said, nodding toward Amaro.

"Yeah," Amaro said. "You woodchucks are used to hunting and shooting and shit."

"I only hunt things what don't shoot back," Clyde said.

The truck drove past the quarry and turned right, following a dirt road that led out toward the hills.

"Do you guys always tool around like this at night?" Amaro asked.

"Whenever Zeppy can borrow a vehicle," Carney said. "The only really safe way to get high is to do it on the move."

"Fucking A," Louie said. "There's more snitches in Chu Lai than there are fucking mosquitoes."

They drove past a new barracks building. Amaro saw air conditioners in the windows. There were men dressed in civilian clothes walking up the outside steps.

"Wow. Who are those guys?" Amaro asked.

"Poop is they're USAID people," Louie said. "Civilian contractors. Got their own mess hall and club. Never mingle with the uniforms."

"They sure live good," Amaro said.

"Yes. Yes, they do," Carney said. "The civilian cover is a bunch of bullshit. I bet they're CIA. The ones who stand by to arm the nuclear artillery shells."

"You're fucked up," Louie said. "There ain't no such thing."

"There certainly is," Carney said. "There are one-seven-fives all around this base capable of firing nuclear rounds."

"I never heard about them," Amaro said.

"Ain't nobody else heard of them either," Clyde said. "Carney is the onliest one in country who knows about them."

"Ignorance is bliss," Carney said.

"You're right," Louie said. "So let's get ignorant." He pulled out several joints. He handed one to Zeppy through the driver's window, lit one, passed it to Carney, then lit another. "This is the complete guided tour of Chu Lai at night," he said.

They passed the joints around as the truck twisted and turned over the dirt road.

"That's the dump out there," Clyde said. "Come sunup there's more fucking birds out yonder than you can shake a stick at."

Amaro saw nothing but darkness.

Clyde said, "I remember back home once there was tree swallows. Good Lord, solid black lines of the suckers just a flyin' from treetop to treetop. Me and my daddy pumped birdshot into the fuckers. We shoveled up truckloads of 'em and burned 'em at the dump."

"Over there is a minefield," Louie said. "Go show us how it works, Clyde."

"I'll toss your bony ass out there good and far," Clyde said.

Amaro saw only a dark, barren patch of ground. The dim lights of Chu Lai faded in the distance behind the truck and disappeared when the truck started downhill. Out the front was black sky, blacker shadows of mountains, and a dome of starspecks overhead.

They smoked two more joints and drank almost a six-pack each. The talk had quieted down as they listened to the sounds of the engine and tires on the gravel. In the dark open area it sounded too loud. It seemed to echo for miles. Amaro felt uncomfortable, making so much of a racket at night.

Carney stood up and pounded on the cab. "Stop the truck. Stop the truck, you asshole."

Zeppy hit the brakes and the truck skidded to a stop. The empty cans rattled across the truck bed. The idling engine sounded as if it was amplified in the heavy silence around it.

"Who are you calling an asshole?" Zeppy yelled.

"Quiet, fool. Talk lower," Carney said.

"What's up?" Louie asked.

"Where are we, Zep?" Carney asked, ignoring Louie's question.

"A couple clicks past the dump," Zeppy said. "Relax, man, you're just too stoned."

"We're a lot further out than that, Zeppy. Look around," Carney said, pointing to the shadows of mountains behind the truck.

"Holy shit," Louie said.

"No, we ain't," Zeppy said. "Relax. I know where we are."

"Oh yeah? And you shit, too, when you eat regular," Clyde said.

"The mountains are in front of us . . ."

"And behind us," Carney said. "We're outside the god-damned perimeter."

"We can't be," Zeppy said.

"Turn this fucking thing around," Louie said. "Let's *di-di* the fuck out of here ASAP."

Amaro sat low in the truck and clicked the safety off on his rifle. He tried to listen to the night noise in the dark, but the idling engine was all he heard.

"There's a turnaround up ahead," Zeppy said.

"Yeah. Yeah, I think you're right about that," Jones said.

"Are either of you sure?" Carney asked.

"I said I think so," Zeppy said.

"Oh. You think so," Carney said. "If you have to think,

then you don't know, asshole. Turn around right here and go back the same way we came."

Zeppy stepped out of the truck and scouted the shoulders of the road. "There's trenches," he said. "Some pretty deep ruts. Jonesy will have to guide me."

"Christ. That's the blind leading the blind," Louie said.

"You got that right," Carney said. "I'll guide. Both of you get back in the truck and listen up."

"What a bringdown," Louie said. "What a fucking bummer."

Carney stood in front of the truck, near the rut on the left-hand side. He waved the truck toward him. He was lit up by the headlights.

"Cut those fucking lights," Amaro said. He jumped off the truck and stood several meters behind Carney, facing the bush.

Zeppy cut the lights.

Louie walked across the road. Amaro crossed with him and entered the woodline. It was dark, full of darker shadows. All he heard was the engine idling, the gears grinding. He felt like he was asking for it.

Louie guided the truck backward. After repeating the move several times, the truck started back down the road in the direction from which it had come.

Louie lit another joint and passed it around in the back of the truck. "Don't give them any," he said, nodding toward the cab.

With the lights out, Zeppy had to drive slowly. He stopped at a fork in the road.

"What's up?" Louie asked.

"I don't remember which way I turned coming up," Zeppy said. "Which way should I go?"

Carney shook his head. "How the hell do you expect me to know? You were driving the fucking thing, for Chrissakes."

"I think it's to the right," Jones said.

"Then make a left," Louie said.

"Maybe we should listen to him," Carney said. "He's probably the only one who was paying attention."

Clyde said, "That sure ain't saying much."

"I know," Carney said. "But what are we going to do? Make the right, Zep."

"Left."

In the dust aura around the beams of light they saw the outline of a guard tower and the spirals of concertina wire and cheered. They weren't far from town. The truck headed for the Strip.

The bars were roaring when they pulled up in front of the Hollywood. The guys bailed out and sauntered in.

The dance floor was enormous. Big enough for separate bars to do business along each wall. And at the bars, perched on stools, were pretty girls dressed the same way the singer had been in the Chu Lai club: miniskirts and spike heels. Most of them were brunettes, but some had bleached-blond frizz. They were pink, electric blue, soft gray, and silky black. These colors blazed by on fishnet legs, and clicked across the floor. The guys dispersed, looking for their regulars.

The band played on a raised stage. Spotlights sliced the smoky space. Americans—airmen, mostly—laughed and grabbed their balls and danced with the slender women. They hung on these pretty girls, whispered loud in their ears. And the girls just wiggled and giggled and ran their tongues over parted lips. "American Bandstand," Asia-style. That's what it looked like to him. Pounding music, flashing lights, laughter—lots of laughter—and made-up girls with almond eyes. Amaro smiled at one. She turned away quickly.

He and Louie ordered a drink. Irish whiskey. "Give me a double Irish whiskey," he said, feeling uncomfortable when he said it. He gulped it down and ordered another. Eighteen years old and on his own in Indochina with a pocketful of money. The music sounded wild. The women all looked hot. The bartender had a gold tooth.

He watched them dancing on the floor, watched American servicemen and Asian ladies raise their arms and shake their asses, trying to keep time with the drummer.

He picked up the drink and walked over to a woman sitting on one of the stools. From a distance, she looked pretty. Up close, she was beautiful.

She had silky hair that broke in black waves over thin olive-skinned shoulders. Firm breasts pushed against a tank-top, and she crossed her legs just the way he would have her cross them in his dreams. Long legs. Slender. One of her shoes dangled from her toes.

"Want to dance?" he asked.

"No dance," she said. At first, he did not hear her. He only watched her lips move. Full lips. Moist and pink like the flower in her hair.

"Want to dance?" he repeated.

"I say no dance," she said.

"How about a drink?"

"You pay. I drink," she said, waving to the bartender. He brought her an amber-filled glass and gave her what looked like a poker chip.

"My name is John. What's yours?"

"My name Din. Hello, John." She swallowed the drink in one piece and set the glass on the bar. "You buy more?"

"Sure," he said.

She waved to the bartender. A refill and another chip.

"That flower in your hair," Amaro said. "Does that mean you're spoken for or still eligible?"

"It mean a flower in my hair, John," she said.

An airman stood next to Amaro and tapped him on the shoulder. "Be careful, soldier," he said. "She's gonna take you for three drinks and split with somebody else."

"What are you talking about?" Amaro asked. He checked the guy's stripes, but couldn't figure out what rank he was.

"I'm talking about those sores on your face, man. The dinks are uptight about leprosy. Bet she won't dance with you."

"I didn't ask her yet," Amaro said. "Besides, it's jungle rot."

"I know it and you know it," the airman said. "But you better spread some bread on sweet pea if you're hopin' to hitch your digger." He took his beer and strolled among the dancers.

Amaro sipped his whiskey. Din stared out at the crowd as if searching for someone she knew.

"I just came in from the field," Amaro said. "You know. I'm here on R and R."

"Me, too," Din said without turning around. "You have money?" she asked.

"Yeah. Listen. These sores. They're not what you think," Amaro said. "It's from being in the jungle. It's not catching or anything."

Din turned and looked at his face. "Once I see people from the island. They have many bumps here," she said, running her fingertips over his cheek.

Amaro reached up and held her hand pressed against his face. "Come with me to a room," he said. "I'll show you. No bumps. Just these frigging sores. You won't catch it, I promise."

"You give forty?" she asked.

"I give forty," he said.

She smiled. "You give fifty?"

"I give forty-five," he said.

"Buy one drink," she said, waving again to the bartender. This time he handed her another chip—no drink—and took money from Amaro's change.

"Come," she said.

Amaro followed her to the back door. She handed a bouncer the three chips. He wrote something on a pad and nodded.

"Where are you from?" Amaro asked as they walked into the back and down a corridor.

She stopped, looked around, then pointed toward the hills. "There," she said, then led him into her room.

"See? No bumps," Amaro said as he tossed his fatigue shirt and pants on a low chair. He kicked off his boots, pulled off his socks. "No bumps. Only jungle rot."

He sat on the edge of the bed and watched Din undress. She pulled her tanktop up slowly, holding it over her head stretched between her arms. Her breasts were red from the weave. Brown nipples, round as berries, stood up on larger brown circles. Her stomach was flat and smooth.

"You like?" she asked, slipping the tanktop from her arms.

"You bet I like," he said.

"Then you give fifty now?" she asked, holding her hand out.

"I give fifty in a minute," he said.

Din stretched out naked on the sheet. One leg straight,

the other bent in a teasing kind of a pose. She still had on her high heels. Her legs were thin, but shapely and strong. Her hips were girlish narrow. For a minute, Amaro wondered how old she was under that hairdo and makeup.

"Here's your fifty," he said.

She smiled, took it, and rolled on one side to tuck the bills in her handbag. There was a fine down on her heart-shaped ass. He laughed.

"You laugh nice," Din said. "Come next to me."

He slid his skivvies down his legs, then reached out and turned off the lamp. He did not want Din to see his hands.

Moonlight fell across the bed in a frosty haze. Amaro lay next to her, touching legs and bellies, her nipples pressing up against his chest. He kissed the wildflower hollow of her neck, flowers in a summer breeze mingled with a trace of body odor. Her scent. Musky and pleasant.

She pulled him over on top of her and kissed him on the mouth. A long, warm kiss. Her fingers felt cool, they tingled on his back wherever they lightly touched.

Up on his elbows, he sucked on her nipples, his tongue making wet circles around her swollen flesh. Her stomach quivered and tensed when he slid his hips over it. She slipped both hands under his hips, cupping his sex in her fingers.

"You no like me?" she asked.

"I love you," he said.

"Maybe you drink too much?"

"Maybe."

She rolled him off her to his side. "Din fix you up," she said.

While she tried to fix him up, her fingers and lips flitting over his skin, Amaro closed his eyes and searched his memory for images to help her out.

He thought of the first time, standing in Linda's parents' basement with his pants around his ankles as Linda did those things to him with her lips. He bent slightly at the knees and held her head, ran his fingers through the tangled curls on her head and whispered her name when his legs buckled and his stomach tightened and he felt turned inside out.

Amaro opened his eyes and watched Din kneeling over him. He rubbed her feet. Ran the palms of his hands over the smooth skin of her legs. He rubbed her pretty ass, then reached under it, stretching his fingers across her stomach. She tightened her legs around his arm and shimmied slowly as his fingertips touched her breast.

He felt her wet and hot against his crotch. She pulled on his nuts and licked the underside of his prick. She nibbled, used her tongue and teeth, sucked it all in, only for it to pop from her mouth and fall limp against his leg.

She moaned. Her body stiffened. Quivered. She parted her legs, released his arm, and rolled over on her side, brushing from her face the wayward strands of hair clinging to her sweaty cheeks.

"You dead soldier tonight," she said, fingering the numb and lifeless lump of flesh between his legs. "Whiskey bad for making much fuck."

He sat up quickly and reached for her throat. He knew how to snap her neck like a dry stick in his hands. Or just squeeze for a minute or two until her lungs stopped.

He pulled his hands back from her throat as if he had touched a hot stove. She glared at him. Slowly, he pressed his thumb against her lips and stroked them gently.

"Get out of here," he said.

Din jumped from the bed and pulled on her clothes with a fluid motion. She walked quickly to the door, opened it, and stepped out into the hall. She did not look back before slamming the wooden door shut.

Amaro lay naked on the bed in the harsh yellow lamplight. He was covered with sweat. His hands felt on fire and his fingers, smeared with pus, stuck together. He stared at the ceiling and felt a dull constant ache deep in his chest, as if something in there was being pinched. He pressed the heel of his hand against his chest but could not reach the aching spot. His breath came in short gasps. His mouth was dry and liquor tasting.

He turned his head and looked at the door. He was glad Din had left. He had wanted to kill her with the same passion he had wanted to fuck her. Both feelings were exactly the same and he could not understand that.

9

Amaro sat with his legs crossed, Indian-style. He leaned forward, flipping the ejection port on the M-16 that lay across his lap.

"Why don't you put that away, man. You're making me nervous."

"Sorry," Amaro said. He picked up the rifle and propped it against the wall, then fell back onto the rug. "I don't want to die in this miserable motherfucker. Shit."

"Take it easy," Louie said. "VC can be cured." He leaned forward and squeezed Amaro's shoulder. "Just take it easy. You're safe in here. Sit up." He lit a cigarette and reached it over to Amaro. "Here," he said. "Get up and take it. I don't want you burning no fuckin' holes in my one-of-a-kind Oriental rug."

Amaro propped himself up on one elbow. He stuck the cigarette between his lips and took a long drag. His lips were dry and split. He couldn't get a good hit. He puffed several times to work up a mouthful of smoke. He inhaled, held it in, let it out slowly with a low hissing noise.

"Tastes like shit," Amaro said between coughs. His shoulders hurt. His neck was stiff.

"Good," Louie said as he stood up and moved backward to sit on the edge of his bunk. "You know what they say. 'A bitchin' soldier is a happy soldier.'"

"Yeah," Amaro said. "And people who say, 'You know what they say,' are a real pain in the ass."

"And fuck you, too," Louie said.

"What month is today?" Amaro asked.

"It's the first August after last January," Louie answered.

"Wake me up in the spring," Amaro said, rolling over on one side, his head back on the pillow.

Louie leaned over and kicked him in the ass. "Hey, fucko. The rug," he said.

"Do that again and I'll shit on your fuckin' rug," Amaro said. "Leave me alone. I got a headache."

"I'll bet. Between them goofballs and all the spooky shit you got crawling around in there, I'm surprised it don't explode."

"I'm sick. My stomach's growling."

"Get up."

"Fuck you."

"Get up," Louie said, letting go with another kick. A harder kick, this time.

Amaro reached behind his back and tried to snare Louie's foot. He winced in pain.

"Get up," Louie repeated.

"Okay. Okay," Amaro said. "But only because I got to piss." He struggled slowly to his feet and stood, shaky on wobbling legs. He reached toward the ceiling, trying to stretch out the kinks. "Wow. I'm really out of it."

"You're telling me," Louie said. He picked up a towel and threw it at Amaro. It bounced off Amaro's chest and fell to the floor. "After you clear the tube, you might try taking a shower. You stink."

"I'm allowed to stink," Amaro said. "Everybody with jungle rot has a right to stink like wormy cheese." He rubbed his fingers through his hair. He growled.

"Feel better?" Louie asked.

"Yeah."

Louie said, "Go take a shower and get human again."

Amaro lumbered to the showers. He hung the towel on a hook in the stall and sat on a commode.

The commodes were separated by plywood partitions, but had no doors. The fronts were open, facing the urinals across the room. The concrete floor sloped down to a large metal drain in the center. Amaro lit a cigarette and tried to push out whatever it was that churned in his guts by tightening his stomach muscles. It did not work. He smoked his cigarette and strained harder. He picked at the painted veneer surrounding a knothole and pulled a long thin strip of it clear, revealing the bare wood underneath. He coiled the strip and let it spring back out.

Amaro recited a poem scribbled on the partition.

"Are you talkin' at me?" a gravelly voice asked. A short, squat black guy with thick eyeglasses stood in front of the open commode.

"You could get killed sneaking up on people like that," Amaro said, startled, feeling stupid getting caught with his pants down. "But no, I wasn't talking to you. I didn't even know you were in the goddamn latrine."

"You wasn't talkin' at me?" the guy asked again, as if in disbelief, as if he knew Amaro had recited the graffiti for him.

"I told you," Amaro said, "I didn't know you were in here."

"Oh yeah? Better be. Better be," the guy said in half-swallowed words. "Better be talkin' to yo'self, grayfay."

"I was," Amaro said. "Fuck off."

"Better be," the guy said. He turned and faced a urinal, the one directly across from Amaro.

The guy reached in front of him and kind of bent a little at the knees, ready to piss. Amaro dropped the cigarette butt in the toilet. It hissed when it hit the water. Then he lit another smoke. He took a long drag and shook his head.

The black guy turned at the waist and looked over his shoulder. "What are you lookin' at, man?" he asked.

"Nothing much," Amaro said.

"Why you be lookin' at me, man?" the guy said. "You lookin' at Hamer?"

"Hey. What the fuck is your problem, chump?" Amaro said, standing quickly and belting his pants. "Why don't you go piss on a tree and leave me the fuck alone."

The guy zipped his fly and pointed a finger at Amaro. "I got my eye on you, man. I know who you be," he said as he walked backward out of the latrine.

Amaro made sure the guy was on his way out the hooch door. He pulled his towel off the hook and walked to the showers. He sat on a wooden bench and pulled off his socks.

He threw them against the wall. "Motherfucker," he said, loud and angry. "I'll be good and goddamned I can't even shit in peace." He ripped his fatigue jacket off, tearing some of the buttons free. They clicked and tapped and skittered on the concrete. He kicked at them with a bare foot. "Ouch, goddamn it, fuck this motherfuckin' army and this country and all the motherfuckers in both. *'I know who you be.'* What the fuck does that mean? 'I know who you be.'"

The black guy stepped out of the deep shadows and aimed an M-16 at Amaro's heart. Amaro stopped dead in his tracks. What a humbug, he thought, after all the bullshit, to be gunned down cold in a hallway by some bug-eyed lunatic. "Oh man, what the fuck," he said.

"I told you I know who you be." The guy said it slowly in a raspy whisper. "I seen you around. You ain't got no function here. But I know where you be at and you ain't gonna bust me, motherfucker."

Amaro smiled. "You're wrong, man. I'm not the heat. I'm not going to bust anybody. Shit. You don't know, man. I'm just visiting. Put that away."

"I'm a put you away, fool," he said. "Just visitin', my ass. This ain't some dumb nigger you be talkin' shit at, ofay."

"Look. You got it all wrong. I ain't what—"

"How do you know?" He pulled the bolt. A live round, locked and loaded. The ejected cartridge bounced in metallic clicks along the concrete floor.

"I ain't what you think I am, man. I'm . . . I'm just hanging out with some friends."

"Yeah? Well you ain't gonna be hangin' out with nobody no more."

"Put that away and let's talk, man. Give me a chance to—"

"Talkin's done."

Amaro felt his heart pounding, his pulse at his temples. It's better not to know. It's better to get it while walking along, cursing the heat and the weight, smoking a cigarette, thinking about something else. He stared into the little black mouth of the muzzle and waited for it to spit something hard through his chest. Something smaller than the tip of his little finger. It would hurt like a motherfucker but only for a second or two.

"What the fuck is going on out here?" somebody yelled.

"None of your business."

Amaro felt someone's hand on his shoulder. He tried to push it away. Louie pushed harder, and Amaro fell against the wall. Then Louie stood between the black guy and Amaro.

"Your only claim to soul, Hamer, is your color," Louie said. "Go ahead and shoot, motherfucker. Kill me, then him, then everyone else in the hooch. Just save a round for yourself."

Amaro stepped next to Louie, faced Hamer. "Go back inside, Lou," he said.

Hamer took a few steps backward. He shifted his point of aim from Louie to Amaro.

"Go ahead," Louie said. "Whenever you feel froggy, take the leap."

Hamer lowered his rifle. He turned and walked away.

"He thought I was CID," Amaro said. "He was ready to light me up."

"You came closer than you know, darlin'," Louie said. "Come on, let's go get loaded."

They drove the coast road south from Chu Lai. The view was familiar: lots of people walking—kids mostly—oxcarts, stands of sugarcane and bamboo poles, strings of sun-dried fish hanging from taut commo wire, motorbikes and lots of dust. Thatch-roof huts lined the roadside. Some of them had no front wall, and Amaro saw old men sleeping on the floor inside. Children played in them. Women cooked. Here and there a shack of scrap wood roofed with sheet metal made from beer cans, stood out among the huts.

"This is still the city of Chu Lai," Louie said. "Part of it, anyway. Suburbs, guess you'd call it."

Children, naked and potbellied, stood staring at the truck. Some of them pissed on the dirt, some waved, smiling nervously as they grabbed at their private parts. Mothers yelled in that harsh but musical way the Vietnamese spoke.

Amaro thought about the way they talked, and he wondered how someone who had those strange noises in his head would think about the world. To Amaro, the Vietnamese always sounded angry, abrupt, in a hurry to have done with it.

The hooches thinned out until they no longer appeared on the roadside, giving way to the jungle shapes and colors that seemed to flow, like slow water, down from surrounding hills. The road widened, and the truck picked up speed, though it still seemed to just crawl along, winding like a lazy snake.

For several miles Amaro watched the jungle, thinking how beautiful it was when he was not part of it. The woodline gradually receded, and flat sections of wild grass and low shrubs appeared. A few stucco buildings in clearings were painted pastel blue and pink, dirty gray where the paint had peeled. Tin roofs, shutters, outdoor tables. Small, carefully tended gardens. Families eating in the shade of tall trees.

Vietnamese walked along the road carrying baskets, bundles, sticks across their shoulders with things tied to either side.

"I'll be goddamned," Amaro said. "Look at that." He pointed to a young Vietnamese guy dressed in dungarees and a loud print shirt. The guy steered his motor scooter around the people on the road, a young girl in back of him, her arms around his waist, her long black hair like a pennant in the wind. She wore a bright silk dress and shoes, and her slender legs straddled the bike. She leaned forward and said something into his ear. The guy laughed and shouted something back to her, and she kissed his cheek. They both smiled.

"Where do they come from?" Amaro asked. He had never seen a Vietnamese his age who wasn't dressed in a uniform or black pajamas.

"City dinks," Louie said.

"How come he isn't in the army?" Amaro said.

"His daddy is connected, probably. A politician, or he's from a wealthy family."

"Ain't this a bitch," Amaro said. "He looks like he's doing okay."

"Are you kidding?" Louie said. "He's doing a lot better than me and you. Look at the ass on that babe. That guy is doing great."

"I can't even afford a motor scooter," Amaro said.

"That guy must be making a fortune in drugs and the black market," Louie said.

"It sure is a lot different out in the boondocks. The gooks out there don't have running water, let alone a fucking motor scooter."

"That's what we're here for, soldier. So they can all have a motor scooter and a hot fox to fool around with."

Groups of children wearing shorts ran alongside the truck. "You give *sop-sop,* Joe," they yelled. "You give can'y maybe."

"Here," Louie said, placing a sack on the seat between Amaro and himself. "Toss some pogey-bait to them."

Amaro reached into the sack and threw candy out of the truck. Some of the kids caught it on the fly. Others stopped and fought for the stuff that landed on the road.

"Just think," Amaro said, "twenty years from now our sons might be over here killing those kids."

"I don't give a fuck what happens over here after my year is up," Louie said.

They slowed as they approached an intersection. There was a white stucco church with a weathered roof and a steeple with a bell. On the opposite corner was a shrine made of stone and shaped like a well, with a colorful statue of a laughing Buddha sitting under a pointed roof.

The kids ran and yelled. Girls smiled shyly. Oxcarts on the side of the road stopped to give them room.

"Do we have time to smoke a jay," Amaro asked.

"There's always time to do a joint," Louie said.

On the road the people were just people, doing the things they did every day for thousands and thousands of years. None of them carried rifles or toted satchel charges. None of them leaped backward, as if pulled by a wire when Amaro willed a round right through their hearts. They acted as if there was no war going on, and Amaro wondered, just for an instant, if the war ever really happened. Maybe he had imagined it all.

"Man, am I fucked up," he said.

"Amen, brother," Louie said, handing Amaro another joint. "Here you go, Johnny Amaro. Just enough to get us around Mars one more time."

"Hey, Lou. Did you know there are rings around Uranus?"

"Only when I nod on the crapper," Louie said.

Amaro took a long poke on the joint. A seed snapped and

exploded, blowing ashes and leaf bits into his face. "That means something, man," Amaro said.

"Oh yeah? What?" Louie asked.

Amaro took another hit and thought about it. He thought it meant that he was special somehow. It had something to do with him wearing this particular tarnished brass buckle at this unique moment in the whole long, never-ending flow of time. In another place, in another time, the brass may have been part of a dead soldier's sword. Or armor. An ornament on a luxurious purple robe. The buckle and that popping seed. They were all too real and interconnected to merely be random coincidence.

"I don't know yet," Amaro said.

"I'll tell you what it means," Louie yelled from behind the steering wheel. "It means you better pass that fuckin' blaster before I smack you upside the head."

Amaro took another poke and passed the joint.

"Goddamn," Louie yelled. "You steamed the fucker up." He lit another ready-roll. "Here," he said, handing it to Amaro. "Keep this one for yourself."

Amaro said, "Be cool with the head tools."

Amaro smoked the joint down to where it burned his fingertips. He grubbed a Salem from Louie, rolled an inch of tobacco from the end, and scattered the shreds in the wind. He slipped the roach into the paper tube and rolled it shut. It took him a while to work up enough spit to roll it tight between his lips without splitting the paper.

He sucked the smoke in and held it down for as long as he could. He always felt that last long hit mushroom upward to his skull. Fallout sparkled behind his eyes. There were pink and blue stucco buildings. Roadside shrines. A whole world moving slowly through a dirt-brown sunlit mist.

Amaro sat back. His fatigue shirt clung to his sweaty skin. Louie, sitting next to him, lit joint after joint and handed them to Amaro. Amaro held on to them, taking pokes until Louie complained out loud. Then Amaro passed them.

His mouth was dry. His tongue felt thick and his lips stuck to his teeth. He blinked and seemed to feel his eyelids scratch over swollen capillaries. But he did not feel high enough. He did not reach that don't-give-a-fuck state he needed to get by.

He could not reach the point where there was no difference between what he saw with his eyes and what he only saw in his head, or the point at which he did not care one way or the other.

He sat in the truck, bouncing hard as the tires shimmied in and out of the ruts. There were cracks in the vinyl seats, the underwebbing showing through in spots. The paint, the light-absorbing paint, was chipped to bare metal. Splotches of mud and splattered bugs clustered on the windscreen. The smell of sweat, of fermenting jungle, engine exhaust, and the sweet top note of primo Asian reefer, clung to him like too much cheap cologne. He wondered how he got there and where he would be tomorrow.

The checkered linen tablecloth was spread with paper plates. Candles flickered from the necks of two empty Chianti bottles. Wax cooled in beaded lines on the straw weave. Forks and spoons were on the napkins. Fresh flowers drooped from a bud vase.

"Have some more," Zeppy said, lifting the gallon to refill Amaro's paper cup. "It's jug wine, but it's good. After all, this ain't Canarsie."

"It's pretty close to it," Amaro said, holding his cup steady. "*Salute*," he said.

"*Salute*," Zeppy replied.

"This tally red ain't that bad," Clyde said. "Give me another hit."

"Don't make a pig out of yourself," Zeppy said. "We got to save some for the pasta."

"Come on, man," Clyde said. "Pour me a little taste."

"Go siphon some diesel fuel," Zeppy said. "That's the shit you rednecks like to drink."

Clyde picked up the gallon and poured himself more wine.

Amaro held his cup out. "I'll take some more, too," he said.

"You got it, partner," Clyde said. "You know, my daddy always says there's just two ways to drink. Alone or with somebody."

"Your daddy makes good sense," Amaro said.

"They're both full of shit, if you ask me," Zeppy said.

"Only ain't nobody askin'," Clyde said.

There was a loud knock on the door, like someone kicked it near the bottom. "Yo, Zeppolla. Open up," Louie said from the other side.

Zeppy unlocked the door. Louie walked in carrying a large serving bowl overfilled with steaming linguine. "Make a space on the table," he said.

Carney came in behind Louie and shut the door. He locked it. Clyde moved the candles and the vase from the center of the table. Louie set the bowl down and smiled.

"That smells great," Amaro said, leaning over into the steam.

"It is great," Louie said. "I put three cans of Carmen Basilio tomato sauce on that sucker. And plenty of hot *salzicci.*"

Amaro said, "Get the fuck outta here—Carmen Basilio tomato sauce."

"Hey. No lie," Louie said. "Yo, Zeppolla. Get me a can from the footlocker."

Zeppy rummaged around in the locker, then stood and tossed Louie a can.

"Here you go, chump. Straight from the States. Carmen squeezed it with his own little hands," Louie said.

Amaro held the label up next to the candlelight. The face was familiar. Thick lips. Splayed nose. The scar tissue around his eyes had been airbrushed and retouched.

"That's Carmen Basilio, all right," Amaro said. He laughed. Basilio used to look like tomato sauce and sausage bits after every one of his fights. But Amaro still admired him.

"Chow time," Clyde said, rubbing his hands together.

"Fuck you, chow time," Louie said. "Chow time is for slopping hogs in the mess hall. Tonight we say *mangiamo.* Give me your plates."

Carney snapped a tape into the cassette player. An Italian aria filled the room. "Don't look at me," he said. "It's Louie's tape."

"Fuckin' A," Louie said. "Di Stefano. The best. We need

just the right atmosphere to capture the mood here in Luigi's Hideaway."

"*Recitar! Mentre preso dal delirio.*"

Amaro knew the opera. He had heard it a thousand times in his father's barbershop. Heard it sung by Caruso. Gigli. Di Stefano . . . *non so più quel che dico e quel che faccio!*

Amaro sprinkled crushed red pepper and grated cheese over his linguine. He twirled his fork in the strands and filled his mouth.

"Christ, you're disgusting," Zeppy said to Clyde. "You look like you're slurpin' worms or something."

Clyde wiped sauce from his chin. "I guess it takes practice to eat this stuff like a wop."

"Years," Louie said.

"Leave him alone, Zep," Carney said. "Tonight's a special night."

They ate and drank. Amaro and Louie took turns sopping sauce from the empty bowl with pieces of fresh-baked bread.

"This is fuckin' unreal," Amaro said.

"It's not over yet," Carney said, placing a covered pot on the table. "I'm not really sure what this is all about, being Irish and all, but Louie wants to perform an ancient guinea ritual."

. . . *tramuta in lazzi lo spasmo ed il pianto* . . .

"I have special dispensation from Don Cheech in Brookaleen to perform this ceremony in front of nonbelievers," Louie said, standing up. He tied a red bandanna around his neck, then lifted the pot lid and uncovered a couple of dozen meatballs piled in a pyramid.

. . . *in una smorfia il singhiozzo e il dolor* . . .

Louie took a clean plate and forked a meatball onto it, the one on top, larger than the rest. He cut the meatball into four equal parts.

"Ahh," he said. "From the position of the *pignoli* beans, I see a short, safe journey for one of us."

"Which one of us?" Clyde asked.

"Shut up, *fidendone,*" Louie said.

"Silence during the augury," Carney said.

"Which one of us?" Louie said. "One who is fucked up for sure, but not a bad guy."

"Thanks," Amaro said.

"Wait!" Louie shouted. "Wait!" He waved his hands over the plate. "Look at this raisin, my brothers. A good omen," he said. "It means one of us will be saved. Spared to live a long and happy life. I see lots of children. A grapevine and a fig tree and a long-legged lady in high-heels and glittery gold panties."

"Hey. If this works out, I'm next on the list for this deal," Carney said.

"Give me a couple of those things," Zeppy said.

"Meatballs for a meatball," Louie said. "Coming right up."

Amaro took a couple and mashed them between two slices of bread. "More wine," he said. "*Vino.* More *vino.*"

Carney walked around the table filling paper cups. He picked up his own glass. "A toast," he said. "A toast to former Sergeant Amaro. A safe and boring war."

They cheered and drank their wine.

The jeep crunched through a gravel bed and came to a stop fifty meters from a long Quonset hut at the base of the operations tower. The airstrip spread in front of Amaro for as far as he could see. Visible heat quivered from the tarmac. Everything vibrated through it: jeeps, trucks, grounded planes. They all seemed to shake apart and float away like water turned to steam.

Carney said, "Some of the guys in there know us."

"Just walk in and show them your orders," Zeppy said. "They'll tell you what to do."

Amaro stood up and jumped from the jeep.

Louie reached behind the seat and picked up a brown canvas AWOL bag. "You forgot this," he said, handing it to Amaro.

"Thanks," Amaro said.

There was a shaving kit, a change of drawers, and an extra pair of socks in the bag.

Louie waved without looking as the jeep lurched away. Amaro listened to the sound of the jeep replaced by the thud of an approaching chopper.

10

The First Brigade of the 101st Airborne Division was headquartered in Phan Rang. To the northeast a small hill separated the camp from the South China Sea. Low-growing shrubs and grass interspersed with occasional palm trees dotted the dusty soil extending east to the coast. To the west lay the ridgelines of the highlands.

Each week the brigade's replacements started P-Training before joining their units. Amaro wondered what the *P* stood for.

The new guys were of all ranks and military occupational specialties. There were NCOs slated as squad leaders and platoon sergeants; second lieutenants, a few from West Point, most from OCS, about to assume command of a platoon; captains hoping to make major by commanding an infantry company; doctors; cooks; artillerymen; demolitions experts; truckdrivers; supply clerks; and the boonyrat eleven bravos. During P-Week they all trained together. There was no rank-pulling or specialty. They were all cherries. They slept in the same tents, ate the same chow, used the same latrines and showers. During P-Week rank had no privileges. Only time in country conferred status. Amaro liked ordering the officers around.

The replacements were formed up between the mess hall and the row of tents used to billet incoming troops. Tent numbers were assigned. They were briefed on procedure as they stood at ease in the sun. Some of them swayed gently, as if the only thing holding them upright was the heavy Asian air. Falling into a single file, they each posed for a Polaroid photo atop a sandbag wall.

They were issued three pairs of jungle fatigues and boots, steel pots, helmet liners, web gear, and weapons. The web gear and steel pots were to be worn at all times, the weapon carried constantly. Each guy was issued two magazines of live ammo with instructions not to seat a round unless told.

After Amaro dismissed the troops, he helped carry some gear to Tent 3 and threw the stuff on an empty cot. It raised a cloud of dust.

"Some fuckin' place, ain't it?" he said to the Spec-5 who lay down on a cot nearby.

"Sure is," he replied. "My name is Spencer. What's yours?"

"Amaro."

"What's your MOS, Amaro?"

"Eleven B."

"Too bad," Spencer said. "I'm a forward observer. Where you assigned?"

"Third of the Three-two-seven. I'm going back to my unit next week. This week I train you people."

"I'm going to Headquarters Company of the First." Spencer sat up and pulled a candy bar from his pocket. "You like chocolate? I brought some with me from Cam Ranh Bay."

"Yeah. Thanks," Amaro said. The candy had melted on the paper. Amaro ate the sticky chocolate off the wrapper by scraping it against his teeth.

The others walked across the wood-planked floor of the tent looking for an empty cot. Conversations started gradually. Within an hour or so the tent was lively with chatter.

"When do we chow down around here?" someone asked.

"Don't make no difference," someone shouted back. "I hear the chow sucks."

The men from Tent 3 shuffled over to the mess hall when they heard the whistle blow. They sat together after filling their trays on the chow line. The chow sucked.

"This is enough to make you appreciate eating Cs," Spencer said.

Amaro pushed the dried-out meatloaf away. The heat had taken his appetite and the brown tile of chopped meat, with its dark red splotch of tomato paste, did not appeal to him. A mulatto E-6 seated across from Amaro forked it off the tray and ate it in two bites.

"Christ," Amaro said. "Is that what happens when you make E-6?"

"A six is a lifer," someone at the other end of the table said. "And a lifer will eat shit and splinters."

"Fuckin' A," the mulatto said. "And chow down on your old lady for a light snack."

Destry, a lanky black kid from Cleveland, winced. "Ya'll don't eat that stuff, do ya?"

"Do the wild bear shit in the woods?" the E-6 replied.

"Some ol' gal back home askt me ta kiss it once," Destry said. "An' I tol' her, I said, 'Girl, what you crazy, girl? You pee through that thing. I shonuff ain't gonna eat no goddamn pussy. Uh-unnh.'"

"Sh-it," the mulatto said. "Show me a man don't eat his old lady nor jackoff his huntin' dog and I'll steal 'em both."

"Well, if you can eat the meatloaf, you can eat any fucking thing," Spencer said.

"Sh-it. Let me tell you something, son," the mulatto said with his mouth full of food. "When you been in Sam's family for as long as I have, you learn that if you can't eat it, smoke it, or fuck it, just piss on it and walk away."

"Some fucking philosophy," Amaro said.

Spencer, Destry, and Amaro left the mess hall and strolled back toward Tent 3. Dusk was turning to dark. They watched the rose-tinted lavender sky turn black above the mountains. Coming from within the tents, loud laughter punctuated rapid phrases.

The three walked along the road, passing OD trailers marked POTABLE WATER and NONPOTABLE WATER.

"Where you from, Amaro?" Spencer asked.

"New York. How 'bout you?"

"Philly. Where were you stationed before you got here?"

"The Five-oh-eight in Panama. I was there for six months while I was going through jungle training. Then I drew the hundred and first here."

"I heard Panama was a good duty station," Destry said.

"I liked it. The women are hot and pretty and the reefer's the best."

Destry said, "I'd like to go to Panama when I get outta here."

"I want to go to Europe," Amaro said.

"This is my second burst of three." Spencer switched his rifle to his other shoulder. "I spent my first tour of duty in Germany. It was fucking great. You'd like it," he said, turning to Destry. "Them big blond German ladies really dig black guys."

"I heard that," Destry replied. "But I think I'd like to go to Panama. I heard that Panama Red is 'bout the best reefer in the world." He looked at Amaro. Amaro shrugged his shoulders.

Spencer didn't, or wouldn't, take the hint so they let the conversation drift to other subjects.

The noise from a nearby Quonset hut grew louder as they approached. They stood in the stream of light at the doorway and peered in at the short-timers who were in Phan Rang for processing out of country.

They had darkly circled eyes and gaunt hollow cheeks. None were fat: there was not an ounce of loose flesh on any of them. Their fatigues were wrinkled and stained; their skins sun-darkened. Their jungle boots, like Amaro's, were cracked and worn ragged.

Some of the short-timers lay on their cots, hands behind their heads, staring at the concave ceiling of the hut. Others sat staring at nothing at all. Off to one side was a high-stakes crap game. The Hispanic with the dice was on a roll. He held a wad of American dollars in his hand, the accumulation of back pay held in escrow. They had all exchanged military scrip for real-world money and now won or lost without thinking much of it either way.

The players sat back on their haunches chewing on cigars, smoking cigarettes, waving fists full of green. They played intensely, shouting and cursing and laughing. The money seemed secondary. The game was just a way to pass the anxious time until they got back to the World. Amaro watched the game silently from the door, then turned around and walked back up the road to Tent 3.

Most of the guys were already fast asleep. Some snored loudly. The rest were huddled in quiet conversation.

Amaro unlaced his boots and, still dressed, fell back on the hard cot.

The sharp and unmistakable report of an M-16 on automatic startled the entire section of the camp. The replacements leaped from their cots, dazed and frightened and still half asleep. Some of the cadre rushed into Tent 3 looking ridiculous in steel pots, boots, and skivvies. They all carried their weapons.

The mulatto E-6 stood at the head of his cot, rifle in his hands and his back against the tent wall. The tent smelled of cordite.

The wooden floor next to his cot was splintered. A new jungle boot was torn to shreds by the rounds he had fired through it. Pieces of gray-black snake mingled with torn canvas and leather and splintered flooring.

"*A krait snake,*" the E-6 shouted, trying to catch his breath. He was shaking and covered with sweat. "I put on my boot . . . felt the fucker with my foot."

"And you lit it up," one of the cadre said.

"What was I 'sposed to do? It was fixin' to *bite* me, god-damn it."

The replacements looked at one another and smiled nervously. The cadre shook their heads and walked out of the tent. The replacements calmed down, relieved that the situation had not been more serious. It was light outside. They all checked out their boots before pulling them on. The mulatto sat on his cot, eyes wide and vacant.

Amaro and Spencer carried hot coffee, buttered bread, and an apple back to the tent. They handed the food to the mulatto.

"Eat something, Sarge. You'll feel better," Spencer said.

"Don't need no food. Ghostas don't eat."

"Forget about it, man," Amaro said.

"It's a omen," the mulatto said. "A fuckin' omen is what it is."

"It was a tired snake," Spencer said.

"A omen," the mulatto repeated, sitting on the edge of his cot, still in his drawers. "God, I'm cold."

They placed the food on a napkin next to his rack and walked away.

After chow the replacements were marched over to the wooden bleacher seats for the start of their orientation. Veterans in starched and tailored jungle fatigues related the advice and myths they had learned and absorbed firsthand. The replacements were instructed in the proper treatment of drinking water with Halazone tablets; they were warned about the incurable "blackwater syphilis" carried by the indigents; they were told to take salt tablets daily and Dapsone once a week.

The instructor said, "If you start freezin' to death in V'etnam, gennelmens, head for the battalion aid station immediately if not sooner."

Leeches were never to be pulled off the skin. That caused infection. "And if you got the shits, eat the fruitcake in the Cs: it's the best cork in the world."

The endless lectures went in one ear and out the other. The replacements sat in the bleachers in the hot sun and heavy air without listening. Most of them, overcome by the climate, dozed insensibly on the backless plank seats. Amaro watched them and thought about home.

"Remember, gennelmens," the instructor said. "Ol' Charlie he say, 'Beware the soldier with the chicken on his shoulder.' Y'all are Screamin' Eagles and your onliest reason for livin' is to kill the mothafuckin' Cong."

After lunch they were returned to the bleachers for a history of the 101st from the Battle of the Bulge through Nijmegen, Holland, to the invasion of Normandy. "The best: run further, fight harder." Reputation, honor, glory, the bodycount, and Robert Ryan dressed as a general.

"Bullshit and manipulation," Spencer said.

"But it works like a charm," Amaro said.

"Yeah," Destry nodded. "I knows what you mean. I wanna get out there and kill me a couple hunnert my damn self."

The next morning the replacements were formed up into a company for a simulated patrol into the restricted area northwest of the camp. Amaro selected a lieutenant to walk point. The man clearly felt confident and in command.

His rifle slung over his shoulder, Amaro followed closely and guided him on the patrol. The lieutenant locked a round in the chamber, keeping the safety engaged. His fatigues stuck to his back as he moved slowly through the bush ahead of Amaro.

Walking along the footpath that paralleled the trail, Amaro said, "You just been blown away."

The lieutenant turned to him, puzzled. Amaro pointed in the direction of a green silhouette target camouflaged next to a shoulder-high shrub five meters to their right.

"You'd a bought the farm," he said. "Next time, light it up. Up here you're responsible for them," he said, nodding back in the direction of the rest of the patrol. "Move out."

The silhouette fell from sight. The lieutenant moved forward, nervous and overcautious. He thought he saw movement in a palm tree directly in front of him, quickly dropped to one knee, and squeezed two rounds into the fan-shaped leaves. The rest of the patrol hit the prone in the foliage on either side of the footpath. The instructor with the main body tipped his steel pot back on his head and laughed mockingly.

"While you was shootin' that parrot, that gook yonder put a well-placed round twixt you and the rest of your life." He pointed to another silhouette on the right flank. "Get your head out your ass, boy."

The lieutenant engaged the safety and resumed point. He looked unsure of himself. It was not as easy as he had thought. The Asian air played tricks. Everything seemed alive and waiting for his next mistake. He heard the silhouette before he saw the motion. He fell to one knee, firing from the hip, walking rounds in the general direction of the sound and movement. He knocked the target flat.

"You might leave here alive yet," Amaro said. Amaro left the path and fell in behind the officer. "Look out for the wire," he said, softly.

The lieutenant shifted his gaze left and right as he slipped carefully through the foliage. He saw the dull gray tripwire snaked across the path. He motioned for the patrol to halt, then slowly moved the leaves and loose dirt to expose the wire. He waved up the trooper behind him, pointed to the booby trap, and continued to move on. Each man in his turn stopped to point out the tripwire to the one behind him. They moved confidently, having detected that tripwire, when somebody triggered the one disguised as a vine. A yellow smoke grenade popped and hissed somewhere overhead.

"You're only as good as the next time," the instructor said. "Remember that."

The patrol moved uphill. The jungle thinned, the air was fresh. They took ten for cold Cs and cigarettes. Amaro sat on the ground, his back against a tree, knees drawn to his chest. He chainsmoked Luckies and thought about the boardwalk in Coney Island, the parachute jump he never rode because he was afraid of heights, the bumper cars, the carousel, the three-shots-for-a-dime shooting gallery.

11

Amaro sat in a web seat on the chopper and buckled the seat belt. Two other guys sat next to him. The guy on the end seemed to be in a daze; he was covered with sweat and shivered a lot. The guy mumbled through chattering teeth and wrapped himself with his arms.

A stretcher case was put aboard and strapped to the deck. The guy on the stretcher had blood-soaked bandages around the top of his head and field dressings over his eyes.

"Hold this," a medic said, handing an inverted IV bottle to Amaro. The medic made some notes on the tag attached to the stretcher. "Okay," he shouted to the crew chief.

The chopper jumped upward. Amaro held on to the wire handle of the bottle, trying to keep the tube smooth and unkinked. The chopper angled to the right, and for a few seconds Amaro stared directly at the ground below as the Huey traveled sideways. When the chopper leveled off, the stretcher case's head rolled back toward Amaro's boots. Blood trickled from the guy's nose and mouth, making stripes across his cheek.

When the chopper touched down, Amaro waited for the medics to take the saline bottle before jumping out the door. In an instant the bird was unloaded and airborne again, and he was back.

"You know where the One-oh-one base camp is?" Amaro asked a guy sitting in a jeep.

"I think so," the driver said. He wore clean fatigues and

smiled a lot. "Your bird get diverted to pick up wounded?"

"Yeah. Can you tell me how to get there?" Amaro asked.

The driver took off his steel pot and ran his fingers through curly blond hair. "It's kind of hard to describe," the driver said. "I know it by landmarks. You know, by sight. Tell you what, though. Jump in. It'll be easier if I just drive you there."

"Dynamite," Amaro said. "I thought I'd be walking around here forever with my head up my ass." He jumped into the shotgun seat and lit a smoke. The jeep took off.

"You guys just got up here, right?" the driver asked.

"A couple of days ago," Amaro said. "They put the company way the fuck out someplace."

"That someplace used to be a minefield," the driver said, "Charlie hit us over there a few times. Mortars and shit. Sappers like to use that area for entry. Recon is always finding these glow-in-the-dark banana-root markers out there."

"Some neighborhood," Amaro said. "Sounds like the one I grew up in."

"With your unit camped out there, that shit'll probably stop now," the driver said.

"Man, I hope so," Amaro said. "So is this what you do? You choogle around town in this short?"

"Most of the time. I drive for my CO."

"That's a pretty good gig," Amaro said. "All we need now is a couple of chicks and a bag of number-one scramble grass."

"That wouldn't be bad," the driver said.

"Well, I guess we can't have everything. But we can get close to a part of it," Amaro said, holding up a joint.

The driver smiled. He pulled out a Zippo and sparked the wheel. Amaro leaned over and lit the joint.

They passed it back and forth in silence, each looking around for people who shouldn't be there.

Sunlight flashed on the brigade sign, that bigger-than-life Screaming Eagle in chipped paint on pitted plywood.

"Here you go," the driver said.

Amaro picked up his rifle and stepped down from the jeep. He handed a joint to the driver. "For the road," he said.

The driver took it and slipped it into his pocket. "Thanks," he said, shifted into first gear, and pulled away.

Amaro walked slowly down the road to his company area. He stopped at the orderly room. Watts looked up from his desk when Amaro walked in. "What are you doing here?" he asked.

"What are you talking about?" Amaro said. "What do you mean, what am I doing here?"

"I didn't expect you back," Watts said, sarcastically.

"I wish you would have told me that before I left. Here you go. Put this in my file." Amaro handed Watts a copy of his orders and his light-duty profile.

"The First Shirt's gonna shit hisself when he sees this," Watts said.

"So what?" Amaro said.

"So he was fixin' to bust yore sorry ass, boy. That's so what. And when he sees this," Watts said, flicking the profile with his finger, "well, the shit will hit the fan, my man."

"That profile is legit," Amaro said. "It's signed by a surgeon."

"That don't make no difference," Watts said. "The Mauler will lay his cross hairs over yore heart."

"Fuck him," Amaro said. "And fuck you, too." He turned and walked toward the tent flap.

"Hey, soldier! It says right here, a week's light duty," Watts shouted. "Since the company's out in the field, there ain't but one little shitbucket needs burning. Now, that sounds 'light' to me. Why don't you tend to that little detail, Amaro."

Amaro stopped at the door. "Did you put my name on the next promotion list?"

"Fuck no," Watts said. "And after the man lays his peepers on this, you be lucky to keep the rinky-dink stripes you got." He opened a drawer and pulled out some letters. "Here's yore mail."

Amaro took the letters and walked out to the latrine. He pulled the full shitbucket to the side and poured diesel fuel into it. He torched it off, then sat on the sandbag wall to read the letters from home.

He held the envelopes in his hand, looking at them one by one. Not opening them, just looking at the names on them. He thought of them, his family. He tried to picture the people whose names appeared on the airmail envelopes, bordered in red, white, blue. The paper was flimsy and thin. Who were they, these people?

He read the address, tried to picture the house. The red shingle siding, chipped in spots with brown fibers, the back-yard, with the quarter and the five pennies pressed into the cement near the drain. The grapevine: hard yellow grapes that made sweet purple jelly. The rose bushes. The sycamore out front with bark like pieces of a jigsaw puzzle. When he climbed to the top he could see the city skyline.

Had he ever really lived there? He did not feel as if he had. It was a house he had seen in a photograph, an old movie, half forgotten. Pete the Barber, Gina the clerk at Sears, Susie who had new glasses. But who lived in that empty middle room? Where was the son, the boy who everyone said would be the first in the family to ever go to college?

Amaro took the unopened letters and threw them in the fire.

Amaro waited for Watts to leave the orderly room. He saw the sergeant, carrying a clipboard, hop into the pickup and drive to the landing zone.

In the orderly room, Amaro ripped open cases of C rations and pulled out cans of pound cake and fruit. He took small rolls of toilet paper; envelopes of cocoa mix, sugar, and powdered cream. He took books of matches and several P-38s; cans of bread, peanut butter, and jelly. He stole half a dozen towels.

He stuffed it all in a laundry bag and carried the bag to the pup tent he had pitched in the far corner of the platoon area. Then he walked to the shower point. He undressed and stood under the water for thirty minutes.

The saltwater showers had helped to clear up his skin. The blisters were drying up, leaving pink-white spots of new skin on his tanned body.

He shaved, dressed, and walked around the battalion area. Wearing new fatigues and clean socks, with his skin clearing, Amaro felt almost human.

"Where have you been?" Watts asked.

"Get off my back," Amaro said.

"Light duty don't mean no duty, soldier. You ain't done shit since you been back."

"I've been burning it," Amaro said.

"Report to the mess tent for KP," Watts said. "And don't give me none of yore backtalk."

"I wasn't going to say anything, Sarge," Amaro said. "Not a fucking word."

"Good. Now move out," Watts said. "Oh. Before I forget. Seems like gook infiltrators or something broke into the Charlie Rats. Stole all the canned fruit and such."

"I'll bet it was the barber," Amaro said. "I heard he just bought a new Caddy."

"Keep outta my shit," Watts said. "Keep your stinkin' ass outta my supply room."

"You won't even know I'm here," Amaro said.

"Don't be messin' 'round, young troop. Don't be dibblin' in my shit. Now double-time to the mess tent, ghost rider."

"I'm on my way," Amaro said. He walked toward the road and the mess tent. When he saw Watts disappear into the orderly room, Amaro turned up the road, coming back into the company area from behind the CP, walking along the path made by the row of NCO tents. Then he swung around the cross-wall and crawled into his tent.

He opened a can of pound cake and a can of applesauce. He ate, smoked a cigarette, and took a long nap.

The company's new replacements paired up to pitch tents in the sandbag rectangles. Amaro had drawn two shelter-halves and set up alone, off to one side, with open spaces between himself and the others.

He picked through the high pile of rucksacks and found one in fairly decent condition. The rest were torn and stained, ripped up by rounds and frag. He carried it back to his tent and began loading it with canned goods he had saved from the hospital package.

He waited for Watts to leave the orderly room, then slipped into it, rifling the sundry boxes for cigarettes and candy and hot sauce.

"What the fuck you doin'?" Watts asked as he walked back into the tent.

"Bustin' your stash," Amaro said.

"You'll never find it. You got mail."

"I'll get it later."

"Why weren't you at formation today?"

"What for? You know I'm present and accounted for."

"To be assigned to a detail. That's what for."

"Fuck that, Sarge. You got plenty of new meat to pull shit details."

"You still gotta fall out for formation like everybody else," Watts said.

Amaro tossed duffel bags from the stack onto the tent floor.

"What did you do with my shit?" Amaro asked.

"I didn't do nothin' with it. It's still there somewheres."

"I can't find it."

"Sorry about that."

"You're just plain sorry."

"Look for it. It's there. Been so much comin' and goin' around here, it's hard to keep up with everything. Know how many personal effects I had to ship out over the past few weeks?"

"Ain't you got it rough."

"And reports to file and form letters to get out . . ."

"You're breakin' my heart. Where's my goddamn duffel bag?"

"Don't bother *me* about that. Look for the fuckin' thing yourself. And make sure that pile is just like you found it when you get through."

Amaro found what he was looking for near the bottom of the stack. He opened it, held it upside down, and shook out the contents. He stuffed several pairs of clean socks and a roll of piaster play money into his pockets, then scooped everything else up and pushed it back into the bag. When he restacked the duffel bags he tossed his on top.

"Hey, Watts," Amaro said, lighting a smoke.

"Hey what?" the sergeant said without looking up from his desk.

"Whatever happened to what's his name—Conroy, I think? What happened to him?"

"What are you, a fuckin' wiseguy?" Watts said, throwing his pencil down and pushing back his chair.

"Don't shit yourself, man. It draws flies. I'm only asking a simple question."

"You mean you ain't heard?"

"Heard what?"

"Heard what went down."

"I ain't heard."

Watts stood and walked around to the front of the desk. He leaned back and sat on the edge.

"I was guardin' the motherfucker and he dropped down on me with a friggin' bayonet . . . what in the fuck are you laughin' at?"

"Nothing, man. I'm sorry. Go ahead."

"It ain't funny. He drops on me with this longass knife, you see, and says, 'I'm a gonna cut your throat, chump.' That's what he says, and he takes my nine-millimeter, ties me up, and books."

"Where'd he book to?"

"Fuck if I know. Just hats up and dismotherfuckin-appears."

"No shit?" Amaro said, smiling.

"No shit. Dickmauler wanted to bust me back down to slicksleeve, son."

"No lie? Shit, Sarge. You might have to earn your living then."

Watts thumbed a black metal insignia on the collar of his fatigue jacket. "Lookee here," he said with a wide grin. "I see your four and raise you two."

"I can't believe an asshole like you made E-6."

"You ain't got much to strut about yourself, trooper. The Dickmauler still got a hard-on for you. He ain't forgot your little to-do."

"All I did was get high with the guy. You let him out the cage."

"Yeah . . . but we been so understrength lately that the First Shirt been humpin' the bush his damn self. The new CO done put it to him and gave him a royal case of the ass, and now he out to put it to somebody else and *you it.*"

"Bullshit."

"Bullshit nothin'. If I'm lyin' I'm dyin'. He said, 'That sorry ass ain't gettin' no more stripes as long as I can still piss a steady stream,' is what he said."

"Put me on the next list."

"No can do," Watts said.

"Don't bullshit me. You can do it. Put me on the next list."

"Won't do any good. He'll jus' cross you off again."

"We'll see. Just put me on the next promotion list."

"You got other things to worry about."

"Oh yeah? Like what?"

"Like when the company comes in for standdown. The first sergeant keeps askin' when you be comin' back. Says you had too much ghost time in the hospital while the rest of us been hittin' the grit and he's gonna do something 'bout that sure as flies eat shit."

"I'll worry about that when the times comes. You just put me on the next promotion list and then we'll see what we see."

Amaro took a saltwater shower and changed fatigues. Then he strolled up the road toward the CP until he found the old barber.

"Cut it short, papasan," he said, pulling at the wild curly tangles with both hands. "Just use the clippers and cut it off, man."

"You betcha, Joe," the old man said, and set to work.

Amaro rubbed the stubble on his head after the old man finished mowing.

"Looks like shit," Amaro said.

"Ahh. Good, Joe. Number-one hakkut," the old man said, smiling.

Amaro smiled back. "Number-one, papasan, you dirty motherfucker, how about if I blow your fuckin' brains out?"

"Ahh. Good, Joe. Number-one hakkut."

Amaro pulled Viet money from his pocket and peeled off a bill to pay for his haircut.

"You want?" Amaro asked, holding the scrip up to the old man's face.

"Sure, Joe. Sure, Joe."

"You bring ten-pack *dinky-dau* smokes and I give papasan."

"Ten-pack. Okay."

"Ten-pack number one or I put boo-coo damndamn on your ass."

"Come back two hour," the old man said, picking up his tools, walking backward, smiling.

"If you bring even one pack that's number ten, I'll kill you," Amaro said.

"Sure, Joe. Sure, Joe," the old man said. He turned and limped quickly up the road.

Amaro walked to the company area. In his tent he made a false bottom in a magazine by wedging two sticks up the sides long enough to hold the guide and six rounds firmly in place. He buried the spring in a shitbucket.

The barber was cutting on someone else when Amaro got back, so he dropped his web gear next to the old man's crooked table, then sat on his haunches in the shade, smoking a cigarette. The old man finished the haircut and bowed to the GI when he got paid. When the guy left, the barber folded his filthy towel and Amaro saw him place a package wrapped in newspaper in his field pack. Amaro lit another smoke and waited. There was no one nearby. He slung the web gear over his shoulder and tossed two thousand piasters on the table. The old man grinned.

"You better smile, you old son-of-a-bitch. If it's shit you won't be able to smile again," Amaro said, pointing at him with an index finger, cocking his thumb.

"Number-one smokes, Joe. You see. You like."

Amaro smiled and patted the barber on the shoulders. "Fuck you and your family," he said.

12

The landing zone became busy after noon. The Hueys shuttled in two, three at a time, and the tired guys in dirty fatigues jumped from them and walked slowly to the company area.

Amaro watched them from the sandbag wall. He watched the movement, heard the clang and bang of tent stakes pounded in the dirt. He liked the company area better when it was empty and quiet.

Tigerbaum and Las Vegas set up in the open space next to him.

"How's things?" Amaro asked.

"Fucked up," Tigerbaum said. "How you feeling?"

"Like homemade shit. How's the work been?"

"Not too bad this trip," Tigerbaum said. "Nothing like the meatgrinder we walked into a while back."

"I heard. I seen Johnny Vanilla in Cam Ranh. He told me what happened."

"It was *bruto*, bro," Las Vegas said. "Ugly as could be."

"It changed things quite a bit," Tigerbaum said. "It's not the same without Malone."

"That's for sure." Las Vegas winced. "The new squad leader is trouble. He's dangerous."

Tigerbaum nodded. "You ain't said snack bar, son. His name is Dugan. 'Mad Dog Dugan' he calls himself. A big sucker. A real *shtarker gesinnt.*"

"He's a sick cat. Gonna get us all blown away."

Tigerbaum said, "The story is when he was here with the One-seventy-third he did something to warrant being recommended for the Congressional Medal of Honor. I can't say for sure what it was. There's a lot of rumors flying around about it. Anyway, he gets back to the World and he's afraid they're going to forget about him, so he re-ups and asks to come back. I guess he wants to show them he really deserves to get it."

"And we get stuck with the dude," Las Vegas said.

"Yeah . . . just our *mazel*," Tigerbaum said. "He volunteers for every dirty fucking job that comes up."

"If it was up to him he'd walk point every day his damn self," Las Vegas said.

"Holy shit," Amaro said. "And they let this guy loose?"

"Not only loose. In authority," Tigerbaum said.

"He's bad vibes, bro. Gives me the creeps."

"That's him," Tigerbaum said, pointing to a guy who looked like a middle linebacker.

"Raised on canned badass," Amaro said, "and John Wayne crackers, eh?"

"*He* thinks so," Tigerbaum said.

"Well, fuck him. After you guys get cleaned up I got the good thing stashed and waiting," Amaro said.

"Awwwright, bro."

"God bless the child that's got his own," Tigerbaum said.

"You got that right," Amaro said. "I got shit stashed around here like a squirrel buries acorns. We be squared away for a while."

"First squad! First squad! Listen up!" Dugan shouted. "Poop meeting after chow."

"Is he for real?" Amaro said.

"Just like a toothache, bro. Like a fuckin' toothache."

Tigerbaum snickered. "The crazy man thinks this is like the Army."

Watts walked up. "The Dickmauler wants to see you," he said.

"I'll see you guys in the mess hall," Amaro said. He walked to the orderly room.

Fluett sat straight up at his desk. He had already showered and shaved and changed his fatigues. Amaro smelled Old Spice.

"Do you know how many good men died while you were hiding in the hospital?" Fluett asked.

"I had malaria, First Sergeant," Amaro answered. "I stayed in the hospital until the doctors felt I was okay to come back."

"You ate good. Slept in a rack. You got a tan. All the while good men, better men than you, were dying."

"It wasn't my fault. I was sick."

"*At ease,*" Fluett snapped. "I don't want to hear any excuses. I sent for you to put you on notice. You *will* make up for all the slack time you took. Is that clear?"

Amaro stared at him.

"I said *is that clear.*"

"Yeah."

"Yeah what?"

"Yeah, First Sergeant, it's clear to me."

"You *will* pay back two minutes for every minute you slacked off. *Is that clear?*"

Amaro snapped to attention and gave a smart salute.

"Yes, First Sergeant, *sir,* I read you loud-and-clear, I read you four-by-five that's a roger First Sergeant *sir.*"

Fluett stood up and pressed his face close to Amaro's. "Watch your step. Just watch your step. Make one wrong move and I'll be on you like stink on shit."

"Anything else you want?"

"I'll speak to you through your squad leader. Now get out of here, you goldbricking punk."

Amaro about-faced and marched out of the orderly room.

He looked for McGee but could not find him. So he went to the mess tent and sat down with Tigerbaum.

"What did the Dickmauler have to say?" Tigerbaum asked.

"The usual Randolph Scott tougher-than-saddlesores lifer bullshit. What he don't know is if he keeps walkin' on the tracks he's gonna get hit by the fuckin' train."

"Hey. You want the rest of that?" Tigerbaum said, pointing to the half-eaten hamburger on Amaro's tray.

"No. You can have it, man."

They left the mess tent, scraped their trays in the trash and dipped them in the drum of boiling water along with their utensils. Then they sauntered toward the tent area.

The squad sat on the sandbag wall facing Dugan.

"Where you been?" Dugan said to Tigerbaum.

"Eating."

"What took you so goddamn long?"

"I was hungry."

"Sit down," Dugan said. "And who the fuck are you, troop?"

"Amaro."

"Oh. *You're* Amaro. I been waiting to meet you. Sit down and listen up."

Amaro sat on the wall next to Tigerbaum and lit a smoke.

"We looked mighty sorry out there on this last operation, gentlemen," Dugan said, pacing back and forth with his hands clasped behind his back. There was shoe polish on his jungle boots. "Too much talkin' and noise and such. Laggin' behind, walkin' slow like a buncha ol' women. That shit *will* stop right here and now. That shit *will not* float in my squad. I'm fixin' to take up the slack so tight your assholes'll pucker up to suck wind. This ain't no Sunday school lah-dee-dah walk in the fuckin' woods pickin' flowers for no slut picnic. This is *war,* gentlemen. This is your *country* you're representin' out here and, by God, you *will* do it with a proper measure of military pride. If need be, every man will carry a extra canteen full of water for *shavin' purposes.*"

The guys groaned. Tigerbaum rubbed his chinwhiskers. "But I'm a holy man," he said.

"If you mean *ass*-holey, I agree," Dugan said. "You *will* shave. Back here, every day. In the field, every other day if necessary. When one of my men gets sent home dead to Mama he looks *good,* goddamn it. He's still representin' his country, dead or alive. Are there any questions?"

"Where do I get a razor, Sarge?" a new guy asked. "I done los' mines."

"That's your problem. Any other questions? . . . No? Good. Now listen up. Feigenbaum, Vegas, and Hiller, you're on bunker guard. Morris and Davis: KP. Peterson and Williams: trash point. Amaro, you burn shit. There will be a full-field inspection for this squad at oh-six-thirty hours. Be standin' tall or don't be here at all. *Dis*-missed."

He turned and started to walk away. Then he stopped.

"You can start your detail now, Amaro. The rest of you are off until after reveille."

"What a fuckin' joke," Amaro said.

"It's no joke," Tigerbaum said. "He's for real. He's out to get that CMH if he has to kill the whole lot of us."

Las Vegas said, "What some guys will do for free beers at the American Legion Hall."

"Come on," Amaro said. "Let's get goin'."

"That's a rog," Tigerbaum replied.

Amaro torched the full shitbuckets and gave them a stir. He took some joints from his magazine stash.

"Ahh. *Bueno muchacho,*" Las Vegas said.

"This'll get us *farchadat* for sure."

"Toke up, GI, tonight you *fly.*"

"Keep your eyes open for Mad Dog," Tigerbaum said. "He's crazy enough to camouflage as a turd and snipe us from the shitbucket."

"That's the truth, bro."

"*Mad Dog.* What a dumb name," Amaro said.

"That's nothing," Tigerbaum said. "The new CO calls himself 'Jungle Jerry.' "

Amaro laughed. "Get the fuck outta here . . . *Jungle Jerry.*"

"No lie," Las Vegas said. "That's his call sign."

"Mad Dog and Jungle Jerry. Sounds like a cartoon show," Amaro said.

"They call me Jungle Jew," Tigerbaum said. "And he's Jungle Joe-Zay."

"And who you be, bro?"

"Call me Jungle Johnny," Amaro said.

"John? Is that your first name?" Tigerbaum asked.

"Yeah."

"I didn't know that."

"But you can call me Leon Rappolo, the marijuana-maimed jazz clarinetist."

"Hey bro. There you go. And I'm Wingy Minnone the one-armed trumpet player. Let's do a set . . . *toot-toot-doodle-oodle-oot-zoots-WEEEEE-ah.*"

"That's bad like a motherfucker."

"It's the *Jungle Jam,* Sam. Newport Gook. Cool blue

riddilly-rebop," Las Vegas said. Then he sang. "'*Ninety-nine guys got eyes for Liza, but Liza got eyes for me . . .*' "

"Hey kids. Quick. Draw a rope on your magic screen so Winky Dink—"

"Winky *Dink?* He's a VC, man."

"Bullshit, too. He's an American adviser. Draw a rope so Winky and Jungle Jerry can pull their stinkin' asses out of the gook ambush."

"Hey. What about Mad Dog?"

"Fuck him. He's dry-humpin' the Merry Mailman's leg."

"Hey, bro. Remember this? . . . *Ho-ho, hee-hee. It's me, it's Pinky Lee.*"

"Fuckin' A. *Strange things are happening . . .*"

"Nah. That's Red Buttons. Another gig."

"Quick kids. Draw a joint for Winky . . ."

"And Johnny, Joe-Zay, and the Jew . . ."

"*Ooo-shew-bee-doo-bee-OOO-OOO . . . OOO-shew-bee-doo-bee . . .*"

They flicked the roaches into the burning buckets and stumbled back up to their tents.

In the field Amaro felt weak. The rucksack seemed to weigh a hundred pounds. He humped hunched over, sweat pouring from him, his knees sore and buckling. He found it hard to concentrate on anything except standing. The muscles in his back cramped tight. His boot soles slipped and he stumbled. With dirty hands he wiped saltsweat from his eyes, trying to keep Tigerbaum in sight.

He barely noticed the terrain. When he did look up, the canopy spun. There was no distinction of form. One color, one shade of green, bled into the other in a swirl of hazy gray. At times he misjudged the distance to the dirt, overstepped clumsily, the rucksack shifting, pulling him off-balance. He could not breathe. He could not think. All his energy centered on placing one foot in front of the other, step by painful step.

When they stopped for chow, Amaro opened a can of fruit cocktail. He squeezed crushed and melted M & M's from the bag. He poured two envelopes of sugar on his tongue and washed it all down with Kool-Aid. But the burst of energy did not come. He still felt tired and dizzy.

He knew it was dangerous to be exhausted, to be at the point where the body just cannot respond and function as it should.

He remembered back to his last Golden Gloves fight, and the feeling was the same. It was a close fight, the men in his corner said, go after him. In the final round a guy named Tommy Fischetti, a guy Amaro had never met before, came out hard, growling like an animal when he threw his punches. And Amaro slipped them and snapped a short left hook off a stiff straight jab and unloaded a right cross and the guy stopped growling and rocked back on his heels. He dropped his guard. His eyes rolled. And the crowd in Sunnyside Gardens knew something was up. Amaro heard the noise they made as he stepped closer to the guy and put everything he had into another hard right cross, but it moved as if held back and it just bounced off the guy's head. Amaro couldn't put the other guy away. He lost the decision.

And now he felt the same way. As if his body could not respond the way it normally would. He became unsure of himself, concerned about not being able to protect himself, to depend upon himself to stay alive. Inwardly he panicked. What if he needed another hard right and bounced a powderpuff instead?

The late afternoon rain cooled the air. Amaro took his helmet off and rubbed the fresh rain on his head and face. He began to feel better.

Dugan assigned him to a position with two new guys that night. Amaro did not like the idea but said nothing to Dugan. When the squad leader walked away, he picked up his gear and moved to the gun position next door.

"Why don't you get your stuff and move over there with your buddies?" Amaro said to Hiller, the new guy in the position with Tigerbaum and Las Vegas.

"Cause Sergeant Dugan told me to stay here."

"Don't worry about it," Amaro said. "If he bitches I'll take the weight."

"Go ahead," Tigerbaum said. "It's okay."

Hiller stared at them, picked up his gear, and moved out.

"Cook some rice," Tigerbaum said. "I got put opp a chicken."

He opened three cans of boned chicken and spooned them into a canteen cup. He laced it with hot sauce. As it simmered on the field stove, Amaro boiled a cupful of rice.

"Wish we had *cominos,*" Las Vegas said.

"And a bottle of white wine," Amaro said.

A flare popped and lit up the space down front and to the left.

Someone was shouting: "Don't shoot! Don't shoot! Dear God don't shoot!"

"What's going on?" Tigerbaum yelled.

"It's me! Don't shoot!" Hiller yelled back.

"Dumbass cherry," Las Vegas said.

"What the fuck is goin' on here?" Dugan said, running toward the position.

"Hiller set off his own flare," Tigerbaum said.

"What's he doin' over there? I told him to stay here," Dugan said.

"I switched places with him," Amaro said.

"You *what?*"

"I switched places with him."

"And who the fuck told you to do that?" Dugan asked, pushing a finger into Amaro's chest.

Amaro slapped Dugan's arm away and stood sideways. "Nobody told me to do it. I told myself. I don't know them guys and I don't know you and I wanted to eat chow with my friends."

"You dumb fucker . . ." Dugan yelled, grabbing at Amaro's shirt. Amaro tried to break his grip but could not, so he made a quick pivot and dug a short hook into Dugan's ribs. It caught him by surprise. He let go and grabbed his side, then lunged at Amaro. Amaro sidestepped, but a roundhouse slammed his ear and knocked him off his feet. He tried to jump up. Someone yanked his collar from behind and jerked him back down.

"*At ease,* goddamn it," McGee yelled. "Both of you . . . *at ease.*"

"He disobeyed a direct order and took a damn punch at me," Dugan said.

"Is that true?" McGee asked.

"He grabbed for me and I hit him," Amaro said.

"Both of you come with me." McGee walked them to a spot out of earshot of everyone else.

He listened to both sides of the story.

"Sergeant Dugan was acting on my orders," McGee said. "I want to keep at least one experienced man in each position. By takin' it on yourself to change places you left three cherries on their own. And you seen what happened. Hiller coulda been killed when that flare went up. There ain't no excuse for what you done."

"That's why I wanted to keep away from them guys, Sarge. I don't want to get splattered with somebody else's shit," Amaro said.

"We're all in this together, soldier. Get that through your head," McGee said. "You fucked up, pure and simple . . . and as for you, Dugan, you fucked up by puttin' your hands on someone in your command. . . . I don't see no grounds for charges against anybody this time, so we'll keep it amongst ourselves. Got it?"

"Got it, Sarge," Amaro said.

"But he risked the safety of my squad," Dugan said. "He took a punch at me—"

"You tried to gorilla me," Amaro yelled.

"At ease," McGee said. "I'm just gonna tell the Old Man about the flare, is all. You get to where he told you to go *on the double,* and don't *ever* do what you did again or your ass be grass and *I'll* be the lawn mower. Do you read me?"

"I hear you, Sarge," Amaro said.

"And you, Sergeant Dugan, will keep your hands to yourself. Military courtesy is a two-way street, or have you forgot that?"

"I ain't forgot, Sarge."

"The next time it's by the book. Do you both hear me?"

Amaro and Dugan nodded.

Amaro picked up his gear and his cup of overcooked chow. Dugan walked over, leading Hiller to the gun. They stood face to face.

"It ain't over, you know," Dugan said.

"You got that right," Amaro answered.

"Watch your step, sucker."

"Watch your back, chump."

"What's that supposed to mean?"

"Just what I said. I ain't about to get bit by no mad dog."

"This mad dog does a whole lot more than bite, punk."

"You may be twice my size but you ain't bulletproof, motherfucker," Amaro said. He turned and walked to the next position. He could feel Dugan staring holes into the back of his head.

The two new guys looked up from their chow when Amaro walked into the position. They glanced at one another, then started eating again.

Amaro dropped his rucksack and sat down. He swallowed a few spoons of cold chicken and rice.

"This tastes like shit," he said. He turned the canteen cup upside down and hit it against a rock. The contents slopped out in one piece. He kicked some loose dirt over it, washed his cup out with some water, and sat back to light a smoke.

Peterson and Morris ate in silence. They stared around the perimeter, stealing glances at Amaro. He saw them. Not directly, because he did not focus on them, but he felt their eyes pass over him.

He turned his head toward them quickly. They both flinched and looked away. He smiled to himself and turned his back to them, aiming his eyes at the jungle.

They both wore new boots. Peterson was the taller of the two, with broader shoulders and a plainer face. But Morris seemed tougher, more compact, more able to kill when he had to. They were both older than Amaro by maybe a year or two. But that would not last long. After a few firefights, age meant nothing at all.

Amaro field-stripped the cigarette butt and scattered the tobacco. He rolled the paper into a ball and tossed it out in front of him. He heard the new guys cleaning up after chow. He heard them talking but could not hear what they said. He felt their eyes on his back.

"What the fuck are you guys looking at?" Amaro said without turning around.

"Nothing," Morris answered. "We're just getting ourselves squared away."

"I know you guys were looking at me, man."

"Hey," Peterson said. "I mean, what the fuck do you expect?"

"I expect you to mind your own fucking business."

"Las Vegas said you've been here a while," Peterson said.

"That's right."

"How long?"

"All my life."

"You must be getting short," Morris said.

"I ain't been here that long."

"You and Tigerbaum been here the longest, right?" Peterson asked.

"We're the only ones left from the old squad. Except for Johnny Vanilla and Spector, the medic," Amaro said, realizing, when he said it, exactly what it meant.

"Yeah. We heard about Vanilla. Is he really as weird as Tigerbaum says?" Morris asked.

"Depends on what you mean . . . What is this, twenty fucking questions or something?"

"Hey, man, lighten up," Peterson said. "We're stuck here living with you. We're just trying to make the best of it."

Amaro spun around and faced them. "The best of it? The *best* of it? What a fucking joke. What a dumbshit thing to say. You been here how long? Two, three weeks?"

"Two weeks," Peterson said.

"Wow. All of two weeks. Well, the *best* of it has come and gone. It don't do nothing but get worse from here on out."

"The best of it is still to come," Peterson said. "What about going home?"

"What about it? What are you, a fucking fortuneteller, you can see the future? You ain't been home. You're still right the fiddle-fuck here, so how do you know it's any better?"

"Come on, man," Peterson said. "It's got to be . . ."

"I don't know what it's got to be," Amaro said. "I just know what it is. And what it is is a motherfucker. Don't be thinking about going home, sucker. We still got to get through tonight. Give me your watch. I'm pulling guard first."

Peterson unbuckled his watch and handed it over to Amaro.

"You better catch some z's," Amaro said. "I'm waking you up at twenty-two-thirty hours."

He took the watch, slipped it into his pocket, and turned to face the jungle. He heard the new guys mumbling as they stretched out on the dirt.

Amaro liked pulling first guard. Most of the perimeter was still awake, with guys whispering among themselves, smoking, or winding down from the long day. He did not feel left all alone.

He checked his weapon, the claymore detonator, and then looked over the black field of fire. He saw branches outstretched, aiming at his head. The bush swayed in exaggerated slow movements, taunting, beckoning him to leave the position and join them where he could be eaten alive. He thought about an orange-haired corpse.

At exactly ten thirty he crawled to Peterson, shaking him awake.

"Your turn, man," Amaro said, handing him the watch.

Peterson sat up, rubbed his eyes, and fumbled to strap the watchband to his wrist.

Amaro clipped the GP strap to a belt loop, propped his rifle against a tree, and lay down. He closed his eyes and tried to lose himself in the shapeless dark.

"*Bon jour, mes enfants,*" Spector said, walking into the position. "Time for your salt."

"Sprinkle mine on a lobster," Amaro said.

"You got a deal," Spector replied. "But only if you bring the Pouilly Fuissé."

"Got it right here," Amaro said, holding up a canteen. "Chateau Jolly Olly Orange."

"Your skin looks really fucked up," Spector said, dropping the first-aid kit and stepping closer to Amaro. He turned Amaro to the light and pressed gently on the pus sacs that covered Amaro's face. "Hopefully they'll seep on their own. I don't want to lance them. Might cause infection."

"They itch like hell," Amaro said.

"I'm sure they do, but don't scratch them. Sit down. Let's see what magic we can perform."

Spector coated the blisters with a thick ointment. "This should help dry them out," he said. "Take these antibiotics. I'll talk to McGee about getting you to Battalion Aid on the next standdown. I'd like to send you back now, but I can't justify a medevac."

"No sweat, Doc. Just powder me with bone dust and do a sacred dance," Amaro said.

"How'd that happen?" Peterson asked.

"It has something to do with the air," Amaro said. "Try not to breathe it if you can."

"It's jungle rot, young cherry," Spector said, replacing his gear. "It only afflicts people who are covered with skin."

Dugan marched into the position followed by his RTO lugging the radio.

"Get ready to move out," Dugan said. "The first squad's got point."

Amaro could hear the childish excitement in Dugan's voice.

"Amaro, you're up in front," Dugan said, with a smile, as if enjoying it. "Morris, you take up the slack. Be ready to move in ten." He turned to walk away, then stopped. "By the way," he said over his shoulder, "you men better shave today. You look sort of scruffy." The radioman teetered after him. Spector shrugged and walked in the opposite direction.

Peterson wet his face and soaped his beard.

"What the fuck are you doing?" Amaro asked.

"You heard the sarge," Peterson said, pulling the razor over his face.

"Yeah. I heard him. So what?"

"So I figured I'd better shave," Peterson said, using his fingers to feel what he could have seen in a mirror if he had one to look into.

"You nicked your chin," Morris said.

"Fuck him," Amaro said. "When he gets impetigo, he can ask Sergeant Douche-bag what to do about it. You ever take up the slack before?"

"No," Morris said.

"Just stay close. Ten meters behind. Or less. It depends. Just don't ever lose sight of me. I'll worry about what's straight up ahead. You keep your eyes on the flanks."

They shouldered their gear and prepared to move out.

Dugan walked up to Amaro and pushed his face close to

Amaro's chin, looking at it with an exaggerated expression of surprise. "I see whiskers, trooper."

"All the time or just when you're sticking your fucking nose where it don't belong?" Amaro asked.

"I thought I told you to shave, raggedy-ass."

"You know you told me to shave, piss-tube."

"I gave you a direct—"

"What's holding up the works?" McGee asked, approaching the head of the column.

"Just some last-minute instructions, Sergeant," Dugan said.

"He wants to know why I didn't shave, Sarge," Amaro said.

McGee looked at Amaro's face and shook his head. He turned to Dugan, started to say something, but changed his mind. He spit on the dirt instead.

"Move out, Amaro. Follow the trail until I give word to change direction," McGee walked back along the column.

Amaro started off the hill. "Sergeant Dugan," he said over his shoulder.

"What?" Dugan turned.

"Fuck you."

Morris laughed. Even the radio humper cracked a smile, but covered it with his hand.

The trail was no wider than a footpath winding through thick bush. It followed the natural contours of the hillside, twisting along where the terrain offered the least resistance. Amaro wondered how long it had been used as an avenue between valleys.

The trail never seemed to run straight for more than ten meters before it disappeared behind a wall of green leaves. It wound back upon itself, changing directions constantly as it snaked downhill in loops. Sometimes Amaro heard the column behind him walking directly overhead. He heard them but could not see them, and it scared him to think of what else was below, unheard as well as unseen.

He was glad Morris was taking up the slack instead of Peterson. He felt safer with Morris; he thought Morris was a good guy, a better guy to have behind him than candyass Peterson. But he missed his partner, Malone. There had been a kind of unspoken communication between him and Malone;

each knew the other's moves, and together they had made a tight point team.

The trail leveled out near the base of the hill and curved gently through the valley. Able to see farther ahead, Amaro picked up his pace. The trail curved around a thick grove. Amaro walked past the top of the bend and started down along the far side.

A VC in black pajamas and conical hat stepped out from among the shrubs on the left flank. Amaro saw the VC raise his weapon. Amaro fired a burst as he dove for cover. The VC fired back, kicking dirt up in Amaro's face. Amaro changed magazines and returned fire, then lay flat and waited for incoming. There was none. He reloaded and emptied another magazine in a wide spray, then waited again.

He rolled quickly to one side when he heard someone approaching from behind. It was Morris.

"What the fuck is going on?" Morris whispered as he crawled up next to Amaro, his eyes scanning the jungle for movement.

"I don't know." Amaro was breathing hard. "Could be a gook on point. Out for a stroll. Taking a shit. I don't know. You see anything?"

"No. Nothing. Everything quiet."

"Let's get the fuck out of here," Amaro said.

They jumped up and ran in a crouch back to the column.

"What was all that about?" McGee asked.

Amaro sat on the dirt, trying to catch his breath. "A gook on the trail," he said.

"Did you get him?" Dugan asked.

"I shot at him."

"Did you hit him, goddamn it?" Dugan said.

"I told you. I shot at him. How the fuck do I know if I hit him? He didn't shoot back after a while. That's all I know."

"What do you think?" Dugan said to McGee.

"Don't know. Might have been alone. Might could be with company."

"Let me find out," Dugan said.

McGee tipped his helmet back and rubbed his chin. "Looks like you're gonna have to," he said. "I can't take a chance on moving into some heavy shit. Take your squad and check it out. I'll form a perimeter right here."

"Airborne, Sergeant," Dugan said. "First squad, drop your shit. We're goin' huntin'."

Amaro cautiously led the squad back to the spot he had fired from. Then he moved slowly toward the area where the gook had taken cover. He thought it was crazy, going out to hunt for trouble like this. It was bad enough when it came to you. To go out looking for it on purpose made him feel stupid.

He found a blood-splattered tree trunk. Bits of things that looked like meat clung to the thick mess. Ants crawled over it, and the dark pools on the ground.

"You hit the motherfucker," Morris said, slapping Amaro on the back.

"No shit," Amaro said.

"Yeah. But you didn't kill him," Dugan said. "You fucked it up again."

Amaro kneeled and checked the dirt for a blood trail. He found it leading off toward bush. "He *di-di'd* that way," he said, pointing away from the trail into heavy cover.

"Follow it," Dugan said.

Amaro led the squad along the blood trail. The pools became wider and closer together. The gook was slowing down. Amaro pushed a branch out of his way, and another swung out, brushing blood on his eyes and mouth. It felt thick and tacky. It was still warm.

He found the straw hat twenty meters farther in the brush. He waved Morris up.

"Go get Dugan," Amaro said quietly. "This is too easy."

Dugan came up with his radioman in tow.

"He's close by and just about bled out," Amaro said, showing Dugan the hat and pointing to the heavy blood spots.

"He should be right up ahead," Dugan said.

"Yeah. He probably is," Amaro said. "Only, who else is with him?"

Dugan said into the radio, "Cougar One. Cougar One. This is Mad Dog, over. Cougar One, this is Mad Dog. We are going to recon by fire, over. . . . Repeat: We are going to recon by fire. Over and out."

The squad spread out in a semicircle. On Dugan's command they opened up on the brush. Tigerbaum fired the sixty from his hip, spraying the trees and bushes. The rest of them spent two magazines apiece probing the jungle. The roar lasted for only half a minute. Then the thudding and whining ricochets stopped, and a thick silence closed in.

"Cougar One. Mad Dog to Cougar One. No return fire. Repeat: No return fire. We're going ahead, over. . . . That's a rog. Mad Dog, over and out."

"I'm going to split the squad," Dugan said to Amaro. "You take Morris, Vegas, and Peterson. Check out the right flank. Meet on this azimuth, a hundred meters up ahead," he said, extending his arm in front of him.

"We shouldn't split the squad," Amaro said.

"He's right," Tigerbaum said.

"We're gonna get us a dink prisoner," Dugan said. "Or kill him and all his friends. You ain't scared, are you, Tough Guy?"

"Scared shit," Amaro said.

"I thought so. Move out, trooper."

Amaro led the detail in an arc around the right flank. The jungle was dense; it was hard to push through.

"The trail's dried up," Amaro said. "The gook didn't come through this way."

"That's good, bro," Las Vegas said. "Why don't we just hat up to the meeting place quick as we can. Fuck Dugan, man."

"Good idea," Amaro said. "Let's go. And stay close."

"Right behind you, Kemo Sabe," Las Vegas said.

There was an explosion. They all hit the ground. From a short distance they heard Tigerbaum yelling. "Amaro. Amaro. Get your ass over here quick."

"Keep hollering so I can find you," Amaro shouted back as he got to his feet and started clambering through the jungle toward the sound of Tigerbaum's voice.

"This is *loco*, bro," Las Vegas said. "The gooks gonna be on us like corn on a cob, my man."

"What else can we do, man?" Amaro said. "Let's get to the rest of them so we don't get caught with our shit in the wind."

Amaro homed in on Tigerbaum's shouts and led the detail to a small clearing. The gook was blown in half. Dugan was lying flat on his back, bleeding a steady stream from the wide rips in his skin. One eye was gone. The other stared upward blankly. The radioman, Davis, was off to one side, screaming. His arms and legs twitched like he was being electrocuted. Hiller tended to him. Tigerbaum and Williams covered the jungle.

"We found the gook face down," Tigerbaum said. "Dugan thought he was dead and got pissed off. He kicked the body to roll it over and the fucking thing exploded."

"Get on the horn to McGee," Amaro said.

"I already did." Tigerbaum's eyes were wide. "They're on their way."

The squad set up a small perimeter around the dead and wounded. Amaro lit a cigarette, hoping the smoke would cover the stink from Dugan's blown-open belly.

"Hey, Peterson," Amaro said. "You shaved for nothing, schmuck."

13

The guys came in from the field for a standdown. Pup tents were pitched in all of the squad areas, and the compound became crowded.

Amaro felt uncomfortable. There was too much talking. Too much movement and grab-ass, long lines for showers, long lines to use the crapper. Music blasted from tape decks, each a different rock hit, and these clashing numbers mixed with the growl of trucks and the throbbing *whopp-whopp* of rotor blades and it all became one big noise.

Some guys could not stop moving. They talked fast and loud, jerking their heads, bending arms and shuffling feet, their hands waving. They cleaned equipment, wrote home. Some guys did not move; they just sat and stared. A few stretched out on the dirt and slept as if they were dead.

"Yo, bro," Las Vegas said, walking toward Amaro. "Tigerbaum's calling a squad meeting."

"Look at this," Amaro said. "Come here and look at this."

"At what?"

"At this, man," Amaro said, pointing at the company area.

"Yeah," Las Vegas said, looking around. "So what?"

"So look at it, man. This is what we do."

"Yeah. Come on, bro. Tigerbaum wants to give us the poop."

Amaro hopped down from the bunker roof. He and Las Vegas walked to the squad bay.

"This is what we do," Amaro said. "This is what we fucking do."

Tigerbaum stood in front of his tent. The squad sat on the ground. Some leaned back on their elbows.

"We're going to have a working standdown," Tigerbaum said. "Nine, ten days at least."

"Aww fuck," Las Vegas said. "I could use some slack time."

"You ain't kiddin'," Morris said.

"Don't shit on yourselves yet," Tigerbaum said. "There won't be any fuckoff time. We're breaking camp."

"Just when I was getting used to the neighborhood," Morris said.

"Where are we going?" Peterson asked. "I hope it's Phan Rang."

"In your wettest dreams," Tigerbaum said. "We're moving the forward base camp up to Chu Lai."

"That won't be so bad," Amaro said. "They got EM clubs with live bands sometimes. There's a PX and a town nearby."

"Outta sight," Las Vegas said. "I can get a good stereo cheap. Any nurses at the Second Surg?"

"Yeah," Amaro said.

"Hot damn! Round-eye pussy," Morris said.

"Probably have to stand in line behind the officers," Amaro said.

"It would still be worth it," Las Vegas said. "At least we won't have to worry about catching cockrot from the dinks."

"You guys can jerk off later," Tigerbaum said. "Let me get this over with so I can catch some z's. Starting tomorrow we'll be packing shit on choppers and trucks. We got to take down the orderly room and the NCO tents and empty most of the sandbags."

"Are we gonna plant any trees?" Las Vegas said.

"Nothing will grow here," Amaro said.

Tigerbaum said, "Some of you will be working in the mess tent or other details around the battalion area."

"Is there a church in Chu Lai, Sergeant?" Johnny Vanilla asked. "The one in Cam Ranh Bay was so peaceful and quiet."

"Knock off that 'Sergeant' shit," Tigerbaum said. "And if there is a church in Chu Lai, I'm sure you'll find it."

"But first," Las Vegas said, "you gotta get stoned and laid before we let you go to it." He stretched out a palm. Amaro laughed and slapped him five.

Johnny Vanilla's face turned red. "What a disgusting thing to say."

Amaro turned to Morris and Peterson. "Does that answer your question?" he said.

"Yeah," Morris nodded. "Guess it does."

"What question?" Las Vegas asked.

"I'll tell you later," Amaro said. "Hey, Saint John, my man. Did you hear God is dead?"

"That's right," Tigerbaum said. "A guy from Graves Registration saw him zipped in a body bag."

Johnny Vanilla stood up. "I won't listen to this," he shouted in his high-pitched voice. "I don't want to burn in hell with the likes of you." He turned and walked away.

"That fucking guy is too much," Las Vegas said.

"What if he's right?" Hiller asked. "Did you ever think of that?"

"Fuck you," Amaro said.

"I'll assign your details to you in the morning," Tigerbaum said. "Hang loose for tonight."

Morris, Peterson, and Hiller walked away together. Two new guys, both tall, black, and quiet, stood up and walked back to their tent.

"What's their story?" Las Vegas asked, nodding in the direction of the new guys.

"They were together at Fort Bragg," Tigerbaum said. "They seem okay. What do you think of the other new recruits?"

"Morris is a down dude," Amaro said. "We should turn him on. Peterson is an asshole. What about the other one?"

"Hiller? I don't know, bro," Las Vegas said. "I don't trust him yet."

"Neither do I," Tigerbaum said. "Fluett wants you to burn shit tonight," he said to Amaro. "Are you holding?"

"Does a bird have wings? We'll be airborne right after dark," Amaro said.

Amaro was assigned to work in the orderly room with Morris and the two new guys. They loaded duffel bags and cartons of supplies on the back of several trucks.

"What's your name?" Amaro asked the thinner of the new guys.

"Timmens," he said. "And that there's Willy Aitch."

"What's the *H* stand for?" Amaro asked.

"Don't stand for nothing," Willy said. "It's my name. A-I-T-C-H. What it is is what it looks like."

"That's cool," Amaro said. "I like that. I heard you guys were together at Bragg."

"You heard right," Timmens said, stopping to light a Newport. "We was slidin' by, ridin' high, till we got popped in Fayetteville."

"Some cracker sold us a ounce of somethin' he done swept up in a stable," Willy said. "Next thing, whambam, they send us to this motherfucker. Know what I'm talkin' 'bout?"

"I know what you're talking about," Amaro said.

"So who's the candy man?" Timmens asked.

"Uncle Ho," Amaro said.

"I told you," Willy said to Timmens, "these white boys are full of shuck and jive. We got to find us a blood who's tuned in to what's happenin'."

"That's square business, hom," Amaro said. "It's the most advanced industry in this fucking country. The gooks sell dope to make money to buy our ammo and supplies on the black market."

"Like part of an eco-nomic program or something," Morris said.

"Fuckin' A," Amaro said. "It's the U.S. Agency for International Development. First you teach them how old John D. did it. Then you build baseball diamonds and sell them three-piece suits. It's un-fucking-American not to get high in the Republic of South Vietnam."

"So how do we contribute?" Timmens asked.

"Be cool," Amaro said. "Just be cool, fool, and you will function at the junction when you get there."

Watts walked into the orderly room carrying his clipboard. "Who authorized a break for y'all?"

"Just taking ten for a smoke and joke," Amaro said.

"Amaro here is the Cougar Company fuckoff," Watts said. "Don't do what he does or yore ass be grass."

"If it was, I'd smoke it," Amaro said. "Watts here is the Cougar Company brown nose. Don't do what he does or you'll die in your next firefight."

"McGee wants to see you," Watts said. "He's in his tent."

"I'll see you guys later." Amaro walked out of the Orderly Room, waddling in imitation of Sergeant Watts. He turned into the narrow space between field tents and stopped in front of McGee's to rap on the tentpole.

"Come in," McGee said.

McGee folded and packed gear into his footlocker and cardboard boxes. Equipment was spread over the floor.

"Sit down," McGee said.

Amaro looked around, but there was no place to sit. He didn't want to disturb any of the stuff McGee had lying around.

McGee closed the lid on the footlocker. "Sit here," he said, and shoved some of the gear onto his cot, clearing a space big enough for him to sit in.

"You wanted to see me, Sarge." Amaro sat down on the footlocker.

"How have you been doing?" McGee asked.

"Could be better."

"That's for sure. You got an extra smoke?"

"Yeah," Amaro said. "Here you go." He handed a Lucky Strike to McGee.

The sergeant flipped open his Zippo and pushed the wheel against his pantleg. The light flared up and he lit the smoke. "Your skin looks a little better. They ever tell you what it was?"

"A rash, they said."

McGee laughed. Amaro smiled.

"You know the First Shirt really has his balls twisted over your getting another light-duty profile, don't you?"

"I figured he wouldn't like it," Amaro said. "But I don't give a shit what he thinks about it. It's legit."

"Yeah. I know. He checked on it. He was fixin' to send you to LBJ."

"I got my ass covered, Sarge."

"Keep it that way. He's like a fuckin' bulldog. Give him room enough to take a big bite and he'll never let go."

"I'll remember that."

"You'll be going back to the doc when we get to Chu Lai. Do your best to convince him."

"Convince who, Sarge?"

"The doc."

"Convince him of what?" Amaro asked.

"Figure it out for yourself," McGee said. He reached over and picked up his fatigue jacket. He took an envelope from one of the pockets. "How have you been doing otherwise?" he asked.

"Okay."

"Have you been getting your mail?"

"Yeah. Watts gives it to me when he remembers."

"Is everything okay at home?"

"Yeah. I guess so. Why?"

"Your family is okay?"

"Yeah. What's up, Sarge? What's on your mind? Why are you . . . Did something happen or something?"

McGee took a letter out of an envelope. "The company commander gave this to me," he said. "It's a letter written to him by your mom and pop."

"Let me see that," Amaro said.

"Later. Your mom and pop are worried about you. They say they haven't heard from you and they were afraid something happened to you and they didn't know about it."

"I didn't realize it's been that long since I wrote home," Amaro said.

"You know, I've watched you since you got here. You're no gallant warrior, that's for sure. Hell, it would be pushing it to even call you a decent fighter. But there ain't many real fighters over here to begin with. Don't know if I would even call myself one. But you do what you have to do, I'll say that much for you."

"Sarge, I . . ."

"Let me finish. I've seen you fuck up all kinds of ways. I know you smoke dope and I can't say as I blame you. We all need something to get us through. But not writing home is the most fucked-up thing you ever did. You got those folks back at home worried sick about you, boy."

"I didn't . . . I don't know what to say to them, Sarge . . . I . . . I can't explain it. I don't know how."

"There's no excuse in this or any other world for it. It's a fuckup, pure and simple."

"You're right, Sarge."

"You're good and goddamned right I'm right," McGee said, handing the letter to Amaro. "Write them. Tonight. That's a direct order. Tell them about your profile. Tell them you're not in the line. Tell them you're okay. Tell them any fucking thing you want. Just let them know you're still alive. I'm sure they'll be glad to hear it."

"Okay, Sarge. I'll take care of it," Amaro said.

"Good. Be sure you do. If the Old Man gets another letter like this one, I'm personally gonna dropkick your young ass clean out the compound. You understand me."

"I hear you, Sarge. I hear you." Amaro stood up and walked toward the tent flap. He stopped and turned around. "Sarge, there's guys over here who . . . who never spent a day out in the boondocks. I mean there's guys right *here* who don't do nothing but bake fucking pies for their whole tour. What I'm saying is . . . you know what I'm saying."

"Yeah," McGee said, leaning back on his cot. "I know. But you're complaining to the wrong man. I been in the field since I got to this motherfucker. I came here an E-7 and, by God, it looks like I'm gonna leave here an E-7. Though at this point, I'll be fucking happy just to leave here. But some other people I know made eight right away. That's just the way it is. Just do what you got to do for yourself, Amaro. Now get the fuck out of here and write a letter to your folks."

Amaro walked out of the tent and crossed the company area. He stopped at the bunkers, tore the letter into small pieces and scattered them.

Amaro spent the morning stacking crates of rockets on the landing zone. Groups of Vietnamese civilians—old men, women, and children—sat huddled in the sun, surrounded by piles of personal belongings. Rope-tied bundles of clothing with buckets, pots, and pans attached, were used for tables and chairs. Children ran around shouting and playing tag. Infants cried. The old stared, rocking back and forth.

Military police walked through the crowd telling people to put their cook fires out. The Vietnamese did not understand that the landing zone was loaded with ordnance. They only knew they were hungry.

The other landing zone used for troop movements was also covered with the displaced and homeless. Choppers landed regularly, bringing more into the camp. These refugees stood on line at Battalion Aid, waiting for medical attention; others walked or hobbled along the roads of the compound.

When the detail was given a long break for lunch, Amaro pulled his jacket on. He walked to the orderly room. It was empty, as he thought it would be at chow time. Watts was always first on line when it came to stuffing his face.

Across from Watt's desk was a poncho draped over an empty rocket crate. On top of the poncho was Sergeant Romo's steel pot. It was exactly as it had been the day it saved Romo's life. The white plastic bottle of mosquito repellent was still behind the elastic band; so was a sealed field dressing and a dirt-stained box of Marlboros. The lighter-sized chunk of shrapnel was still embedded in the steel of the pen-and-ink *Playboy* bunny drawn on the camouflage cover. The chunk of metal had all but wiped out the rabbit's head, yet it had not so much as scratched Romo's scalp.

The guys in the company paid tribute to the helmet, slipping into the orderly room to leave small devotions. They called it "Pisspot, the Patron Saint of Ass," as in pool players who shoot eight ball without calling their shots, sinking impossible combinations on luck, on pure ass.

The guys who knew Romo, and were there when he got hit, brought tokens to Pisspot in the hopes of having some of its luck rub off on them, so they could ass-out the way Romo had. On the poncho under the sacred hat they left half-eaten bits of green Chuckles, mold-covered M & M's, tiny tar-stained roaches, grenade rings, Vick's Inhalers, bullets, condoms, worn-out socks, a pair of satin panties with the word *Tuesday* embroidered on them, little sickle-bladed P-38 can openers,

Tiger Balm labels, peace signs, piasters, rosary beads and love beads, Tigerbaum's mezuzah, and anything else they felt was worthy.

The Dickmauler hated the mess. He raved about how it was against all military standards. But Jungle Jim, the new CO, realized its importance to the men and gave orders to leave it be. Watts had to tidy it up once in a while when the donations piled up too high. He would police the stuff and toss it all into a cardboard box next to the altar.

Amaro's personal sacrifice that afternoon was a paste made of pound cake, applesauce, Tiger Balm, dirt, reefer seeds, and drops of blood taken from a slit on his thumb. These he had mixed together in a bread can and spooned over a heat tab. He placed the offering under the steel pot, touching his fingertips to the shrapnel, then closed eyes and whispered, "Kiss my ass."

When his private ritual was completed, he opened two boxes of sundries and dumped them out on the floor. He tossed all the writing paper, envelopes, and shaving gear into one box and pushed it to the side. He placed all the candy, cigarettes, and soap into the other, and lifted it to his shoulder.

He carried the box to the landing zone, laying it down on the corner of the sparse hedgerow. The children stopped playing and watched him with curiosity. Amaro reached into the box and pulled out a handful of candy. He opened a bag of M & M's and popped them in his mouth. He smiled, nodded, and rubbed his stomach with his hand. He tossed the rest of the candy to the children, pointed to the box, and waved them toward it. They came slowly.

Amaro stepped through the crowd gathered around the box and walked along the road leading away from the company area. He walked past the battalion aid station, the movie screen, and battalion headquarters. He turned onto a wider road, a road busy with trucks, jeeps, and wandering civilians. There were motor pools behind barbed-wire fencing—a sign said CANNIBALIZATION POINT—large Quonset huts used for storage, an officers' club decorated with palm fronds.

The center of the camp was laid out in a wide circle around a tall flagpole. Along the sides of the road, stacked rocks served as curbing. Each of the large tents had a small rock border out in front of a low sandbag wall. Amaro walked into one of the tents. He did not remove his helmet as he was carrying a rifle.

"I'd like to talk to the Inspector General," Amaro said.

The Spec-5 behind the desk looked up at him. The specialist was clean, close-shaven. His fatigues seemed new.

"What's the problem?" the specialist asked.

"Are you blind?" Amaro said.

The specialist tossed his pencil down on a stack of paperwork. He leaned back in his chair.

"First of all, there is no 'Inspector General,' soldier. It's not a person, it's a thing. It's the name of this section. Second, this section is administrative, not tactical. You look as if you need a doctor. You should go to your battalion aid station. We can't help you here."

"Look. I've already been there," Amaro said. "And they haven't done any good. They gave me the same stuff my platoon medic gave me, then sent me back to the line."

"That's SOP."

"I want to talk to somebody in charge."

"If you've already received treatment, what else do you want?"

"I want to see a real doctor, damn it. Battalion aid is for guys shot and bleeding. They're not interested in things like this," Amaro said. He held his hand over the desk and made a fist. Thick yellow pus oozed from the sores on his knuckles. "But I'm interested in it, man. I'm the one who's rotting away."

The specialist handed him a form. "Fill it out," he said.

"Shove it up," Amaro said.

"You were AWOL this afternoon," Fluett said, leaning forward with the knuckles of his clenched fists white against the desktop.

"From here, maybe I was," Amaro said. "But I was accounted for. I went to see somebody about my medical problem."

"You violated the chain of command."

"I'm getting fucked by the chain of command, First Sergeant."

"You sorry yard bird. Just who do you think you are, going over my head?"

"I was trying to get around that rummy at the aid station."

"Watch what you say, trooper. You're in enough trouble as it is."

"It's true. Spector's done more for me than—"

"At ease! This is a war, trooper. War. This unit does not have the time to pamper minor aches and pains."

"I'm just trying to—"

"Shut up. Just shut your mouth. I've seen a million malingering punks like you."

"It wasn't—"

"At ease!" Fluett said. "What did you want with Sergeant Watts?"

"Nothing important," Amaro answered. "I can take care of it tomorrow."

Fluett stood up and walked to Amaro. "What did you want with Sergeant Watts?"

"I wanted to return this," Amaro said, taking a file from his trouser-leg pocket. He handed it to Fluett.

Fluett snatched the folder from Amaro's hand. "And what piece of shit is this?" he asked, as he moved closer to the cone of yellow light cast by the bare bulb over Watts's desk.

Amaro did not answer.

Fluett shook his head as he read the file. He said, almost in a whisper, "I don't fucking believe it. You slimy greaseball. Who is this doctor, some candyass draftee?"

"It's a legitimate profile, First Sergeant," Amaro said.

"Legitimate? *Legitimate?* Who the fuck do you think you're fooling? You must think I'm the dumbest stump jumper to ever come down this pike, don't you. Well, don't confuse me with this asshole doctor of yours. You can fool him, but no snotnose punk like you will ever pull the wool over my eyes. Not in this or any other life. Just who the fuck do you think you are, goddamn it."

"It's a legitimate profile, First Sergeant. I got problems with my skin," Amaro said.

"The only problem with your skin is the yellow stripe down the middle of it, you son-of-a-bitch city-scum greaseball."

"Up yours, motherfucker."

Fluett took a step toward Amaro, then stopped. He ripped the medical file in his hands. Tore it and threw the pieces. Amaro watched them flutter and twist to the wooden floor.

"That's what I think of you, you spineless skin bag, and that jerk-off doctor," Fluett whispered. "You're a fucking disgrace."

"And you're a fucking asshole," Amaro said softly.

Fluett took another step closer. Amaro clicked off the safety on his weapon.

"Come on, scumbag," Amaro said. "Come on and push a little harder. I'll fucking cut you in half where you stand."

Fluett stopped in his tracks. He wiped his palms on his trouser legs. "You don't have the guts," he said.

"Try me and find out," Amaro said.

Fluett did not move.

"I thought so," Amaro said. "Without those stripes to hide behind you ain't nothing. You're a fart in a windstorm, you lifer cocksucker."

"I want you here first thing tomorrow morning, with all your gear, soldier," Fluett said. "The battalion surgeon assures me that light duty does not prevent your being attached to Headquarters Company. Your candyass won't melt guarding a forward perimeter, but you can get dusted just as easy."

Amaro engaged the safety. "Suits me," he said. "As long as I don't have to see your ugly fucking face."

"Oh, you'll see it again, you chickenshit little prick. You'll see it again and it will be the last thing you see on earth."

"Maybe," Amaro said. "Maybe that's the way it'll go down. Who knows? But I'll die with my teeth sunk deep in your fucking heart."

Fluett stepped back to his desk and scribbled something on a form, crumpled it into a ball and threw it at Amaro. "Your orders. Take 'em and get out of my sight."

Amaro picked up the crumpled paper and squeezed it in his hand, then backed slowly out of the orderly room.

"Yo, bro," Las Vegas said. "You sure gave the man a royal case of the ass. I heard him yelling from way out here."

"I was trying to bust a blood vessel in his head," Amaro said.

"Then you shoulda tried harder, bro. You woulda done us all a big favor."

"Maybe someday I will," Amaro said. "Come with me. I want to get something."

They walked out to the perimeter wall. Amaro stood at the cross-wall and counted off sandbags.

"Keep your eyes open," Amaro said.

"We're cool," Las Vegas said, scanning the company area.

Amaro dug up the preserve jar and took some joints out of it. He rewrapped the rest of the stash and buried it back in the same hole.

"Pretty slick, Rick," Las Vegas said.

"I ain't no fool, O'Toole," Amaro said. "Listen up. If I don't come back sometime, help yourself."

"What do you mean, if you don't come back?"

"There's about thirty number-one joints in there. Split them with Tigerbaum. Turn Morris on, too. I think he's a good guy."

"Hey, Ray. You gotta have busted bones or something to get sent out of here."

"I got to get out," Amaro said. "If not out of the country, at least out of the line. I've had it, man. I've seen it. I did what I had to do. I'm losing it, man."

"Shit, Amaro. We all already lost it. Just go with the flow, bro."

"I don't want to die in this motherfucking place."

"I hear you talking, man," Las Vegas said. "I know what you mean. It's like, who gives a fuck, right?"

"Yeah," Amaro said, checking the wind. "Like who gives a fat rat's ass. You got it." The breeze blew from the east. "We can do one of these right here. Only the gooks up in the mountains will be able to smell it."

14

The battalion landing zone in Chu Lai was bigger and busier than the one in Duc Pho had been. Interlocked strips of steel PSP covered the dirt, cutting down on dust and mud in the rainy season.

Amaro sat on the metal, leaning against his rucksack. Two replacements for Headquarters Company, new guys in country, sat at Amaro's side. They were quiet. They seemed nervous. One of them chainsmoked and tapped his foot in a rapid four-four beat.

Cigarette smoke rose and bent in the gentle morning breeze. It was already getting hot. Amaro broke a sweat just sitting on the open landing zone.

He thought about getting even with Fluett for sending him back out to the field. It was a dirty trick, but it had happened too fast for him to do anything. So he decided to take the ride, see what it was like. The AT platoon in Headquarters Company had to have it easier than the grunts out humping the line. Just go someplace and set up. That's all. No search and destroy. No walking point. Maybe some hot chow once in a while.

A Huey came in for a landing. Amaro watched a couple of guys jump from the door and run bent over at the waist, holding steel pots and weapons. Some other guys ran to the chopper and carried back empty chow cans.

"That's your bird," an NCO shouted. "Get aboard on the double."

Amaro and the new guys picked up their gear and trotted to the chopper. They tossed their rucksacks on the deck and climbed aboard. The new guys looked around, confused, and said something to each other. Amaro could not hear what they said over the rotor and idling engine but he knew.

"Just hold on to something," Amaro shouted.

One of the guys looked at him.

"Just sit on the deck and hold on," Amaro shouted, gesturing.

They did what he showed them. A ground crew loaded cases of ammo and grenades on the deck. The crew chief gave a hand sign and the chopper took off.

From the air, the terrain around Chu Lai looked just like any other Amaro had seen. The lush green jungle; the white-ribbon waters; the play of light and shade. He had learned to watch the sun so he knew he was flying north.

The chopper banked left, following a river to the north-west. Down below were bare-chested men wearing conical hats, standing waist-deep in the water. Several small boats paddled midstream, trailing the cork floats of homemade nets. These men moved quickly, they tugged on ropes, pointed at the riffles.

The Huey lost altitude and flew low over a treeline. A wide, open area appeared beyond the canopy. Amaro saw C-130s parked along an airstrip carved in the jungle. Two planes and several choppers. Quonset huts on line along the runway, and field tents pitched in the distance. One tent had a white circle with a red cross painted on the roof. There was some truck traffic, and jeeps, and dozens of walking soldiers. The camp was encircled by sandbags and concertina wire, and bunkers were positioned along the outer edge. Tall towers stood on the hilltops along the western perimeter of the camp. The riverbank formed the opposite flank.

Across the river, on a hill, Amaro saw an artillery battery: a ring of howitzers, 105s, aimed in every direction. Crates of shells were stacked within the perimeter, and in the center of the circle was a command post made up of several pup tents pitched around a field tent. A shallow valley separated the artillery position from another, wider perimeter. The chopper touched down inside this wider cordon.

Amaro grabbed his gear and jumped from the Huey. He ran toward a guy who carried a clipboard and stood next to a stack of supplies. Amaro knew these were the guys who could answer all his questions.

"My name is Amaro," he shouted over the noise of the chopper. "From Charlie Company."

The NCO checked the papers on his clipboard. "Yeah," he yelled. "We were expecting a cripple. We get all the fucking rejects, like the Statue of fucking Liberty. Send us your humble, your weak and lame, your gimps, the ones who sprout yellow feathers."

"Hey," Amaro said. "Fuck you. Just tell me where to go and save your bullshit for the cherries." He nodded at the two new guys. "Maybe they'll be impressed by a real hardass like you. I sure as shit ain't."

The NCO looked around the landing zone. "Hey, Fatman," he shouted. "Come here."

A tall, heavyset hightone walked slowly to the NCO.

"We got us a hotshot gunman from a line company to replace Higgins," the NCO said. "He's supposed to be a real gunslinger. Take him over to your position and get him squared away."

"Okay, Sarge," Fatman said. He turned to Amaro. "Come on with me."

Amaro stared at the NCO, then followed Fatman.

"Leave that here," the NCO said.

Amaro turned around. "You talking to me?"

"Yeah, I'm talking to you," the NCO said. "Leave that with me." He pointed to Amaro's rifle.

"What are you, fucked up or something?" Amaro said. "I ain't giving you my piece. Get fucked."

"You're my new machine gunner, Hardcore," the NCO said. "Give me your rifle so I can send it back on the chopper."

"Fuck you and your machine gun," Amaro said. "Let somebody else play Guadalcanal."

"You're it, Hardcore. Like it or not, you're it," the NCO said. "When we hit the shit, Charlie always takes out my gunner first. With you here, I don't got to waste one of my own men. Give me your rifle."

"It's cool," Fatman said. "We got Higgins's forty-five back at the gun. You can pack it as your sidearm."

Amaro slipped the GP strap from his shoulder and handed over the piece. The NCO took it and smiled. He turned and walked away.

"Let's get to where we're going," Amaro said. "I feel naked."

"It's just out behind them trees," Fatman said.

"Is that what they call you? Fatman?" Amaro asked.

"Yeah," Fatman replied. "The name sort of fits. What do they call you?"

"Amaro," he said. "What do you guys do out here?"

"Spread shade for battalion field HQ," Fatman said. "Sometimes run cover for the artillery. It ain't bad. After we set up, the work's all done. At least we don't gotta hump all day long. Some patrols now and then. Once in a while a ambush. But nothin' too heavy, y'unnerstan'."

"Sounds okay," Amaro said.

"That's good. 'Cause you ain't got a choice. You here, and that's that."

They walked past some low shrubs into a wooded area. The ferns were dense and the bush thickened out beyond the foxhole.

The gun position was a hole. A shallow hole with sandbag sides. The M-60 rested on the bags.

The first thing Amaro noticed about the guy sitting in the foxhole was the lightning streak of pure white hair growing out from his hairline. It was combed back, blending gradually with the dark brown curls on the rest of his head.

"A spooky motherfucker, ain't he?" Fatman said to Amaro. "He's Valdez, the assistant motorman. This is Ammurrah, the new trigger."

"Hello, man," Valdez said.

"How you doing?" Amaro said. "Where's the forty-five?"

Fatman pointed to a pistol belt folded in the corner of the hole. Amaro dropped his rucksack, unhooked the holster from the pistol belt, and attached it to his web gear. He drew the automatic, removed the magazine, and cleared the chamber.

"It's clean," Amaro said.

"It's clean, okay," Valdez said. "Higgins, he take care of that fucking thing."

Amaro loaded the .45 and slipped it back in the holster. He found a dozen loaded magazines and two cleaning kits—one for the .45, another for the sixty—wrapped in a cloth bandolier. He was sorry he didn't meet Higgins. He would have liked him.

"If you guys don't mind, maybe you could run me through cleaning the gun," Amaro said. "I ain't fucked with one in months."

"It's clean, okay," Valdez said. "Higgins, man, he clean that fucking thing like he was gonna eat it or something. *Conio,* that fucking guy he was a nut, yes or no, man?"

"Higgins was a far-out dude," Fatman said.

"I know it's clean," Amaro said. "I just wanted to get to know it better. That's all."

"Well, go ahead, okay," Valdez said. "*Conio,* who the fuck is stopping you, man. Knock yourself out. Just don't break my balls about it."

Amaro spread a towel on the bottom of the hole and broke the machine gun down. It was spotless. Everything had that magic light coat of oil always talked about but never seen. He reassembled the gun, then broke it down, several times over. When he felt sure that he could do it in a hurry—when he could do it the way he had seen Vernon do it—he reassembled it, adjusted the bipod, and positioned it on the sandbags.

"Where's our field of fire?" Amaro asked.

"*Conio,*" Valdez said. "Hey, you hear that, Fatman? 'Field of fire'? Holy shit. Where the fuck you from, man? Field of fucking fire. Damn, Sam."

"Just point that motherfucker at anything that moves," Fatman said. "The whole fucking country is our field of fire."

"You a funny guy, man," Valdez said. "*Conio.* Field of fire, okay. You believe that shit?"

"Fuck you," Amaro said. "I was only asking. How the fuck am I supposed to know what the SOP is around here?"

Valdez laughed out loud. "Essopee? Goddamn, you a funny motherfucker."

"You keep busting my chops and I'll blow white hair all over them fucking trees," Amaro said.

"Be cool, man. Be cool," Fatman said. "You'll get used to Juan Valdez. It's just the way he is, man. It's his way, you dig?"

"His way, huh. Tell the *muchacho* he's headed for a karma kickback he keeps fucking with me," Amaro said.

Valdez laughed louder. "You hear that, Fatman?" he said, out of breath. "*Conio corrajo,* 'a karma kickback,' okay. This is one funny motherfucker. Goddamn my belly hurts."

"So you're Juan Valdez, huh," Amaro said. "Ain't you the guy that picks coffee beans out of his nose?"

"Goddamn, y'all have met before," Fatman said. "He always be diggin' in his snotlocker."

"You bleach your hair or what?" Amaro asked.

"Bleach your ass," Valdez said, patting his hair in place. "Is a birthmark, *puto.* Makes me somebody special." He stopped laughing.

"I knew a girl used to bleach her pussy white so we could find it in the dark," Amaro said.

"Valdez does it so he knows where to scratch when his ass gets itchy," Fatman added.

"What the fuck is this, man?" Valdez said, taking a corncob pipe out of his pocket. "A fucking mutiny or some shit whatever you call it? Why you sidin' with the gray dude for, eh, you tub of shit. *Conio,* you gringos stick together like a virgin's knees, okay." He held his legs together and crossed his arms over his chest.

"What's the pipe for?" Amaro asked. "Do you do Popeye as good as you do Ricky Ricardo?"

Fatman laughed. "Fucking Ricky Ricardo. He nicked you that time. He done peeped yore hole card."

"Shut up, Lucy. I show you fucking Popeye, okay," Valdez said. He pulled a plastic tobacco pouch out of his field pants pocket. "*Da-dada-da-da-da-dum.* Here's the fucking spinach, okay."

Fatman glanced at Amaro. Then he looked back at Valdez.

"Don't worry, okay," Valdez said. "This fucking guy is too funny to be heat. You want some fucking muscles, man?"

"Spinach is my favorite food," Amaro said.

"See? See? What I told you, Fatso? *Conio,* you worry too fucking much, man. You gonna get a mulcer or some shit like that," Valdez said. He stuck his hand in the pouch and ran his fingers through the reefer. The leaf crumbled and flaked. It fell through the screen, separated from the stems and seeds. Valdez reached the pipe into the bottom of the pouch and thumb-loaded the bowl. He folded the pouch and jammed it back into his pocket.

"You're kind of loose with the stash, ain't you," Amaro asked.

"No sweat," Valdez said. "Nobody fuck with you out here. Everybody just do his own thing. Nobody hassles nobody."

"It's cool," Fatman said. "Layin' back. Cuttin' slack. Like tokin' in yore own crib."

They passed the pipe around.

"This ain't bad for loose shit," Amaro said. He coughed. His eyes teared.

"What, you got better?" Valdez asked.

Amaro pulled out his magazine stash and slid the bottom open. "Ready-rolls," he said.

"*Conio,* Fatman," Valdez said. "This fucking guy he's a machine gunner for real."

Fatman and Valdez walked to the landing zone to get a hot lunch. Amaro stayed in the position, heating water for cocoa. He opened some pound cake and applesauce.

The area seemed safe to him. The sandbagged hole, though cramped, felt like a fort. It was something to get behind; something between him and whatever was out there.

The perimeter was busy. Choppers went in and out constantly. Although he couldn't see them from his position, Amaro knew the artillery was close by, and a little farther off was the Special Forces camp. He had never been in the field with so large a unit, sitting in one place ready to defend instead of attack. It wasn't too bad, being attached to Headquarters Company.

Amaro spread out a poncho and broke down the machine gun again. It was easy to do. Big parts. Everything sturdy. The barrel separated from the stock with just the twist of a lever. It had a big bore, made to fit rounds also used for the M-14s.

The gun always worked. Amaro was convinced if it had been buried in mud, he could load up, squeeze the trigger, and put out some heavy firepower. He liked the confidence he felt behind the gun. He cleaned it, oiled it, and towel-wrapped the reassembled gun.

Carrying it in the line he wouldn't like, not carting another twenty-one pounds around in the boons. But here, all he had to do was set it up, leave it there, pull maintenance, and get stoned.

He found a bayonet on one of the rucksacks. He didn't know if it belonged to Fatman or Valdez. He pulled the bayonet from its scabbard and started to whittle on a branch. Then he kneeled in the shade of the tall tree directly behind the foxhole and began to carve on the trunk. He didn't know what he wanted to carve. His initials. Maybe his name. Amaro worked carefully, carving quarter-inch strips, using the knife tip to pry away the layer of soft wood under the bark to expose the bright yellow hardwood. A sticky sap dripped tearstains from the cuts.

He sat back and stared at the NYC in yellow six-inch letters on brown bark. He stared at it and wondered why, of all things, that was what he carved.

"New York, New York," Fatman said. "The city so nice they named it twice."

Amaro turned quickly. He did not hear them approach.

"Ah, *si*," Valdez said. "The corner of Broadway and Four-two Street. Now clean that sticky shit off my shiv, okay?"

Amaro wiped the blade on his pants, then flipped it at Valdez. It ripped a divot in the dirt next to Valdez's boot.

"You want to play stretch?" Valdez asked, picking up the knife.

"Why not?" Amaro said. He stood up and faced Valdez.

Valdez leaned to his right and buried half the blade with a quick snap throw. Amaro slid his left boot until it touched the blade. He balanced himself with his hand and pulled the bayonet up.

"You had it now, motherfucker," Amaro said. He switched the knife to his right hand and steadied himself for a throw. His legs were spread apart, almost in a split, and a sharp pain stabbed his back. He tried to aim, but couldn't concentrate. The bayonet hit the dirt too far forward. It stuck for an instant, then fell on its side.

"*Conio,*" Valdez said. "You can't do nothing right, man."

Amaro stood up straight and leaned backward with his hands pressing on his hips. He saw a C-130 climbing up above the treeline in the distance. The ground shook when the artillery started a fire mission. Amaro dove in the foxhole.

"Relax," Fatman said. "It's outgoing. Happens all the time. You'll get used to it."

Amaro kneeled in the foxhole. He watched the C-130 bank in a wide half-circle against the dreary sky. He listened to the outgoing, felt the shock waves in his gut. The C-130 climbed.

Even before the volley reached his ears, Amaro saw the plane break in half. Cartons, crates, boxes, even a jeep, tumbled out of the torn-apart sections. Amaro saw the silhouettes of three guys free-falling, spinning, legs moving like they were trying to run in midair. A chute opened from the back of one of them, but the guy streamered into a hillside. The two plane sections twisted end over end and crashed somewhere out of sight. The artillery fired another barrage.

"Did you see that?" Amaro asked, climbing out of the hole.

"Fuckin' A," Valdez said. "*Conio corrajo,* what a fucking humbug."

"That's the first thing them One-oh-fives ever hit," Fatman said. "Ain't that some shit."

He left the position and walked toward the center of the perimeter. He saw guys playing cards on ammo boxes. Others pulled maintenance on equipment. They all seemed to be doing something, and Amaro wondered just what it was he was supposed to be doing. His function—what was his function? That old lifer line, what a fucking joke.

Amaro walked past the aid station set up next to the landing zone. Some GIs were being treated; none of them seemed seriously hurt. Out behind an unmarked tent, Amaro saw a gook lying on a stretcher, one of his legs black and swollen twice the size of the other. Flies swarmed it. The gook wore only a pajama shirt.

Next to the stretcher, another gook was lying on the ground, his hands tied behind his back and a rope pulled tight between his bound ankles and his neck. An ARVN officer in starched fatigues stood over the prisoner. Several members of an American LURP team squatted on their haunches nearby, smoking cigarettes, watching the ARVN do his job.

The ARVN was crazy, running between the two prisoners, kicking. He waved a pistol. Jerked on the rope. Barked.

Amaro wanted to kill the three of them, just to stop the noise. He looked at the LURPs. They smoked cigarettes and ate candy bars. Two of them were betting on which prisoner would crack first.

It started to rain. Amaro jogged back to the position, but he was soaked by the time he got there. He found Fatman and Valdez huddled in the foxhole. They had covered the gun with Amaro's poncho. He left it there, where it would do the most good.

"I told you this fucking guy he ain't got the sense enough to come in out of the rain, okay," Valdez said.

"Maybe he needs a shower," Fatman said.

" 'Maybe'? *Conio,* what the fuck you talking about, 'maybe,' " Valdez said.

Amaro sat up against the tree, the same tree he had carved on, and lit a Lucky. He cupped the smoke and listened to the raindrops pelt his steel pot. He felt cold and wet and sick to his stomach. *What the fuck was happening?* No need to know. Can't know. Just do it. Do whatever. Go with the flow. He leaned against the tree, drew his knees up to his chest, wrapped his arms around his legs, and lowered his head. "I don't mean nothing," he whispered. "Nothing means nothing."

The rain stopped as if someone had shut the tap. The sun came out. It was hard to breathe.

Amaro stretched his fatigues over some branches in a patch of sunlight. He wrapped himself in a towel. His crotch felt sticky and raw. His sac stuck to the inside of his leg. He opened the towel and saw a wide raw circle of skin on the inside of each thigh. Wetting a corner of the towel with canteen water, he soaped and rinsed his crotch. Then he covered the spots with salve and wrapped the towel around his waist.

"What the fuck you doing, man?" Valdez asked. "You douching or something?"

"Cleaning my balls," Amaro said. "Something you don't got to worry about."

"*Conio,* man," Valdez said. "Back home the girls they write poems about my balls, okay."

"Hip little ditties about birdseed and BBs," Fatman said.

"Hey, Fatso, watch your mouth, okay," Valdez said. "Or I eat the pieces I kick off your ass, motherfucker."

"I'll bring the crackers," Amaro said.

"You should talk," Valdez said. "Walking around here in a towel like a *puta* or some fucking thing. What's that shit, man?"

"What's what shit?" Amaro asked.

"On your back, man. Them skeevy things. What, you fuck with a frog or something like that?" Valdez said.

"What's he talking about?"

"You got blisters or some shit on your back, man," Fatman said.

"Fucking jungle rot," Amaro said. "I'm getting it on my nuts, too."

"*Conio,* keep away from me," Valdez said. "Things are bad enough without that shit."

"Too late. I rubbed pus on your canteen cup," Amaro said.

"That's ugly, man. I think I'm gonna be sick," Valdez said.

"What are we gonna do about tonight?" Fatman asked. "It's gonna rain like a motherfucker."

"Fatso can always tell when it's gonna rain," Valdez said. "The stitches in his pussy start to hurt. *Conio,* he's like a old fucking cunt."

The sun started to set. Amaro pulled on his fatigues. They were still wet. He hated the idea of his skin rotting while he was still alive. It was an evil omen. He hated the way his wet clothes felt cold and clammy, the way it must feel in a grave.

"We gotta make some kind of a hooch," Fatman said. "Come on, Ammurah. Give us a hand."

"Fuck you," Amaro said. "I'm already wet. Make you own fucking hooch."

"Hey, motherfucker. You do your share, okay," Valdez said.

They snapped ponchos together and tied the hoods tight, arguing all the while.

"Use rocks to hold it down?"

"No, rocks won't do it. Get some rope."

"Use a couple of sticks to pitch it so's the water slides off."

"What the fuck, you building a house? Just stretch the shit over the sandbags and tie the fucker down."

"It won't work."

"Fuck you, it won't."

They argued and carried on until the sun set and night covered the camp.

15

It rained hard all night. Amaro curled up in the corner of the foxhole, trying to get away from the water leaking in down the center of the hooch. Puddles formed in the hole and the mud got deep. He looked up, saw the hooch sagging, rolled over, and tried to sleep.

The sound of snaps ripping apart woke Amaro at the instant the water poured in. It hit him like a cold shower. Amaro stood up.

"You motherfucker," he yelled at the top of his lungs. "Just leave me the fuck alone."

His voice carried over the dark and quiet jungle. Valdez laughed loud and hard.

"I told you this fucking guy he's crazy, man. You're funnier than fucking television. Now shut up and go to sleep, okay."

It rained every day at exactly three in the afternoon. The blue sky went gray and heavy raindrops, big as marbles, poured straight down for maybe fifteen minutes. Then the clouds drifted somewhere else to dump their buckets, and the sun came out again. It rained the same way at night for two weeks in a row.

Amaro could not take saltwater showers out in the field. Humid heat and wet fatigues caused new eruptions on his skin. His crotch was covered by a glistening, sticky ooze. He had trouble walking. Trouble sitting still. The constant burning itch made lying down impossible. When he complained, the senior medic smiled and gave him a new tube of salve.

Amaro stopped eating hot chow. He stayed in the position and ate pound cake and applesauce from his rucksack. He spoke only when Fatman or Valdez asked him a question. He answered these questions with as few words as possible, just enough words to let them know he didn't want to be bothered.

Whenever he could, he walked off by himself to lower his pants and sit with his legs spread far apart. The air, though hot and humid, felt better than cloth or skin.

Even when word came to break camp, Amaro kept to himself. His rucksack was packed, the gun cleaned and ready. That was all he cared about. Fatman and Valdez gave him a hard time about not helping to empty the sandbags and fill up the foxhole. But Amaro just sat near the tree, his eyes unblinking, his hair wild, his face unshaven. His skin was covered with drooping sacs.

Amaro heard them talking about Tam Ky. They spoke of a heliborne assault, an attack on an enemy position. But Amaro did not care where he went, or how he had to get there. It would all be the same. The same fucking thing. He would just leave another rotting piece of himself behind.

The landing zone was hot so the chopper pilot brought the Huey in at treetop level, hovered for a second tipped to the right, and dropped the troopers quick out the door. One guy broke his leg on impact. Some others floundered on their backs, rolling on their rucksacks, trying to get up, move out, avoid the incoming. One guy had died in midair.

Those that could, double-timed into positions ringing the taller of two hills. Those that could not, crawled for cover wherever they found it. Wide trees and big rocks were best, but the body of a dead buddy worked too. More choppers came in and dropped more troopers. More ran and crawled and a couple never moved. The guy with the broken leg fired bursts at the emptied choppers as if they were the enemy.

There were enough paratroopers now to tighten the perimeter around both hills. They shook off rucksacks and from the prone fired at the jungle that was killing them. Some shouted and screamed but no one seemed to hear them over the steady *crackacrack* snapping of small arms fire. Medics snaked among the living and the almost dead, doing for each whatever they could. Smoke grenades popped and purple smoke bent over the hills.

Amaro hugged the dirt, sucking in the cordite air. The machine-gun barrel was hot. Too hot. It had to be changed but he was too scared. So he slowed his rate of fire instead. It seemed as if everyone else did the same. The tempo slackened. The noise eased up to an occasional sharp *pop*. Then even that stopped. The ejected brass tinkled against the ammo links. It was strange, after all that noise. It terrified him, filling him with more fear than the sight of blazing tracers. On the hill there was the smell: the purple-gray drifting smoke. The moans and screams of wounded: *Dear God. Please. Help me.*

Amaro and Valdez changed the barrel on the sixty. Using a towel from his pack, Amaro flipped the locking lever and pulled the almost melting steel out. Valdez replaced it with the cool spare barrel. Then they lit cigarettes. They looked around the hill. Faces familiar and strange returned stares.

"*Conio,*" Valdez said. "This is some ugly shit."

Squad leaders searched the perimeter for their men. The re-formed squads shifted into platoons. Positions were taken up and some order restored. Up on the hilltop the dead and wounded were dusted off by Chinooks bringing in the 105s by canvas strap slings. They unloaded supplies. The guys drew ammo and grenades. Crates of shells were stacked neatly next to the gun battery.

Amaro's position was on the higher hill, the one the artillery was set up on to provide support for the rest of the battalion. On the smaller hill was the command post. A down-curving ridge between them completed the saddle. The hilltop was relatively flat, sloping steeply on three sides. Dry, waist-high grass covered the crest. Amaro scanned his field of fire into the valley. The jungle was not thick.

"We'll dig in after chow," Amaro said.

Valdez and Fatman, who had returned with full ammo cans, agreed.

There was an E-5 from artillery in the next position. Amaro watched as the guy made a field stove from a bread can. The guy placed a blue heat tab in the can and struck a match to it. As he leaned to pick up a rice-filled canteen cup, the toe of his boot kicked over the stove. Orange-yellow flames raced in a fanning line on the flattened grass. The guys in the position tried to stomp it out. They could not control it. Amaro and Valdez joined them along with several others nearby. They stomped on the flames. Tried to smother them with ponchos. But the dry grass caught like seasoned tinder.

Two men from each position were sent to put out the fire. They heaved shovelfuls of dirt on the flames. Used ponchos until they melted. Black smoke curled above the hilltop. Men from the CP were sent to help out. But the flames spread, reaching higher than the troopers were tall. Soot-faced, they ran back and forth, choking in smoke, eyes tearing, skin about to blister.

Amaro saw someone double up like punched in the chest, his legs lifted from the burning grassy hill. He ran to pull the guy from the flames. The guy was dead. A round had gone right through him. Dirt kicked up in spots around Amaro. He could not hear the incoming but he saw it in the faces of the guys who got hit. When the CP opened up into the valley, the shots could barely be heard over the sound of the fire.

Then the flames reached the stacked ammo. The howitzer shells exploded, blowing guys into the black smoke cloud in pieces. The dirt was too hot to stand on. There was no air, no cover, no way to fight back. Amaro looked toward the position. Valdez was gone. So was Fatman and almost everyone else. An explosion lifted Amaro from the ground, throwing him into the fire. He rolled in the dirt, slapping his sides to put out his fatigues. He crouched, low-crawled, and tried to find a place that did not burn where he could breathe. He ran downhill. Behind him he felt the hilltop explode. He felt whizzing bits of metal hit him in the back. A green tracer splattered against a stone next to his foot. A VC gunner had him in his sights. Amaro dove flat and rolled. He jumped up and ran. He was short-winded from smoke and fear. The lower hill seemed miles away. Amaro sprinted and dove, jumped up, tripped over vines, and fell. He ran along the down-curved ridge, keeping below the skyline, his arms crossed in front of his face. He pulled himself up the incline of the smaller hill, gasping for air, not hearing, not knowing.

The medics poured water on him and covered him with burn grease. Only when his hearing returned did he realize it had been missing. Now he heard as well as felt the explosions on the other hill. They rumbled under the sharper sounds of rifle fire.

The first of the resupply choppers appeared in the distance. Two others followed. When the chopper was over the hill, the rotor seemed to freeze. It just stayed still and the chopper started to spin. It spun around like a kid's toy and slammed into the rocks on the hilltop. A squad pulled a survivor from it and boxes of ammo. The other two choppers veered sharply and backtracked. When they returned, they stayed high up, dropped supplies from the door. A five-gallon can of water hit a guy and crushed his skull.

There was no way to dust off the wounded, so the medics dosed them with painkiller. The dead were stacked in a pile near the rocks. Everyone was stuck right where they were.

The fire on the taller hill burned itself out. There was just a lot of smoke and the stink of burned bodies. The gunfight seemed about over. More choppers came in to evacuate the casualties. The VC in the valley brought down two.

Amaro scrounged a couple of cans of pound cake and applesauce. He could walk, there were no broken bones, so they gave him a dead man's rifle.

"The fucking barrel's bent," he said.

He walked around the perimeter and found Valdez with the sixty.

"Where's Fatman?" Amaro asked.

"I don't know," Valdez said. "I don't know what happened to him."

Amaro unloaded the rifle and flung it off the hilltop. He sat behind the gun and started to clean it.

Amaro and Valdez were part of a makeshift company detailed to return to the higher hill. Late in the afternoon they moved out and traversed the ridge. There were orders to protect the burned-out artillery tubes. Amaro carried the gun and as much ammo as his sore shoulders would allow. He had two canteens on his pistol belt, the same pistol belt he had the .45 hooked onto.

He was too dry to spit. He dreaded going back.

There was a triangular rock sticking up out of the ground near a burned-down tree. Amaro set the gun up behind it. He and Valdez, and a third guy neither one of them knew, began to dig in. They scooped dirt from behind the rock and stuffed it into sandbags. The hole was wide enough and long enough for three to lie in. Not too deep, but the sandbag sides helped out.

Amaro quickstepped around the perimeter, collecting ammo cans and bandoliers. There was some incoming sniper fire. He kept low, crouching next to a charred corpse. Amaro thought it looked like Fatman, but he could not be sure.

Valdez clipped bandoliers together. He arranged the cans in line behind the hole. A round cracked and pinged off the rock and Valdez wormed deeper into the duff. Amaro and the third guy sat low in the hole and wrote home. Amaro told his parents everything was fine. He apologized for not having written more often. Before he closed the letter, he told his folks he loved them.

At sundown a breeze blew, fanning the still-smoldering log next to the machine gun. The log glowed orange. When the breeze increased the log glowed brighter. As the sky darkened, the position was silhouetted as if spotlit. Amaro crawled over to the log with an entrenching tool and drew sniper fire. He lay behind the log and shoveled dirt over it. The spikelike grass stubble cut him. Blisters on his hands broke and seeped. All he could hear was the ringing in his ears. Two rounds thudded into the log and showered him with orange cinder sparks. Amaro ate dirt. The log glowed red in the moonless night.

Amaro knew it was coming. He stared out into the black jungle and listened to the gunships growling overhead. He flinched when it started, when the silence exploded and the green and white tracers arced inward like the screaming neon lights in a madman's dream. And the orange tracers shot back. Some straight. Some bending. Others shattering into a million glittering pieces. The *crackacrackem poppoppop* loud, then lower, then louder still like uneven waves in a storm. The gunships dropped flares. The bright white fading to gray light made unnatural shadows in the eerie landscape. Palm trees came to life. Spit green-and-white streaks. The gunships flew opposite one another in a circle wider than the perimeter. They breathed red fire, the tracers waving down from a black spot somewhere in the sky to a blacker spot somewhere on the ground. So far away, the dotted lines were seen first, then the sound, seemingly unconnected—a mournful groan, as if some rusted hinge creaked as the door to an unused corner of hell was opened to swallow the hill and everything on it. But the VC were tucked in a pocket inside the bullet fence from the gunships and the perimeter. And they came shouting, they came from all sides.

There was a gradual slope for fifteen meters in front of the gun. Then the land pitched downward. Amaro kept the gun trained on the edge. Valdez cracked a case of grenades and he and the third guy lobbed them over the ridgeline. A VC mortar zeroed in on the glowing log, walking rounds toward the gun. First a distant *phhooomp*. Then the dread explosions raining dirt on their steel pots. And chunks of speeding jagged metal tore into everything. Including the third guy. He was kneeling, throwing a grenade, when the mortar chewed him up. The grenade rolled in front of the rock and went off. Blood streamed from Amaro's ears and nose and mixed with specks of bloody flesh from the third guy.

More VC came over the edge. Now they climbed over the dead, those dead hopping jumping like alive when machine-gun rounds slammed into them.

"Get a fucking grenade launcher," Amaro screamed. "Who got a seventy-niner? Who got one? Light up that mothafuckin' mortar. It's gonna kill us all. Light up that fuckin' mortar. Light 'im up, light 'im up. Goddamn it, light 'im up. Light up that mortar!"

He walked tracers into the spot he thought the mortar was set.

Phhoomp it said.

"*Die,*" he screamed.

Phhooomp . . . phhoomp.

The explosion blew him upward. He slammed back down hard. His finger numb on the trigger. The barrel glowed. While he cursed the mortar, they came over the edge. Valdez punched Amaro's arm.

"Turn that fucking thing around," Valdez yelled. "*Conio,* here they come."

Amaro swung and fired. Some ran past him. Over him. He drew the automatic and somersaulted one with a round high in the back. He turned and mowed the edge.

The perimeter pulled back to compensate for casualties. But Amaro could not move. He was frozen in place, too scared to get up or move out. He saw his name carved on the stone. He had dug the grave himself. He was not going anywhere until it was over between the mortar and him.

The firefight continued through the night. Acrid clouds hung like a shroud over the saddlebacked ridge. The night sky brightened from black to dark gray. The rifle fire sputtered. Amaro covered Valdez with a poncho because blown-open heads looked ugly. He ate pound cake and applesauce. It tasted like cordite.

He lit a cigarette and tried to count the bodies on the edge. Lost his count. Started over. And over again.

He stood up and stumbled over a dead gook, the one with that big hole in his back, beetles eating on the skin. Pulled a wallet from his pocket. There was some scrip in it and the picture of a woman. A woman and a young boy. He stole the guy's dope, some fat ready-rolls like Pall Malls with clipped straight ends, and fired one up. He took a few deep pokes. Then puked a day's worth of bitter cake and canned fruit.

He sat down shivering in a cold sweat, cramped and aching and sick. Valdez under the poncho. Only half of the third guy left. Amaro sucked in a deep breath, picked up the gun; with an ammo belt around his neck, he staggered up to the rocks on top.

Choppers came in to evac the wounded. The dead from the day before had turned from ash white to purple-black. They were rolled into body bags. They stank in the heat. The fresher kills did not.

The burned bodies fell apart when touched. Replacements came in on the choppers and policed the pieces. Some of them wore handkerchiefs around their noses and mouths.

There was a stone well off in the distance. Amaro saw someone in black run behind it. Balancing the bipod on a rock he jerked the slide. Orange tracers waved outward, cutting a path toward the target. They shattered and sparked. Amaro held tight the trigger. He would not stop firing until the well was dust and he was the guy behind it.

The gun jammed. Amaro was out of ammo. He pulled the automatic and fired a full clip, laughing, cursing, running back and forth in front of the rocks.

Someone tackled him from behind. Amaro clubbed him off with the barrel of the .45. Someone else punched him in the face. Amaro spun around and pulled the trigger. The piece clicked twice; then Amaro threw it at the crowd behind him. He felt something hard hit him across the shoulders, on his neck, under his steel pot. Amaro fell to his knees. He felt them kicking his chest, his stomach, his back. He could not move his arms. He could not see their faces. Then even the pain went away.

16

The new base camp was too tight, too crowded for fifteen hundred troops, too far from the sea. Newly filled sandbags, still plump and unsettled, seemed not to belong where they were stacked. Amaro was glad to get away from the camp. Glad to get away from the lifting, the digging, the constant confusion of getting it all done right now.

He checked in at the main building of the Second Surgical Hospital to pick up his routing slip. Then he walked to Tent 7.

"How have you been?" the young doctor asked.

"About the same," Amaro said as he hopped on top of the table. "The backs of my legs feel cramped."

"Have you been resting? Taking it easy?"

"We've been working like mules. Packing. Loading. Setting up. A lot of work."

Amaro lay on his back. The doctor picked up Amaro's right leg and pushed the knee up toward Amaro's chest.

"How does that feel?" the doctor asked.

"Not too bad," Amaro said.

The doctor repeated the action, this time bending Amaro's left leg. "Your skin condition looks better."

Amaro winced.

"That one hurt, did it?" the doctor said.

"Yeah," Amaro said. "That one hurt."

"Where?"

"Right here." Amaro pulled his thumb across his lower

back. "I felt the pain in here, too," he said, rubbing his hamstring.

"Nothing turned up on the X-ray. All I have to go on is what you tell me."

"I'm not bullshitting you, Doc. My back really is fucked up. I can't go out to the field like this. I don't feel sure of myself. I'm scared, man. You know what I mean? I'd be putting myself and everybody else in danger."

The doctor smiled. "It seems to me that, even if you were one-hundred percent, you and everybody else would still be in danger out there."

"That's not what I meant, Doc. What I mean is—"

"I think I know what you mean," the doctor said. "Relax, soldier. You'll still have a light-duty profile. But I'm going to send you over to the physical therapist before you leave here today. He'll give you some exercises—some stretching exercises—which may relieve the pressure."

"Sounds good, Doc."

"Sit up and cross your left leg over the right."

Amaro did as he was told. The doctor tapped Amaro's left knee with a rubber mallet. Nothing happened. The captain tapped it again. Harder. Still, nothing. The doctor held Amaro's left heel in the palm of his hand and stretched the leg out straight. "Do you feel this?" the doctor asked, pulling the mallet handle upward on the sole of Amaro's foot.

"Yeah. I feel it," Amaro said.

The doctor pressed a little harder, and pulled the handle upward. Amaro felt his toes clench involuntarily.

"That's a good sign," the doctor said. "Get dressed."

Amaro pulled on and buttoned his fatigues. He laced his jungle boots. "Do you know what time it is?" he asked.

The doctor looked at his watch. "Two thirty," he said.

The doctor handed the routing sheet and the signed profile to Amaro.

"Take this to Tent Four," the doctor said. "They'll show you the exercises."

"Thanks, Doc," Amaro said. "I really appreciate this."

It took longer at the physical therapist than Amaro had hoped it would. He wasted most of the time waiting. But that was the Army. He was used to it.

They showed him how to touch his toes; how to stretch up, all the way up, standing on the balls of his feet; they told him to sleep on the floor. He thought that was funny. Sleep on the floor. The floor was the only place *to* sleep. Stretched out flat on the dirt like a log, or a rock, or a stiff. The exercises were familiar: side bends, torso twists, all the old PT routines. They wrote the exercises down in order and numbered the repetitions.

Sergeant Watts walked through the company area to the spot where the first platoon bivouacked. Most of the tent spaces were empty. Amaro's tent was pitched in a corner. Towels were stretched out over it to dry in noontime sunlight. Empty ammo boxes, rusty magazines, web gear, and Charlie Rat scraps littered the front of the tent. Watts kicked the stuff to one side, leaned over, and opened the flap.

"Drop yo' cock and grab yo' socks," Watts shouted. "Time to rise and shine, young troop."

There was no response.

Watts bent lower to peek inside. Amaro was not there. From a pile of empty pound-cake and applesauce cans, a claymore mine, set up as if ready to trigger, faced Watts.

"Jesus."

Crumpled packs of Lucky Strikes, hand grenades, machine-gun rounds, dry socks filled with captured rice, and a couple of balled-up pairs of fatigues were scattered inside the tent as if dumped from the open rucksack that lay gutted in the corner.

Watts stood up and walked along the sandbagged perimeter wall. He waved to a bunker guard. "You seen Amaro?"

"Say what?" the guard said.

"No never mind," Watts said. Across the flats was a place in the wall that turned in front of a hedgerow. There, in a shady spot, was Amaro sprawled on a poncho.

"Get up, goddamn it." Watts kicked the soles of Amaro's boots. "Look alive."

Amaro rolled over on his side. "Get fucked," he said without opening his eyes.

Watts kicked him harder. "Ain't no time to play fuck-around. We got birds coming in with wounded. The Dick-mauler hisself gonna be here soon, jaws tight, ready to bite."

"Come on, Watts. Leave me alone." Amaro curled up on the poncho.

"I'm doing you a favor, chump. The First Shirt he see you slackin' up while the unit be hittin' shit and he gonna bring it down hard. No *lie.*"

Amaro sat up and leaned on his elbows. His back ached. His head felt heavy. He rubbed his fingers through tangled hair and over the stubble on his face.

"I'm up. Okay? Now leave me alone," Amaro said. He stretched. Took a few deep breaths. Tried to muster enough energy to stand up and walk to the crapper.

The medevac touched down near Battalion Aid. First Sergeant Fluett and Sergeant Malone jumped off, then helped medics wrestle wounded onto stretchers and into Triage. They walked separate ways when they finished. .

When Malone looked into Amaro's tent he saw his friend on his knees searching through the mess of discarded gear.

"Lose your mind?" Malone said. "You'll never find it here."

"A joint," Amaro said. "I'm sure I dropped the fucking . . . hey. What are you doing here? You okay or what?" He scrambled out of the tent.

"I'm fine now," Malone said. He dropped his gear. "I was going to crash with you. I don't feel like pitching a crib all alone. But, Christ, what a fucking slob you are."

"I can clean it up."

"I don't have enough time for that," Malone said, smiling, doing a quick little dance with his elbows, knees, and hips. "Twenty-one and a wake-up, motherfucker. I'm so short I can sleep in a matchbox." He held his hand out, palm up. Amaro slapped down on it.

"I thought the bird was for the wounded," Amaro said. "You ain't hit."

"Fuck no, I ain't hit. But I can't say they didn't try." He sat on a sawhorse. "We went on a water run this morning and walked into a bunch of dinks. The wind blew and shit flew.

When it was over I told McGee there was no fucking way I was going to stay in the field for another fucking minute. Too short to get stung by the humbug."

"For sure," Amaro said. "But how did you get past Fluett? When he's in the field he wants everybody out there."

"That's the beautiful part," Malone said. "Did you find that joint?"

"Not yet."

"How about a butt?"

"Got one right here close to my heart."

"Fire it up," Malone said. "Anyway, that scumbag Fluett wouldn't cut me any slack. Kept my ass on the line. So today I told McGee I was getting on that chopper one way or another. Dig this. Know why Fluett came in?"

"A bullet between the eyes, I hope."

"Not quite as good as that," Malone said.

Amaro handed the cigarette to Malone. He took a deep slow drag and watched the smoke curl skyward when he exhaled. "His rifle jammed," Malone said.

"Yeah," Amaro said. "So what?"

"*So what?*" Malone said. "Don't you hear what I'm saying? You smoke too much shit. Fluett took himself out of the field because his M-16 automatic rifle jammed in a firefight. When McGee asked him if I could split, the fucking prick was stuck. He had to let me come back."

"Look," Amaro said, pointing.

Fluett was striding in a straight line toward the orderly room. Amaro and Malone followed at a distance.

Watts was behind his desk fussing over a form. He sat at attention as Fluett walked in. Amaro and Malone loitered outside, listening.

"Airborne, First Sergeant," Watts said.

Fluett ignored him. He walked past Watts, past the magic helmet and the rows of piled duffel bags, the stacks of cardboard boxes and wooden crates. He dropped his rucksack next to his desk, ran an arm over the desktop to clear it, then sat down. Immediately he began breaking his M-16 apart.

Watts was used to being ignored. He pretended to read a form and glanced at Fluett cautiously. Never had Fluett come back from the field without heading straight to the shower point. The first sergeant never sat at his desk without being showered and shaved, Old Spiced, dressed in the clean fatigues he kept folded in his footlocker, those fatigues with black-on-green name tags, insignias, heavy chevrons, master-blaster wings, and his combat infantryman's badge with a star between the wreaths.

Fluett broke the weapon down with a vengeance and spread it on the desk. He checked the chamber, the rifled barrel. Held the firing pin up to the light. Felt the cere, searching for worn spots. He examined the bolt, the ejector, the receiver, the spring. Picked each piece up a second time, then a third, touching, looking, shaking his head.

He stood up and held the barrel toward the light, sighting the bare bulb overhead through the narrow tube. He turned it around, gripped it like a baseball bat, then slammed it hard on the desk. He smashed the trigger housing. The rear stock flew against the tent wall. He swung the barrel down in ax chops. Chips flashed from the gouged desktop.

Then he attacked the duffel bags, striking them with the rifle barrel, kicking them with his boots. Stacked crates crashed to the floor and Fluett kicked at the boxes of candy and cartons of cigarettes. Ammo boxes split apart and bullets skittered on the planking.

Watts stood up quickly and walked out of the orderly room as Fluett worked his way toward him. The first sergeant said nothing. There was no expression on his face. He just kept swinging that rifle barrel, hitting everything he could reach. He knocked Romo's magic helmet from the altar crate. He stood there pounding straight down on the trinkets, smashing them, sending them flying in all directions—the fragments of some garbage bomb.

He stopped suddenly, out of breath. The rifle barrel fell from his lowered arms. He turned, kicked the stuff out of his way as he walked back to his desk. He hoisted his ruck-sack, dropped his steel pot on his head, and walked out of the orderly room toward his tent as if nothing at all had happened.

"You think he's upset?" Amaro said.

Amaro chased Malone around the company area. Malone moved side to side, made cuts like a wide receiver, straight-armed Amaro away from the reefer. They pushed and shoved and played like boys in a city lot.

"*At ease,*" Fluett shouted from somewhere behind them.

Amaro grabbed the roach from Malone, field-stripped it, and scattered what was left.

Fluett had returned from the shower point. He was dressed in clean fatigues and polished boots and carried a leather shaving kit. A towel was draped over one arm. The air around him smelled of soap and cologne.

"You're not fooling anyone," Fluett said.

"I'm not trying to," Amaro said. "The both of us know what's going on. Besides. What are you going to do about it, anyway? Take another stripe? Fuck. You can have them all, for all the good they do me here."

"Stripes may mean nothing to you," Fluett said. "But be advised they mean quite a bit to me. There are other ways to teach you proper respect."

"Is that a threat?" Amaro said.

"I don't have to threaten. Malone," Fluett said, "report to the mess hall. You're still a part of this unit, and not too short to wash trays or wind up with your ass in a sling. Get over there on the double and make yourself useful. It will keep you out of trouble."

"See you later," Malone said to Amaro. His hands shook as he tried to light a cigarette. He was too short to hassle with Fluett, too short for any of this. He turned and walked toward the mess hall.

Fluett stared at Amaro. "You can get busy doing the only thing you're capable of," he said.

"And what might that be, First Sergeant?"

"Burn shit."

"My profile says no bending, stooping, or prolonged standing. Go find somebody else to do it."

"If you do not burn that shit within the next fifteen minutes, I will personally haul your sorry ass to the battalion commander and give you a direct order in his presence. You will be marking time on a stockade wall instead of chasing your tail up here."

"You know, you been on my fucking case since the day I got here," Amaro said. "I don't know who or what the fuck you think you are, but I'm telling you to your face that I'm not impressed with you, your stripes, your Army, or your whole fucking war. All you are is a dumb-fuck lifer, because if you didn't have those stripes to hide behind, you'd of been shoveling cowshit all your fucking life."

"Woulda's and coulda's don't mean a fat rat's ass," Fluett said, slowly, in a flat voice. "Fact is, I have these stripes, and you don't. That means I do *not* have to shovel cowshit. I *order* insignificant little assholes like you to burn barrels full of it. That is what it is all about. You are a snotnosed malcontent gumming up my unit. Smooth operation is vital. Lives depend upon it. There are one hundred twenty-six troops in this company, and nearly two thousand in the brigade. Every one of your immature fuckups endangers and hinders."

"You are a sick motherfucker," Amaro said. "Do you ever stop for a minute and listen to what you're saying?"

"Never. I don't have to. There are procedures. Programs to get with. The machinery has to function smoothly in order to be successful."

"Your fucking machinery turns people into hamburger. People, man. *People.* Don't you—"

"Soldiers . . . are soldiers," Fluett said matter-of-factly. "Soldiers are not lardass civilian *people.* You've never understood the difference."

"I understand that you go out of your way to break my balls every chance you get, and I've had it with you and this whole fucking deal."

"That is not my concern. As long as my unit does what it is supposed to do, I am doing my job. When it malfunctions, it is my responsibility to identify the problem and correct it. Simple. Right now, the smooth, hygienic operation of my unit requires you to burn its shit. Get to it." He turned around and walked away, then stopped. "Shave and take a shower when you're finished," he said over his shoulder. "You stink worse than you look."

Malone carried greasy pots from the mess tent out to the slop buckets. He poured water into empty garbage cans and lowered the gas heaters in place to boil water to wash the things in. He tightened the clamps on the heaters, securing them to the rims of the cans.

Amaro walked out of the tent. "I was looking for you," he said. "Cookie told me you were out here."

"Got to clean this fucking mess," Malone said. He pointed to a pile of utensils, pots, and pans. He shrugged. "Better than being in the line. Poor bastards. If I wasn't so happy, I'd feel sorry for them."

"Want to smoke a joint?"

"Not right now. It would be a bring-down to do this when I'm stoned out totally."

"When you get through, meet me at the crapper."

Malone laughed. "You got that detail again?"

"It blows my mind," Amaro said. "You got to clean up the mess from cooking the food and I got to clean up the mess from after the food."

"Yeah. So?"

"When you stop to think, it's just so fucking crazy."

"I know," Malone said. "But it's all the same old shit to me. Pardon the pun." He picked up the five-gallon can of diesel fuel and filled the tanks on the heaters. "Let me finish this and I'll meet you at the crapper. An hour. Maybe less."

"Okay," Amaro said. "How much is in that can?"

"About half." Malone opened the small metal door that covered the pilot on the first heater. He adjusted the fuel flow knob and struck a match.

"Let me take it, man. Save me a trip."

"Go ahead," Malone said. "Just go do what the fuck you got to do and let me get started over here."

Amaro tightened the lid on the gas can, picked it up, and started out for the latrine.

The explosion shook the ground. Amaro hit the dirt and rolled sideways. He turned. There was a loud *whoosh* and a column of black smoke and blue flame shot up. He jumped up and ran to it.

187 :

The earth burned where the fuel had splattered. Garbage cans lay flat. Malone's fatigues were wrapped in flames. His face was white in places where the charred skin curled up and pulled away from what was under it. A flat piece of sheet metal stuck up out of his forehead.

Amaro ripped off his fatigue jacket and beat at the flames. He cleared a path to Malone and tried to smother the blue fire that crackled on his friend's body. It was no use.

"Get the fuck outta there," somebody yelled. *"The other one's gonna blow."*

Amaro ran back through the flames and dove behind some sandbags. Another explosion sprayed fiery diesel fuel.

Guys shoveled dirt. Poured water from cans. The fires were put out one at a time.

Amaro ran back to the body and fell to his knees. He stared, then sat back on his haunches, holding his singed fatigue shirt. Malone sprawled flat, arms and legs spread, the piece of sheet metal in his head upright like the rudder of some capsized boat.

Between the garbage cans, rising above them, half-concealed by smoke, was Fluett. He stood with his fists pressed to his hips.

"Motherfucker," Amaro screamed. Tears made mud on his face. *"Order him to stand up. Order him.* You're so fucking good at giving commands. Order him. *Order it.* You mother-fuckering stinking asshole cocksucker son-of-a-bitch."

His voice trailed off, mumbling, scooping dirt. Fluett exchanged words with the mess sergeant, then disappeared inside the tent. Somebody wrapped a wet towel over Amaro's shoulders.

17

Sergeant Watts sat behind his desk in the orderly room, pretending to be busy. He shuffled papers, pulled open and shut file drawers.

Fluett leaned back in his chair, his hands clasped behind his head. He stared at the tent roof, then lowered his eyes to Amaro.

"I knew if I gave you enough rope you'd hang yourself," Fluett said.

Amaro stood in front of Fluett's desk. His hands were in his pockets. He looked at the wooden floor. He studied the cuts and scratches on the toes of his boots, looking for a pattern. He thought one series of marks looked like a star. Maybe a snowflake. He tried to remember the number of points on a snow crystal. No two alike. Billions of trillions of snowflakes and no two ever alike. Amaro wondered how that could be true.

"You fucked up real good this time," Fluett said. He leaned forward and slammed his hands on the desktop. "Stand at attention when I talk to you, troop."

Amaro kept his hands jammed deep in his pockets. He kicked a small white pebble and watched it skitter across the floor.

"I said stand at attention," Fluett yelled.

"I am," Amaro said. "Now why don't you get to the point so I can get the fuck out of here."

"The point. Get to the point. That's very good," Fluett said. "Because that's exactly where you're going."

Amaro turned. "Hey, Watts. You got a smoke?"

"No, he does not," Fluett said. "He has nothing for you. No one in this company has anything for you. You look at me when I am talking to you."

Amaro stared hard at the first sergeant. "Happy now?" he asked.

"Almost," Fluett said. "But not yet. I have a hunch, though, that I will be, soon."

Amaro laughed.

"I'm glad you think it's funny," Fluett said.

"I was just thinking about what would make a miserable motherfucker like you happy," Amaro said.

"Well, you don't have to wonder about it anymore. I'm going to tell you. What will make me happy is to send your malingering candyass back out to the line."

"I've got a profile. You can't."

"Not as far as this unit is concerned. According to Headquarters, you like to fight. You like to fight so much they sent you back here because they don't want to have *any*-thing to do with you. We know just the place for guys who like to fight. You are going to the field tomorrow morning. You will walk point every day. You will walk point until you go nuts, or get dusted. Either will make me very, very happy."

Amaro started to say something, but changed his mind.

"I thought you'd like it," Fluett said, faking surprise. "That will be all. Now . . . get out of my sight."

Amaro walked toward the tent flap.

"Wait a minute," Watts said.

"What for what?" Amaro asked.

Watts pointed to an M-16 rifle. The rifle was propped upright against his desk. "Turn in your sidearm and take this with you. It's yours."

Amaro picked it up. "Where's my ammo?"

"I'll issue it to you in the morning, right before you leave."

Amaro shouldered the rifle and walked out of the orderly room.

He found a usable rucksack and packed it with C rations and extra socks. He filled his canteens and clipped them to his gear with D-rings. Out of habit, he broke the M-16 and started to clean it. The bolt did not have a firing pin. He reassembled the weapon and snapped a GP strap to the carrying handle.

Amaro stayed hidden in his tent while the others went to chow. Then he walked over to the third platoon area, where some replacements had pitched their tents. In one of these he found grenades and a full magazine in a rucksack. He carried these back to his own tent.

There he smoked a joint while he cut a towel into long, thin strips. He tied several together at the ends, then rolled up the homemade rope and shoved it in his pocket, along with a grenade.

Behind the stacked supplies in the orderly room Amaro found extra weapons chained to a gun rack. He pulled the useless bolt from his M-16 and replaced it with a live one from a rifle standing in the rack. Then he walked back to his tent.

Amaro stood outside and lit a Lucky. He followed the curve of the road downhill. In a wide flat space at the bottom he saw the brigade's new replacements in ranks in front of the tents.

They stood uneasy in new jungle boots. They sweated in stiff new fatigues, shifting their weight from foot to foot, pulling damp skivvies out of their cracks.

Amaro could only watch them from a distance. When he was near them he felt uncomfortable. In the mess hall he had noticed their eyes were not dull but clear, as if eager to look around and see. They talked too loud and too much. They found things to laugh about. At the table with them he felt as if on a bus in a foreign country, eavesdropping on conversations in a language he did not understand. The words all sounded familiar but they did not seem to mean the same things to him as they did to them. Yet he realized he meant more to this load of total strangers than he meant to anyone else in the world. They were linked by the same space and time. The strongest of all possible ties.

The new ones moved too quick. They were lively, in a hurry, as if they had someplace to go, someplace pleasant. So he avoided them. Kept as far away as he could. He just did not understand them. How can they be the way they are? he thought.

He saw a crowd gathered behind some tents near the top of the hill. He field-stripped his cigarette butt as he walked toward the crowd, scattering tobacco shreds, rolling the ripped paper into a tight ball and tossing it out in front of him.

Amaro stood on the edge of the sprawling group and tried to see over their heads. Most of them were taller than him and, with their steel pots on, he could not see over them even on his toes. He shouldered his way through the crowd ignoring the "Hey, watch it, man" and "Where the fuck do you think you're going?" and pushed to the front.

A long snake, a python, with zigzag black stripes making diamond and hourglass patterns, lay stretched across the sand in a big chicken-wire cage. The lower part of it coiled on itself. The upper part rested in a wide curve.

"What's the big deal?" Amaro asked.

"They're going to feed the brigade mascot," someone said.

"So what?"

"So how much do you weigh?" a guy behind him asked.

Amaro did not know how much he weighed. He had noticed his belt was four inches tighter. He could tell by the line the bar of the brass buckle made on the web.

"I don't know how much I weigh," Amaro said quietly.

"I figger about one-twenty," the guy said.

"If that much," another guy said.

"What the fuck?" Amaro glanced about. "Are you crazy or what? A hundred and twenty my ass." He used to weigh one-sixty-five. He knew that much.

"Yup. 'Bout one-twenty is all," the guy said.

"So what?" Amaro asked.

"So that snake yonder could swaller you whole," the guy said. "Helmet, fatigues, your stinkin' boots and all, then sleep for a year."

"Coming through! Coming through!" guys yelled and the crowd separated to let a three-quarter back up to the cage.

The piglet was fat and ugly. It had mud-colored splotches on it and thick bristles and a long face with a snout. It did not look the way Amaro imagined a pig to look. The skin was neither pink nor smooth. The head was long. And it grunted. He had to ask someone what the thing was.

The animal ran into the chicken-wire, bending it, shaking the posts like the cage was going to fall apart. It lowered its head, the snout pushing furrows in the sand. Amaro was surprised to see the squat thing move so quick.

The snake flicked its tongue and kept its head on the sand, listening.

"That sucker smells bacon."

"Pork chops."

"Spare ribs, motherfucker."

The grunts started betting on how long it would take.

The pig stopped in its tracks, twisted, ran. It fell on its chest, dug its snout in the sand, rolled to all fours, all the time grunting and snorting.

In slow, sideward waves—pushing sand in front of it— the snake inched forward in utter silence, keeping its head on the ground and flicking its tongue as if unaware of anything else being in the cage. It slid forward, cutting the cage in half, taking running room from the pig. The curves in its body deepened as it grew closer.

The pig rumbled, rubbing its hide against the cage. The snake closed down the space, an inch at a time.

A Vietnamese civilian walked on the road.

"Let's feed it a fuckin' gook," somebody shouted, and others cheered, "Catch that dink. Don't let him get away!"

Amaro stared intently at the scales that moved in ripples down the python. The slight muscle movements caught the light as curves tightened and narrowed in its body.

The pig turned and charged the moving tube. One curve looped over the other and the snake slipped around the pig, then looped again twice around.

The pig grunted.

"Why don't it oink?"

"Ain't it gonna squeal?"

After each grunt, the coils around it tightened and it grunted again.

"That's what Jodie be doin' to your ol' lady," somebody yelled.

"Up yours," somebody else answered.

"Nope. Up *hers*."

"Talk about a main squeeze. Gaww-aww-damn."

Another grunt. The coils tightened. A soft hissing sound from the pig. The snake lay there, its head on the sand. It was coiled twice around the ugly thing, flicking its tongue. It never blinked once. Its muscles rippled gently as the pig's hind legs jerked, then stopped.

Slowly the coils loosened. The pig fell still. The snake tongue flicked it. Pushed the pig with its head. It yawned, its jaws unhinged. With rapid biting motions, it started to push the pig into itself even as it pulled itself over the pig. Little by little the pig disappeared into the slime tube until there was just a big lump in the snake, right behind its head.

The python lay still. Only the scales around the lump moved.

Amaro crawled along the sandbag wall. He stopped at the corner, close to the orderly room, and stayed low in shadows. He slipped the straps of his rucksack off his shoulders, leaned his rifle and steel pot on the pack. Scanned the company area.

Amaro saw the replacements walking up the road. They followed Sergeant Watts to the flick. It was almost dark. The movie would start when it got dark.

The space around Amaro was quiet and still. The dry dirt felt warm from the sun heat it retained. The sky turned dark. It seemed deep. The stars were clear and bright. Shooting stars slid by like slow tracers.

He stared down at the dirt and saw every grain, every separate grain, each in its own place, each with its own shape. Each speck held its own space against all the others next to it. And all the gritty specks made up the dirt, as drops make up a cup of water or a river or even the South China Sea. Specks of grit, drops of water, the stars shining in the deep well overhead.

Who gives a fuck if you disappear, he thought. It just slides in and fills your empty space.

He stared at the dirt and tried to listen. He heard sounds in the distance—muffled sounds. There was nothing moving, nothing making noise, in the space he was concerned with. He thought about the space around First Sergeant Fluett's tent.

He was sweating now. His heart pounded hard in his chest. And from the silence all around him he heard a ringing in his ears, a faint, steady ringing. He thought maybe it was the sound that specks of dirt make as they cling to one another. Maybe, when there was nothing else to hear, a guy could listen to the sound gravity made, or light as it sped by. And then Amaro knew the faint, steady ringing was only in his ears. It was the sound he heard when there was nothing else to listen to. And when his eyes were closed there was nothing else to see but the insides of his eyelids.

He lowered his face to the dirt. He smelled it. He felt it on his skin. All he wanted to listen to was the ringing in his ears. The insides of his eyelids were all he wanted to see.

A crunching sound caused him to flinch. He opened his eyes and looked up. He saw Fluett leave his tent, heard Fluett's boots displacing specks of dirt as he walked past the orderly room and headed for the road.

Amaro waited, then crawled around the outside of the orderly room and into Fluett's tent.

He used a short strip of towel and tied the grenade to the wooden frame under the cot. He tied one end of a long length of towel to the runner on the other side. He pulled it taut so it followed the contour of the canvas under the cot. He tied the loose end to the ring on the grenade.

Amaro was on his back under the cot and sweat ran in his eyes. He wiped his palms on his fatigue jacket.

It was dark in the tent, darker under the cot, so he closed his eyes trying to adjust to the darkness. He listened hard to hear if anyone approached. There wasn't a sound. Only the ringing. The ringing sounded loud.

He opened his eyes. He slowly straightened the pin on the grenade, holding tight, with one hand, the towel tied to the ring. He pulled the pin until only a small part of it stuck out beyond the safe side of the handle.

Keeping one hand on the ring, he followed the stretched towel with his fingers, making sure it was in place, making sure it was smooth and in contact with the canvas. He checked the grenade a last time. The pin was a fraction of an inch from pulling loose.

Carefully, he let go of the ring and rolled quickly out from under the cot. He jumped to his feet and sprinted back to where he had stashed his gear. He dove behind the sandbag wall and flattened against the ground. Just in case.

The space around him was quiet. Nothing happened to shatter the stillness. Amaro pulled his rucksack on, dropped his steel pot on his head, picked up his weapon, and ran up the road toward the landing zone.

Amaro stopped at the cage and stood panting, watching the snake. He would spend the night on the bare landing zone and take a chopper out at dawn. He lit a cigarette with the stub of a match and wiped the sweat from his face. He saw the oval-shaped thing move slowly—very slowly—through the tube. Slick shiny skin glistened. The eyes stared. He took careful aim and squeezed the trigger.

Copyedited by Margaret Wolf.
Designed by Frank Lamacchia.
Production by H. Dean Ragland,
    Cobb/Dunlop Publishers Services, Inc.
Set in Garamond by Kachina Typesetting, Inc.
Printed by the Maple-Vail Company on acid-free paper.